THE FUTURE

THE FUTURE

CATHERINE LEROUX

TRANSLATED FROM THE FRENCH
BY SUSAN OURIOU

BIBLIOASIS
WINDSOR, ONTARIO

FIRST EDITION
4 6 8 10 9 7 5

Library and Archives Canada Cataloguing in Publication
Title: The future / Catherine Leroux ; [translated by] Susan Ouriou.
Other titles: Avenir. English
Names: Leroux, Catherine, 1979- author. | Ouriou, Susan, translator.
Series: Biblioasis international translation series ; no 42.
Description: Series statement: Biblioasis international translation series ; no 42.
Translation of: L'avenir.
Identifiers: Canadiana (print) 2023019785X | Canadiana (ebook) 20230197884
| ISBN 9781771965606 (softcover) | ISBN 9781771965613 (EPUB)
Classification: LCC PS8623.E685 A9413 2023 | DDC C843/.6—dc23

Edited by Stephen Henighan
Copyedited by Rachel Ironstone
Cover designed by Natalie Olsen
Typeset by Vanessa Stauffer

   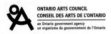

Published with the generous assistance of the Canada Council for the Arts, which last year invested $153 million to bring the arts to Canadians throughout the country, and the financial support of the Government of Canada. Biblioasis also acknowledges the support of the Ontario Arts Council (OAC), an agency of the Government of Ontario, which last year funded 1,709 individual artists and 1,078 organizations in 204 communities across Ontario, for a total of $52.1 million, and the contribution of the Government of Ontario through the Ontario Book Publishing Tax Credit and Ontario Creates.

PRINTED AND BOUND IN CANADA

TO MY CHILDREN

_____

…like words in the mother tongue, like recollections in memory, or like children in childhood, none can be recovered

ÉVELYNE DE LA CHENELIÈRE

AUTHOR'S NOTE

This novel is a work of speculation and invention. Although I have kept many of the geographical and historical characteristics of the city of Detroit and of Southwestern Ontario's Francophone community, I have also invented large portions thereof, including a regional French dialect particular to the Fort Détroit of my imagination, which is represented here in English translation.

I

I've seen the future, brother
It is murder

LEONARD COHEN

Ten days after Gloria's arrival, her neighbour is killed on the street.

It's the noise that roots her to the spot at first, a crash like a hacking cough, a beam giving way after years of wear and tear. A sound both swift and deafening. In that contrast, she realizes just how serious this must be.

When Gloria steps outside, the woman from next door has already reached the twisted figure in the middle of the street. Gloria wonders how she made it there so quickly. Only thirty seconds earlier, she had heard her muttering to herself as she stood in her backyard pinning jumbo-sized T-shirts to the clothesline, a structure of concentric squares, dimensions within dimensions. She must be the kind of person capable of reaching unheard-of speeds when a loved one's life is in danger.

All that remains is a mound of clothing, as though the force of the impact had dissolved the man inside. The woman bends over, her hands clutching at the fabric. Since arriving in the city, Gloria has witnessed countless scenes between this woman and her father. One time, he hid behind the hedge and wolfed down an entire birthday cake. Walked out of the house carrying a flaming tea towel. Sat, naked as a worm, behind the steering wheel of the old

Pontiac parked in the alley. Every time, his daughter came running, grabbed the old man by the arm, and led him back inside, scolding him all the while. He wasn't to go out on his own, she reminded him, it was too dangerous. Fate has proved her right.

Crouched on the street, the woman wails, "Papa! Papa!" Gloria feels as though someone should walk over, lay a hand on her shoulder, murmur words of comfort. But there's no one else in sight on Avenue Clyde. She looks down at the half-rotted steps and her feet striped with veins. Then a man with a greying beard comes at a run. He bends over the old-timer and reaches into the shambles his body has become. Noting his efficient gestures, Gloria assumes he must be a doctor. She sees him bow his head without a word and begin compressions on the downed man's chest even though he, the woman, and Gloria all know there is no hope. The downed man's daughter cries soundlessly, her mouth gaping wide as though trying to swallow the horror. She is in that space where events still seem reversible, where death is still so close you think you can call it off. The shadow of a bird passes overhead, and Gloria can see it is the old man's soul. She turns. Her legs carry her inside. Her whole body feels shrouded in something like ether. Death has invaded the sky.

Through open windows, she hears what ensues—the sobbing, the phone calls, a few family and friends arriving, their hushed conversations. The sounds of the kitchen, of papers being shuffled, of objects being picked up and put down based on a new order. What she does not hear is an ambulance or a police car, nor anyone mentioning the driver who fled the scene or demanding that justice be served.

So it's true. Fort Détroit has become a place devoid of faith or law.

* * *

The next morning, islands of mist waft over the vast wild field that stretches like a prairie behind the house. Young deer stand poised on the horizon like so many tightrope walkers. Gloria steps onto the rear porch carrying a cup of chicory root tea. She thinks back to what used to stand there. She has only ever been to this house once before, fifteen years ago. The year of her first grey hair. At that time, the porch looked over a row of decrepit yet still-standing buildings. Abandoned, burnt, they have since collapsed, and the earth is busy grinding down their remains.

A creaking echoes on the other side of the fence with its missing slats. The neighbour is also outside, fleeing a too-quiet house.

Gloria walks over to her. "I'm so sorry," she murmurs. "About the accident. I…My condolences."

Her neighbour acknowledges her words with a nod, keeping her sturdy body half turned away.

"It's crazy," continues Gloria. "They should put in speed bumps."

Her neighbour snorts, the kind of laugh people give when they no longer believe something is possible. "Who are *they*?" she retorts. "The city? The blue-collar workers? Even the undertaker doesn't come to the house anymore. We had to pay some guy to take him in his pickup 'cause the funeral home hasn't got a hearse left. Motor City, my ass."

The neighbour looks away and her anger fades, spent. Gloria tiptoes back to the yellow house.

* * *

Shadows dribble from the light as it passes through the fan on its way to the table, to Gloria's fingers. She hasn't budged for an hour. She stares at her hands, dappled by the fragments of night raining from the ceiling. If only she could do nothing but this for days. Stay on at the table where Judith no longer sits and contemplate this pelting free of pain.

Eventually, however, she reaches for the phone. This time, the line works. She dials the number she knows by heart by now, the one burning her fingertips. *You have reached the Fort Détroit police station. We are unable to . . .* Gloria hangs up. She knows the message by heart, too, even the voice delivering it so tentatively, as though it had run out of excuses to serve up to citizens.

Gloria comes from a slow-moving world where events occur one after another. It would take more than a single lifetime to assimilate everything that has gone on in this house. Where she comes from, things change so imperceptibly it's even hard to mark the passage of days or years. With no sign of transformation, time stagnates. Here, the opposite holds true, time gallops ahead. Gloria feels as though she has aged another decade since arriving. There's nothing like the death of a child to project you into an age beyond your years.

All of a sudden, a tiny shadow appears beneath the pantry door. Advancing swiftly, it sniffs the air, detects the human presence, and freezes as though to make itself invisible. With its pointed head and fur as grey as a dust ball, the rodent bobs over the tiles' faded pattern, then scampers away, not making a sound. Gloria opens the door to the pantry she has yet to fully explore. It's a long, well-organized cupboard. Narrow shelves for spices, medium ones for cans, and large ones for flour and sugar and bags of dried peas. A space meant for abundance, designed for generosity. Gloria breathes in the scent of brown sugar and mustard that clings, out of sheer nostalgia, to the flaking paint. Because other than calcified stains and insect wings in the corners, these shelves have been bare for decades. The kitchen is an empty vessel. What can a field mouse possibly find here? On the table, shadows cast by a sudden sunbeam striking the fan transform into stunning reflections. One escapes, climbs the wall, and attacks the wallpaper like the flame from a lighter. Before she fully grasps what is going on, Gloria finds herself moving to extinguish the spark igniting the wall's warped covering.

* * *

On her way out to do her groceries, Gloria hears a sudden commotion from inside the green house next door. The soft thud of objects being thrown every which way. An exasperated litany of dull thumps. Rage has resurfaced. As she starts down the avenue, she sees her neighbour bring out a box full of clothing and toiletries. Without sparing a glance for Gloria, she drops the whole lot onto the sidewalk. Some feel the need to get rid of every last trace right away. Others want to keep living with the traces even when that means walking around with a house on their back.

Petals rain down on the streets, the fluttering of tiny, imprecise wings. The indulgence of May blossoms. Their future of bitter fruit. Gloria loiters, hoping a few will lodge in her hair. She wants to walk into the store and have someone mention the spring shower; above all, she wants someone to say something beautiful to her.

On the way there, she thinks of the cities she has known. None like this one. None as honest, she realizes. Continually monitored, restored, rejuvenated, the other cities perpetuate the fable of immutability: that human constructions are eternal. In Fort Détroit, that myth no longer exists. The impermanence of things, their fragility in the face of the elements, is on full display. Pavement disappears in chunks, sidewalks crumble. The naked trunks holding up electric cables welcome the new life that climbs and grafts itself to their porous wood. Houses are gutted, torn apart by fire and neglect. Nature has returned to occupy them; they let themselves be consumed.

Gloria walks for over half an hour, dreaming of Mason jars filled with rice, beans, flour, all arranged by colour. There is only one convenience store in the whole of the city's west side that still occasionally sells mushy fruit and vegetables. Once there, she notices a structure resembling a scrap-iron skeleton in the parking lot. It's a huge matchstick figure built out of disparate materials. Its left arm is raised, as though to greet passersby. At its feet, two young children in blue school uniforms return its greeting under their father's amused gaze. On the wall behind them, torn posters reveal fragments of words—*HAVE YOU SEEN THEM?*—the missing and their faces, gone from each poster, like fallen teeth.

Once inside, Gloria hopes to unearth bread somewhere but finds only pancake mix. No eggs. Lukewarm milk. Black bananas. She settles for two cans of bacon and beans, a jar of marinated beets, raisins. In any case, for weeks now, eating has become a chore for her. Food tumbles around in her mouth like gravel.

She returns home at a leisurely pace, admiring the houses that are still standing; they are modest, even the most comfortable of them, and, for the most part, abandoned. But each looks grateful to still be here. They breathe; they close their eyes. They ask for mercy.

* * *

The next morning, Gloria sits down to her bland bacon and beans, pecking away as she flips through *Le Citoyen libre*. The meal reminds her of her grandmother, and the newspaper reminds her of the city's forebears. The paper denounces the proposed demolition of the Tour de Lys. It says the tottering monument was commissioned by Cadillac himself, yet only completed a decade or so after the death of the founder of Fort Détroit. It contends that the structure is Francophone America's Leaning Tower of Pisa. Who would ever suggest destroying Pisa's famed monument?

She is on the horoscope page when Francelin knocks. Gloria doesn't need to look through the peephole to know who it is. He's the only one who comes to visit. She hides in the pantry to wait for his steps to retreat. Then she opens the front door. A small pyramid of lemons appears on the doorstep.

It was Francelin who came to open the door for her the day that she arrived. Stepping inside, Gloria wondered why he'd bothered to lock it. Clearly, the lock hadn't stopped anyone. All the windows were broken as was pretty well everything on the main floor, which wasn't much. The worst mess came from the stuff that had been brought into the house after it was trashed. Food wrappers, cigarette butts, empty bottles, a disgusting stench.

"That's typical Fort Détroit. Leave a place empty for thirty seconds and you can be sure someone'll take a shit inside," said Francelin, pointing to a pile of excrement in a corner of the living room.

At Gloria's stunned expression, he made quick work of removing the pile with a shovel, taking pity on the grieving woman in her sixties.

Young and robust, his vitiligo making his expression elusive, Francelin had appointed himself guardian of the neighbourhood's abandoned homes. Hence it was with a certain authority that he set out to offer Gloria a grand tour as though she had no connection to the place. She turned him down flat when he suggested showing her the second floor and assured him she would rather clean the rest up herself.

That didn't stop him from returning the next day with new windows, which he installed with amazing ease. She tried to pay him; he refused.

"I took them from a dead one."

"A dead person?"

"A dead house. An abandoned place nobody goes to anymore. The opposite of one that's alive."

"Oh."

"These're a standard model, easy to find," Francelin said as he wiped away the prints his fingers had left on the panes. "Just like for any other doors, sinks, light fixtures . . . All almost the same."

"And bathtubs?"

"Tubs too," Francelin said, averting his gaze.

He left her a brush, some soap, a broom, and a few garbage bags. He felt sorry for her.

* * *

Gloria presses the lemons using a crooked fork. She dilutes the juice, adds a bit of sugar and a pinch of salt, pours herself a glassful, then steps out onto the back porch. Instantly, condensation forms beads on the glass even though the heat is not actually all that extreme. It's the humidity, thinks Gloria, all that water rising from water. She sits and thinks of Lac Sainte-Claire, Lac Érié, Lac Huron. Of the Détroit and Sainte-Claire rivers, their narrow passages like birth canals. She thinks of the forces that originate there, redefining the climate and borders.

An arrival interrupts her thoughts. Across the way, her neighbour lollops in her direction, carrying a pink box. Gloria waves.

"Don't know why folks are so bent on bringing me dessert. Here. Some pastries for ya."

Gloria accepts the box and pours lemonade for her guest, who sits down on a step and lets her gaze linger on the gouged porch and the broken glass in the flowerbeds.

"They really did a number on this place! Mind you, it's already a miracle it didn't go up in flames. The malefactors showed some mercy."

"Malefactors?"

"The druggies, the junkies. There's a whole gang of 'em round here."

Gloria offers her a pastry, but she shakes her head. "I'm a diabetic, no sugar for me. That stuff could kill me. But your lemonade's great. Not too sweet."

She looks to be well over forty, with broad shoulders, steely eyes, and a mouth made for smiling. A good, obstinate, honest woman. She drums her fingers on the glass.

"So," she resumes in a curt tone. "How much did ya pay for it? Eight thousand? Nine thousand? Make me laugh with the great deal you got."

"I didn't buy it. It's my daughter's house."

The neighbour sets her glass down. The air slows.

"I'm sorry," she murmurs.

She truly is. Her body shifts, goes from hard to soft. She has recognized something familiar where least expected. She lays her hands on her thighs, leans in. Evening settles in slivers of blue onto the city.

"You'll see, there's not much left round here. A buncha crooks, a coupla good eggs—Theo, the guy who tried to revive my dad, he's one of 'em. He's a nurse, helps people with what ails 'em. You already know Francelin, he's always helpful but a bit thick at times. A lotta crooks though . . . You'll need to get yerself a weapon."

Gloria shrugs. She's never held a gun in her life.

"My name's Eunice. If you need anything, I'm just next door."

* * *

By the glow from the bulb, Gloria studies the crumpled words. It's as though they flee any reading. She does manage to make out Libra. *Your sleep is under assault. Don't let guilt overcome you; forgiveness begins with yourself. Watch out for a chill in the air.* Her eyes shift further down the column to Leo. *Stop running. An unexpected friend comes to you. It's time to unclench your fists. Lucky numbers: four, thirteen, twenty-two.* Surprised, she shakes her head but continues on to Aquarius, her sign, the only one from which she expects no miracles. *You are poised to enter a new world. Don't be afraid; ghosts do exist, but they wish you well. Carve out your place. Your colours are green and blue.* She finds the astrologist's name, one that is both sibylline and appropriate: *Father Pontchartrain* she reads at the top of the column. The bulb's light flickers then fades. Another power failure.

She gets up from her makeshift bed in the living room. There must surely be a more decent mattress than this dirty, sagging couch somewhere upstairs. But Gloria can't bring herself to venture there. Outside, all the streetlights are extinguished; the darkness is as dense as well water. Although she has trouble seeing, she's positive there's something moving out there. Like a rustling in space, a startling in the tranquility of night. Stray dogs bark. She remembers Eunice's advice to carry a firearm. She thinks of all the stories she has heard about Fort Détroit and all those she has yet to hear. Once attention is paid, one tale follows another like scarves from a magician's sleeve. The city of revolts, bankruptcies, injustices, and stray bullets, the city of curses, pyromaniacs, and poltergeists. Gloria presses hard against the glass as though to keep every one of them out.

Across the street, a rundown house seems to cough in the night. A whining sounds, one she takes at first for a shrill laugh, but it could be a rattling instead. Then silence cloaks the night again. It was probably just a beam collapsing, or a remnant of some kind giving way. Where she comes from, people name houses, and once baptized, they neither crumble nor empty. What is this one's name? she wonders, listening to the creaking from the second floor. But soon she plugs her ears. She doesn't want to hear the answer given by the ghosts.

* * *

The morning is biting as though air from the freezer had blanketed the place overnight. Gloria takes advantage of the blackout to thaw what had become an icy, impenetrable grotto. Once defrosted, the freezer loses its cavernous look and its aura of mystery. It stinks of freon and swallows all sound. Gloria sticks her head inside and cries, "Ho!" Her voice is cut off midway. She murmurs "Cassandra, Mathilda." The words disappear, sucked into the void. Like her two granddaughters.

Once she has finished her chore, she turns to the cans of paint Francelin brought over the day before. She opens them to reveal the turquoise inside. It's as though two large aquamarine eyes are staring back at her. Or perhaps at the wall that was once white and is now covered in dirt and water damage.

A few strokes and she can't take any more. The brush is instantly coated in disgusting grime, and the stains are even more visible than before. As with certain faces and certain cities, some rooms show more wear when an attempt is made to spruce them up. Gloria scans her arms, her bare feet. There's more paint on her body than on the wall.

Since her arrival in Judith's house, she has had only sponge baths, shivering in front of the small sink in the half bath on the main floor. The thought of sliding into the tub upstairs is unbearable. But today, a washcloth won't suffice. After seven minutes weighing the pros and cons and two minutes spent staring at her horoscope, she decides to knock on the door of the green house.

"I can't use my bathroom. And I really need a shower."

The neighbour frowns for a few seconds, then her forehead unknots. She has understood. A towel beneath her arm and slippers on her feet, Gloria enters Eunice's house.

It's one of those homes that forever brings vegetable stew to mind. The furniture, the rugs, the colour of the walls, everything has a hint of stew, the very essence of stew. Comfort, force of habit, a certain blandness coupled with a feeling of safety. Gloria finds herself transported back to her village and to the houses of her childhood friends, their mothers with bouffant hairdos, the counters smelling of vinegar. Eunice leads her to a beige bathroom that complements the brown reigning elsewhere. On their way, Gloria catches sight of a table groaning under all the various electronic parts and tools.

"That's my bread and butter," explains Eunice. "I fix old radios."

The water pressure is strong, and Gloria can feel herself melting under the steaming jet. Her body is stiff with aches and pains whose onset she never felt. The shower releases some of her tension. For a moment, putting her clothes back on, she experiences the buoyant state that used to be hers. But then, the weight returns to her shoulders.

Eunice invites her to sit down to salad with her. Stunned, Gloria stares at the gleaming tomatoes, the velvety shoots of arugula, the tiny balls of garlic flowers, the chopped basil. She turns her astonished gaze to Eunice.

"I know people," she states, pleased with herself.

Gloria shuts her eyes as she bites into her first tomato. A burst of life explodes onto her tongue. For the first time in weeks, the beginning of an appetite quivers inside her.

"So, think you'll stay for good?"

Gloria looks hard at her hostess, who adds, "You're painting the place, got new windows ... Looks like you're settling in for a stretch."

"For a while, yes," says Gloria, wiping her mouth.

Eunice lowers her eyes and purses her lips as though to lessen the question she's about to ask. "The two girls, Cassandra and Mathilda…we haven't seen 'em since…since their mother…Where're they at?"

Gloria downs a mouthful of soda. The bubbles fizz madly in her throat, a swarm of scalding words. "I don't know. They disappeared the same day as Judith … That's why I want to stay on."

Eunice nods gravely, serves Gloria a second helping. Tomato seeds glisten on the plate like so many nuggets of gold. Neither woman touches on the possibilities. That Mathilda and Cassandra may have been kidnapped by the same person who killed their mother. That they, too, may be dead. That what happened prior to that was no doubt worse than all the rest.

On her way home, Gloria catches sight of something moving in the opacity of a cedar grove. It looks like an ermine's belly, or a snow fox, a creature of blinding white. One that flees with a metallic clatter.

* * *

From the bottom porch step, Gloria scatters sunflower seeds. She thought she saw the tiny grey silhouette of her field mouse under the shade of a beech tree. The seeds fall close to the steps at first, then she throws them farther and farther, hoping to draw the animal out from its burrow. But the rodent doesn't budge, refusing to surface from beneath the dead leaves where its movements are barely visible. After a while, Gloria is no longer sure she did actually see it or that the infinitesimal breath under the vegetation is truly that of a living being and not just the wind, the season turning, the earth yawning.

At the foot of the stairs, ants have built a sand palace, only its outer pyramid visible. Gloria imagines the embryos for which the stronghold was designed and the secrets kept by the microscopic creatures. Their dreams of warfare, their incalculable army of twigs and glass. The weight of a billion insects marching in step, speaking with one voice. Relishing the same long poem brimming with code. A code that Gloria, close to illumination, almost manages to decipher. She wakes with a start, having dozed off sitting on the steps watching the anthill. Bending over again, she notices that the movement criss-crossing its surface has stopped. The worker ants have disappeared. The sand is damp as though someone had just dumped water there. Who could have come here to drown a nest of insects?

* * *

On the day of the funeral, Gloria makes her way to the neighbourhood church. Its corroded bells chime in showers of rust. Up at the front, Eunice's shoulders weep, yet the woman herself doesn't make a sound. Gloria hasn't tried to untangle the web of people related to her neighbour, the result of successive breakups, widowhoods, and second marriages. She shakes hands, pays her respects, then takes her leave, forgoing the procession to the graveyard. On the way home, she thinks of Judith's ashes, the urn at the back of a kitchen cupboard awaiting a more permanent resting place that Gloria has yet to find. Nothing is certain here, nothing is final, not even the ones who are gone.

Back at the house, she tries again to call the police. This

time, a woman answers and agrees to transfer her to the detective in charge of the case. But as she transfers the call, the line cuts out. Discouraged, Gloria sinks to the ground on the back porch. A single tulip has blossomed at the far end of the yard. It quivers like the shadow of a terror-stricken animal. Gloria feels a sudden affection for the flower's velvety petals, its supple stem. Then she remembers: She was the one who planted the tulip there fifteen years ago. She had dug up bulbs from her own garden. She clutches her head between her hands. Now the garden's warm fragrance is unrelenting. She feels an ache in her belly, her breasts, the tips of her toes. She wants to lie down on the ground, bury herself there.

She looks up. Something has caught her eye, an object cutting through the air above the field. Brushing away a fly, she advances slowly, her hand a visor above her eyebrows. A whip? More like the rod of a giant metronome marking time in slow motion.

She perches on top of a blackened mound that looks as though someone burned their bad memories there. From her vantage point, she notes that the end of the rod is bent. She squints. A hand. A brown, knotted hand wields the hooked object as it swings back and forth in the field. The metronome is a man, and the rod, a hoe. Someone is weeding the wilderness.

For several minutes, she watches the movement back and forth. Almost imperceptibly, the hoe shifts eastward as though following the clouds. A yellow butterfly flutters toward the man. A good omen, Gloria thinks. She decides to follow the insect through the tangle of saplings, quack grass, prickly bush, and other vegetation. The greenery is home to a host of insects and reptiles whose presence Gloria can sense, not see, through the mineral vibrations emanating upward.

The man has long greying hair that falls in dreadlocks to the small of his back. Despite the cool air, he's wearing a light pair of shorts and a drenched undershirt. Through his exertion, he has created his own microclimate. He doesn't seem surprised to see her appear. His rod stops as though forgetting to swing up again after touching the ground. Dazed, Gloria notes that he has hoed a patch some four by ten metres and weeded an even larger area. He turns to her, eyes sparkling, sporting a broad smile.

"You don't look like the kinda person's gonna tell me I got no right to be here."

"I just wanted to see up close."

"I'm not a crook, not a madman. I'm gonna start growin' food in your backyard."

"It's not really my yard."

"All the better. Belongs to no one. It's mine, it's yours. Do you like rhubarb?"

"Not really."

"Perfect, me neither."

She laughs, surprising even herself. The man smiles and returns to his task. After a moment's hesitation, Gloria retraces her steps. A small trail is already taking shape amid the whispering of plants.

Two hours later, sitting on the back porch, she bites into a pastry in the shape of a bear's claw that tastes of sugar and dust. Putting it down, she catches sight of the farmer following the same path she'd made earlier on. He waves with a level of familiarity that seems to come naturally to the two of them, as though there were a third person holding each of their hands.

He sits next to her. His name is Solomon. His family has lived in Fort Détroit for seven generations. He resides in one of the dead—now resuscitated—houses whose former solarium he has converted into a greenhouse. Thousands of plants wait to extend their roots through the fields he's cleared here and there round the city.

"I know your neighbour well…Eunice. She's the one told me 'bout this lot. She loves tomatoes. Soon as I'm done breakin' ground, I'll plant you some, then cucumbers, then cantaloupe. You'll have to water it, mind. Eunice knows, I told her. If you give her a hand, I could add more seeds. Carrots, pea vines, romaine lettuce…How's that sound?"

"Sounds good, I think."

"Perfect, perfect…Meantime, look on this."

He hands her a paper bag in which she finds a large cucumber and a handful of small purple fruit. She bites into one, and her mouth fills with a taste of night sky.

"What is it?"

"Wild cherry. Ripened early this year. There's a tree a block away, no one ever picks 'em, don't think it's edible. That's the problem with Fort Détroit. People think there's nothin' good here, so the good stuff goes bad. Slice that cucumber up for me, would ya? Add some salt. Then a glass of water, if you don't mind. I'm parched."

As she pulls out a knife, Gloria blinks. There is not a single spoon left. She checks the sink, the other drawers. Nothing. A cardinal's song draws her back outside. She casts an anxious glance at the cedar grove where, she'd now swear, it was the clink of cutlery she'd heard.

28

"You okay?" Solomon asks.

"This might sound crazy, but I don't know where my spoons have got to."

"Ah, that's another Fort Détroit specialty. Things go AWOL."

He shoots her a knowing glance, then empties his glass in one gulp. When he leaves, Gloria watches until he vanishes into the field, then follows the swaying of grasses where he has walked long after he's gone, sometimes in more than one spot at once, like two halves of the same motion. The quiet is vast, as though the sky itself has fallen silent. She realizes the voices of children are what's missing. There are so few.

* * *

In the middle of the night, she's wakened by terrifying cries. A cross between the howling of a wolf, a starving baby, and a woman being tortured. Wrapped in the thin armour of her sleeping bag, she shuffles out to the front porch. The sound, though distant, is horrifying. Gloria feels she must do something. Plug her ears. Scream even louder. No longer hear the calls. Terror glues her to the spot. She has no recollection of when or how she falls asleep, her head inside, her feet outside.

At dawn, a rustling has replaced the screams. A family of squirrels has made themselves at home while she slept. They're celebrating round a ripped bag of walnuts. The minute Gloria stands, they scamper out the open door. She studies the floor, remembering the first thing Francelin told her. The linoleum is covered in droppings.

Cradling a cup of chicory, she reads her horoscope from yesterday again. *Life unfurls around you, beneath your feet, above your head. Accept it in whatever shape it is offered. Heels and toes are vulnerable spots.* Gloria lays the paper down. Can the orgy of violence and distress she overheard last night be described as *life unfurling*? It sounded like a massacre. She reflects on the article's astrological wisdom as she cleans up the squirrels' leavings. Hearing the garbage truck pull up, she runs barefoot outside without a thought for either her heels or her toes. In the half-light, the truck slows with a wheezing rumble. The garbage man, who looks to be a century and a half old, empties Gloria's trash can into the hopper, then gives a cheerful whistle for the driver to continue. But another whistle, a shriller one, interrupts him. Eunice appears on her porch and, with extraordinary precision and strength, hurls her bag directly into the container under the trashman's approving gaze.

"Bang on target, Nini!"

"Have a good day!"

Grinning like someone who has just hit a home run, Eunice turns, only to catch sight of Gloria.

"Oh!" she exclaims. "You're up early—good thing! I've got plans for you today."

Gloria invites her inside. She offers Eunice some chicory tea, which her neighbour accepts with a grimace, then a bowl of Cream of Wheat that Eunice stares at blankly.

"You read the horoscope? Let's see what it says . . . *Aries: Mysteries abound this season. Your questions will find answers where they themselves emerged. Lucky numbers: two, eighteen, and thirty-three.* A lotta nonsense!"

"I'm curious about the astrologist. Father Pontchartrain . . ."

"It's a buncha lies. There's only one way to get fate to talk. And that's what we're gonna do. Get dressed, neighbour, we're off to investigate. We're gonna find your little girls."

* * *

Night is still moulding the air as they step back outside. Birds chirp incessantly as though it's their responsibility to hoist the sun above the city. Eunice walks at a good clip, barely noticing the two hares like spectres on Avenue Clyde.

"You seem kinda sluggish," she says after a while.

"I didn't sleep too well. Did you hear, last night?"

"What?"

"The screaming…howling, really."

"Oh, the coyotes? Don't get yourself worked up, they're asleep by now."

"Coyotes? In Fort Détroit?"

"'Course! Haven't you heard 'em before? They're a real pain! At least they shut the damn dogs up."

"But it sounded like a…a woman who…"

"Yeah, I know," says Eunice, slowing down to glance at Gloria. "It wasn't though. C'mon, we're going to Marina's, then Alain's right after. They're the only ones who've got jobs, so we gotta catch 'em 'fore they leave."

Eunice's plan is to go door to door. She saw the police when they came to write a report on what happened in Judith's house. According to her, all they did was take a few pictures and notes.

"Even if they did speak to the neighbours, they wouldn't've got much. Not many people round here like talking to the cops. Me and my dad were okay with it, but there wasn't much we could tell 'em. We were at the hospital when it happened. My dad had a weak chest, we spent the day there. He was always sick," she adds as if by way of apology or to underline the inevitability of his passing.

Gloria notices an alignment of the dandelions in the

cracked pavement that forms something like an arrow pointing north.

"Did you know them well? My daughter and granddaughters?"

"So-so. I'd often hear Judith singing. Other'n that, she wasn't too talkative, as you can imagine. The little ones a bit more. Always busy the older one was, wiping stuff up, she's the one kept things clean. The little one was more on the wild side."

"Wild side?"

"She did whatever she felt like. Marched to the beat of her own drummer, as they say. Her sister was the only one could make her stay on the straight and narrow. She sure listened to her ... Like two bum cheeks in the same pair of underpants, those two."

Gloria doesn't have time to ask anything more. They've reached a house somewhat more spruced-up than the others. The unwarped boards, the clean white, the doorknob shining like an oft-touched object. A tall brunette opens the door. She's wearing a mouse-grey suit and tired high heels. Behind her, a young girl is busy buttoning up her school uniform.

"Hi, Marina. Hi, Lili. This is Gloria, Judith's mom."

Immediately, Marina's face crumples like a map being folded. Her heart, too, must often be touched.

"Her two grandkids have been missing since the day ... well, the day of the murder," Eunice explains. "We're making the rounds of the neighbourhood to find out if anyone saw anything. It was April twenty-fifth, you might remember. A Thursday."

Marina shakes her head as she looks at Gloria. "I'm so sorry. It's awful what happened. I'd often see your little ones.

Their school was near where I work. They were always outside, you'd've sworn there weren't any teachers there."

"There never were," Eunice interjects.

"Sometimes I'd give 'em a few bucks for their lunch. You know how skinny they were, you'd've sworn they never ate."

Beside her, Gloria could almost hear Eunice choke back the words, "They never did either."

"As nice as could be, mind you. The youngest, Mathilda, had quite the personality. In a fight, I'd see her get all feisty, don't mess with me like. But good at bottom, you could tell," she's quick to add.

"And what about April twenty-fifth?" Eunice reminds her.

"I saw Judith on her porch on my way to work. I remember 'cause that's what you always say to yourself after, 'I just saw her not six hours ago, how can this be...' She waved at me and looked...uh...tired, ya know? I didn't see hide nor hair of the girls, not here, not at school. I figgered they'd been placed somewhere. I didn't know they'd gone missing. It breaks my heart."

"Nothing strange or suspicious in the days before?"

"Well..."

Marina looks at Gloria, then at Eunice, then at her worn-out shoes.

"No need to beat round the bush, Marina. Gloria knows her daughter was a user."

Gloria stiffens; Marina steps forward, half-closing the door behind her as though to shield her daughter from the conversation.

"Well, uh," Marina continues, "you know how it is, she was messed up, weird people'd drop by all the time, the little girls suffered. You know how it is."

"If you think of anything else, come find us. Gloria's here for a good spell."

Returning down the walkway, Eunice glances at Gloria. "You didn't know…'bout your daughter…?"

"I had a suspicion," she says quietly. "There were too many needles for it to have been just that one week."

"But before? You didn't know?"

"We weren't in touch much anymore."

After a few steps, Gloria stops. "Wait! Why didn't we ask her daughter? She must go to the same school as Cassandra and Mathilda."

"Uh-uh. Marina's little one goes to a private school in the suburbs, like three-quarters of the city's kids. She hardly spends any time in the neighbourhood."

They make their way past the lots with their straggly yards. Here, no one mows their lawn anymore. Lawn-mowing is an act that belongs to another world, where the border between the domesticated and the wild is well defined. At her daughter's place, there's not even any grass left.

Eunice points at another house. Its paint has peeled off so much it almost looks iridescent. The minute they approach, a huge dog runs out from the backyard barking. Immediately, a baritone voice shuts it down. "Hugo! Be quiet!"

Alain steps out onto the porch. Seeing him, you'd never guess he'd have a voice that deep and resonant. He has a slight build and a youthful face despite his wrinkles, which are forgotten the minute he engages.

Eunice exclaims, "Phew, we caught you before you headed out to work."

Alain laughs. He doesn't work anymore, he was laid off two weeks ago. "Looks like the shop's about to close.

They've kept on twenty employees for the sake of appearances."

Alain saw nothing out of the ordinary at Judith's, either in the days before she died or those following. "There was a big party o' malefactors 'bout a week after, but I figger it was just more of the usual. The thrill of an empty house."

His dog looks like a cross between a boxer and a dragon. It circles Gloria, whining. Alain sends it round to the backyard. "You should ask Raquel. Last time I saw her, it seems to me she told a story 'bout Judith's girls."

They find the old woman in her backyard, bending over green arrows sprouting from the soil. One after another, Raquel grabs hold and, in one quick tug, snaps them off at ground level. Catching sight of her visitors, her body unfolds like a rusty pocket knife. With her right eye shut tight to keep out the sun, she raises a shoot to her mouth and bites down.

"Asparagus already?" Eunice asks.

"Uh-huh. End of May's asparagus season."

Raquel rolls her *r* as though its taste was particularly delicious. She holds two shoots out to Eunice. "Give one to your friend," she orders.

Gloria receives the asparagus the way she would a flower, delicately.

"Go on, give it a taste," Raquel urges. "It helps you pee!"

Although she has no real desire to eat a soil-spattered vegetable this early in the morning, Gloria obeys with the docility of a three-year-old. Chewing on her own crunchy stem, Eunice explains the reason for their visit. Right away, Raquel's eyes light up. "Oh, yes. I saw the two little girls one day in April. About a week after I caught sight of Nain Rouge."

"Nain Rouge?"

Raquel turns to look at Gloria with piercing eyes. "The red dwarf who foretells catastrophes."

Eunice lets out an exasperated sigh. "Local folklore," she clarifies. "And the little ones?"

"They were in the fields wearing big backpacks. Running away."

Eunice ponders this, her brow broader in the sunlight. "Not necessarily...Maybe they were off to the laundromat."

Raquel sends her a stern glare. "Girl, I've been round long enough to know the difference between a trip to launder clothes and a couple of runaways."

"Okay. Thanks, Madame Raquel."

"They were heading west."

"Uh-huh."

"Walking real fast."

"Perfect, thanks."

"Don't mention it. They were decent little girls—a bit wild, but decent. And you," she continues, addressing Eunice, "how're you doing without your father? Finally getting a bit of rest?"

Eunice shoots her a look of outrage.

"Hey, there's no crime in saying it! Old people are a source of all kinds of trouble! I should know. Listen, you come see me, I'll get rid of those knots for you," she adds, wiggling her crooked fingers.

"You're...a masseuse?" Gloria asks.

"No, 'course not. Look at me, I couldn't massage so much as a worm. I've got the gift in my hands is all."

Then, her eyes like a vise on Gloria, she adds, "You'll come too. You've taken on way too much grief."

A flustered Gloria joins Eunice on the sidewalk.

"Crazy old bat," Eunice mutters.

Gloria looks at her, eyebrows raised. "She doesn't look all that crazy to me."

"Eating raw asparagus, really!" Eunice stops, her gaze frank. "Raquel is one to exaggerate. She earned her living using the 'gift in her hands' on all the fellas in Fort Détroit—it was johns she had, not patients. I've got serious doubts 'bout her powers as a healer. And I'd take anything she says with a grain of salt. Who knows, maybe all she saw was your girls taking out the garbage and she turned that into two runaways."

* * *

Next, they find the nurse Theophilus, busy tending to the wound of a man who looks to be in his fifties. A crackling of violin music comes from the back room, providing a soundtrack to the caregiver's gestures. Before his next patient's turn, Theo confirms the decline that Judith and her family had experienced over the past months and advises Gloria to go to the police station in person.

"You'll get nowhere by phone. They don't make much of an effort."

"Too busy bashing our young'uns!" his patient sputters.

The other rounds aren't that helpful. Two women in their mid-thirties won't even answer their questions. The larger of the two, whom Eunice calls Block, fires a hostile look at Gloria, stating she knows nothing. The last house, belonging to a man named Jonah, is empty. Eunice tells Gloria she should try back later. "Used to teach elementary school. I think he and Judith shot up together. He knew the family well. Might be of some help."

Gloria steps inside as though she'd never been in her house before. The holes in the wall stare back at her, weeping an ochre seepage, the damaged ceiling resembles pockmarked skin. Even the smell contradicts everything she has tried to persuade herself of since her arrival. The stench of shit, urine, and mould has been erased, but something lingers underneath, a sour, pungent odour. Gloria breaks into sobs that engulf her like a landslide. The world turns muddy and blurred. The weight of the Great Lakes, of straits laden with heavy metals, of five weeks of paralysis, and of a lifetime of passivity hits her. She finds herself on her knees, mouth stretched wide as though trying to swallow the horror.

She remains there for a long time, until the angle of daylight changes. When she finally gets to her feet, the morphology of her body has changed, her limbs no longer fit together the way they used to. A dislocation or shortening, a slight shift in every fundamental axis. Little by little, sounds rise from the ground where they'd been tethered by pain. A creaking, the wind, her breath. The words of the ghosts upstairs. Slowly, she stands, and, for the first time since returning to Judith's place, she climbs the stairs.

Once on the landing, she catches a glimpse of something moving at the window, a white, winged body—an almost-angel, if not for the odd filth coating its pallor. A stunned Gloria rubs her eyes, but when she opens them again, she sees nothing but a cottony sky and butterflies chasing each other.

The three bedrooms are almost bare. Gone are the mirrors, trinkets, vanity, and rug she remembers from her last trip to Judith's fifteen years ago. The pink room has not a single piece of furniture left and is no longer really pink. In the two other rooms, a mattress lies on each floor. One is stained, with rumpled sheets surrounded by cigarette butts. Her daughter's. The other bed is clean, well-made, its blue quilt without a single crease. Two pillows touch at its head. The girls slept here together. The image forms a bubble in her mind. In an attempt to curb her anguish, she walks over to the closet. Empty hangers, a pair of rubber sandals with a broken strap, an old ballcap. Next, she heads for the half-staved-in dresser. The drawers stick out like soldiers saluting. Like the closet, they have been emptied.

In a sudden frenzy, Gloria races downstairs. She grabs her travel bag still full of her belongings. Back upstairs, she throws her clothes into the dresser and slams the already bashed-in drawers. She throws her bag to the back of the closet and leaves to fetch a mop and broom. For three hours, she scrubs the floorboards furiously. She rolls her daughter's sheets into a ball, which she stuffs into a garbage bag that she throws down the stairs. She opens wide the big window and, without hesitating, tips the mattress outside. Once everything is clean, she tackles the main floor. She pulls every container of rotten food from the refrigerator, then scrubs it down. The oven, the cupboards, and the counters are scoured as well. Once the dirt is gone and the floors have changed colour and the secrets that haunted every corner have vanished, only one room remains.

Gloria stands for several minutes in the doorway to the bathroom. The floor is covered in footprints going every which way. All have the same sole in different sizes. The police seem to have spent a good deal of time here. With the same effort required to face a headwind, Gloria forces her gaze onto the tub. Neither dirty nor clean, tarnished with age. Like a huge seashell, an open, empty palm. The image that has haunted her for weeks lies inside. The naked, lifeless body of her daughter. Rather than let the apparition fade, this time Gloria allows herself to look long and hard at every detail. Her protruding ribs, the skin of her stomach stretched by the memory of pregnancies, her thighs, beige and wiry. Slowly these features are superimposed on the contours of a pink, plump child. As though opening a book forgotten for decades, Gloria bows to the feeling that used to come over her when her daughter was little, one that all mothers experience at some point. The conviction, watching one's child, that one is witnessing a lifeform more alive than any other. A surplus of life concentrated, against all logic, in a tinier being. An observation accompanied by its opposite: The fear of that child dying. The very idea that such an exponential life could come to an end. Gloria blinks back the tears that threaten to attack her cheeks, and Judith disappears. Above the sink, the mirror sends back a reflection of the full moon of Gloria's face, her thick curls. Stars in the corners of her eyes, unfathomable blue beneath.

She weeps softly as she turns on the taps, first the hot then the cold. Her clothes fall, loose, her skin doesn't shiver. When the tub is three-quarters full, she slides into its warmth with reverence and apprehension. The water caresses her chin. She says, "Judith. Speak to me."

Then she ducks her head underwater and listens.

A few hours later, crickets chirp and chime, sounding like a flute crossed with a guitar. Gloria's hair drips onto the linoleum as she considers tackling the last stage in her overhaul. A brushed-metal object no taller than a bouquet of flowers, as deep as an open fault. In the darkness, it reflects nothing; a dull presence, impossible to interpret. She had hoped to find a place for her daughter's urn—the living room shelf, the back of a closet, six feet underground—and bring this day to an end, to a verdict. But all is still left hanging.

A noise from the backyard scatters her thoughts. Facing the night, the windowpane sends her back a darker copy of the kitchen's interior. She opens the door and sees, quite distinctly, Judith's mattress floating above the fields, farther and farther down the trail, before vanishing into the night.

* * *

A defining feature of Fort Détroit is the park along the Rivière Rouge. Gloria has no idea how she made her way here; it's more than a half-hour walk from the house. The huge park teems with murmurings. Beaks that snap, teeth that bite down on thin air, the spirits of women who have left it all behind. The vibration of a never-seen river. Overhead, the sky hangs low like a bird of prey about to claim a life. Gloria watches as the storm's descent batters the landscape. Grasses and leaves flip and spin. The downpour seems to drown out shrill cries that sound like those of children leaping into water. A legion of snails files out from the woods. Gradually, Gloria realizes she isn't wet; she's standing beneath a bower. Once again, she has no memory of taking shelter here. An image comes to her of a gazebo with long spider legs racing over to position itself above her head. She smiles. Once the rain shower has passed, she walks home down streets smelling of wet pavement and the pollen of birch trees. Then, increasingly, of smoke. As she draws closer to Avenue Clyde, the air thickens with it. Fires are an almost daily occurrence in Fort Détroit, yet none has ever broken out so close to the yellow house, at least not since her arrival.

She steps up her pace, feeling guilty as though she has just skipped school. When she reaches Clyde, her gaze is drawn immediately to the other end of the street, mesmerized by the blazing inferno. The flames give off so much light that all else is obliterated: the trees, the street, the houses. The yellow house is invisible, too, engulfed in red and orange. A police car with a dented fender is parked diagonally across the road. Running now, Gloria reaches a small crowd that, from a distance, could be mistaken for a huddle of concerned neighbours. Up close, it instead resembles a group of vacationers attending an outdoor concert. Lawn chairs have been pulled into the middle of the street. Chips and beer are passed from hand to hand. Children run everywhere, brandishing licorice sticks. The intensity of the fire, the sorts of materials it feeds on, and for how long are all topics for discussion. The police officers, meanwhile, lean back against their vehicle, impassive as they observe the scene.

"No firefighters?" Gloria asks as she joins the others.

"We called 'em an hour ago," Alain answers. "They've only got half a dozen trucks to cover the whole city. The storm set off fires all over the place."

"The police show up for form's sake," adds Theo, "but unless they can piss farther than us mere mortals, they're not good for much."

"At least they're not beating up innocent bystanders," Alain says under his breath.

Gloria looks at the motley and unruffled crowd. They have left a distance of several metres between them and the officers. The memory of riots and ongoing police abuse is never far off. On the horizon, plumes of yellow smoke rise here and there. Everything is burning.

"You're lucky," Raquel sputters, chewing on a licorice stub. "Your house is set back from the street. Fifteen feet closer to the sidewalk, and its front would've been scorched."

Squinting, Gloria can just make out the shape of gables and windows reflecting the wild bursts of flame. Her house has been spared. The dead house across the street has disappeared in one seething roar. Remembering the forecast of heat from this morning's horoscope, she drops into the chair Theo offers her and, like the others, gives herself over to the spectacle.

* * *

The flowers that grow along the railway tracks are almost painfully beautiful. Amid the mineral heat of trains and the smell of tar, they rise next to where carriages pass, tousled and ardent, inundating embankments, transforming silence into a whispering.

Gloria would have liked to stop and pick a bouquet, but, in a hurry to get to where they're going, Eunice seems indifferent to the surfacing of yellow hearts and white corollas. She's busy cursing the authorities.

"We asked them for spots to cross the railroad. Twenty years later, we've still gotta carry wire cutters in our purses to get through fences."

Gloria looks left then right. Judging by the number of breaches in the chain-link fence, there's little chance they'll need Eunice's tool. The tiniest lane has its own private access.

"Wouldn't it have been easier to just call Solomon?" Gloria asks as she steps over a pile of old newspapers.

"Uh-huh, but I've been without electricity since yesterday, so no juice ..." Eunice responds, waving her cracked cellphone.

On a utility pole, Gloria's attention is caught by a word in red capitals: *MISSING*. Her eyes widen in astonishment. From the coarse-grained paper, Mathilda and Cassandra look out at her as though through a dirty screen.

"Francelin," states Eunice, answering the question Gloria has yet to formulate. "He nailed some seventy of 'em up in the city."

"That's kind of him."

"But maybe not all that helpful," adds Eunice, pointing out a half-dozen older posters calling for the return of others with tattered faces and scribbled names. "No news yet, I'm guessing, 'bout your little girls?"

"No. I mean, yes. Not much. After talking to the neighbours, I went through the girls' room."

Eunice gives a slight nod. Overhead, a squirrel sets a young linden tree to quivering.

"Their drawers were empty. The closet too. I don't think they'd have taken the time to gather together their clothes if they'd been kidnapped. Or if..."

"Uh-huh."

"Raquel might be right. They could have run away."

Eunice gives her head a vigorous shake as though to reorder the information inside. "If so, that changes everything."

"They could have gone anywhere. They could have taken a bus to Toronto, Montreal. Or to the US."

"I can guarantee you those girls had no passport. Or even a bus ticket ... I don't know where they'd have come up with the dough. If they did run away, they can't be far."

A warm wind gusts behind them, causing Gloria's wide purple skirt to billow like a parachute. The two women come to a stop by a street more well-off than the others, and Eunice seems almost disappointed to see her cutters won't be necessary. A large gap has already been opened in the fence. Someone has even posted a sign that reads: *Perlemère*. They've reached Solomon's neighbourhood.

If the gardener's home was a person, it would be schizophrenic royalty. Despite its wear and tear, the Victorian residence still has a majestic look, yet Solomon has built all kinds of annexes out of ill-assorted scraps: recycled planks, sheets of plastic, cardboard, bits of string. The single-gabled roof, apparently destroyed by fire, has been replaced with Plexiglas panels. Through every window, green stems are visible, some of which escape through broken panes, along with a blinding light likely powered by a small wind turbine attached to the chimney stack. The whole place is a many-storeyed greenhouse.

"In the fall, we all get together here to do the canning. You'll see, it's fun working as a group. Tomatoes, pickles, fruit in syrup…"

Gloria follows Eunice along the south side toward a glassed-in shed. She steps inside without knocking. Immediately, the smell of black loam envelops them. The air is damp and astringent, almost green with chlorophyll. Hundreds of sprouts at various stages of development surround them. Little fairies made of sap.

"Solomon!" cries Eunice so loudly the fairies fold in on themselves.

The place is deserted. With an exasperated sigh, Eunice announces they will have to do the rounds of the other greenhouses to find the farmer and the tomato seedlings he promised her. Before leaving the hodgepodge house behind, she grabs a deep wheelbarrow that she pushes just as impatiently as she would walk a lazy dog.

"You know," suggests Gloria, "if you like, we could ask around about your father too. Try to find the person who ran him down."

Eunice shrugs.

"We could canvass the neighbours again," Gloria insists.

"Theo already did. No one saw a thing."

"We could call the auto repair shops. The car that hit your father must have been damaged, and there might be a mechanic who remembers working on it…"

"That's not a bad idea. Maybe. But not now. I can't do it now. Anyhow, my dad's dead. We need to focus on the living."

In the face of her friend's pragmatism, Gloria refuses to formulate or even entertain the thought that her granddaughters, too, may no longer be among the living. On the side of the road, pineapple weed—that she used to call chamomile when she was little—unfurls its delicate green hands. She picks some, rubs the round flowers between her fingers. A fragrance of apple peel fills the air.

The trail they follow ends in a huge vacant lot. In the middle stands a long shack built following the same model as the annexes to Solomon's manor: an eccentric one. Through the fogged-up Plexiglas, they can make out shapes darting about like fish in an aquarium.

"Hmm. That's not Solomon."

As they enter, they barely have time to glimpse three small heads—one black, one red, one blond. Kids. The children take to their heels, their too-big, hole-ridden clothing floating behind them, their skinny arms laden with young strawberry plants.

"Hey!" Eunice shouts.

Gloria doesn't budge. In the mind-numbing heat of the greenhouse, her heart races as the children disappear. Eunice clucks, then she grabs some strawberry plants herself and thrusts them at Gloria before taking the same number for herself.

They leave via the fields, battered by the noonday sun. A half an hour's walk later, they finally reach their destination. Gloria is parched and overheated, and Eunice is in a foul mood. A modest bungalow lies ahead, half of which seems to have been sheared off to make way for a semicircular greenhouse about fifteen metres in diameter. The second structure fits so well into the first it's as though the greenhouse sprouted from the house, an impressive outgrowth.

Solomon sits between two old men wearing patched jackets spattered with dirt. The three talk comfortably, taking sips of a sparkling drink. One of them strums a mandolin. The recently watered plants fill the greenhouse with their perfume.

"You're here! We've spent two hours looking for you! We're dead tired!"

Solomon, seemingly unperturbed by Eunice's bad mood, opens wide his arms. "Eunice! Come try our homemade kombucha! Thanks to Ulysses." He points to one of the other two men. "He used the wild cherry crop to make several gallons' worth."

After a few sips, Eunice softens and Gloria feels a spark of life returning to her very fingertips. The place is a peaceful jumble. Various canning jars border the rows of seedlings. Books, newspapers, a record player, and a tarnished trumpet take up the rest of the space. The old men smoke and laugh quietly.

Solomon introduces them. "My partners, Ulysses and Caesar. We founded the IAO."

Eunice rolls her eyes at the sheer pretentiousness of the acronym.

"The IAO?" Gloria enquires.

"The Interlopers Agricultural Organization. We've got no official authorization. We do everything on the sly. Four greenhouses in other parts of the city, plus the ones here!"

The men invite their guests to taste different greens: mustard, sorrel, watercress…Eyes closed, Gloria listens to the scrunching each mouthful makes in her head.

"We've borrowed a wheelbarrow," Eunice announces. "And a coupla strawberry plants. Till our tomatoes are ready . . ."

Solomon laughs. "Yeah, yeah, Nini, you'll get your love apples! We'll drop 'em by tomorrow."

"We saw some other folk helping themselves in your greenhouse on Rue Cécile-Tousignant," Eunice adds. "Three kids. The sight of us scared 'em off."

"Yeah. They come, they take. They're gatherers…"

"Why do they do that?" Gloria asks.

"'Cause they're hungry! There are lots of kids left to their own devices in this city. With all the cuts to child welfare…"

Gloria is dying to find out more from Solomon, but Eunice is already busy planning their day tomorrow. A draft lifts up a corner of the newspaper lying on the table. Out of habit, Gloria finds the horoscopes. *You're a skiff on a swift river, no sail or centre-board. Let yourself be swept along. Any faults in the landscape are fertile. The number fifty pro-*

vides support. Looking up, she gives a start to see Solomon beside her.

"Astrology's a lotta hogwash," he states. "To know the future, try Tarot. I'll drop by with my cards. I can guess you've got all kinds'a questions."

Gloria stares at Solomon, who gives a kindly wink before loading the tomato seedlings into the wheelbarrow. "Eunice, hon, since you're so hungry for tomatoes, take these. We'll load the rest into the pickup tomorrow."

* * *

An exhausted Gloria makes her way home, her skin stretched taut from the burning sun. She downs two tall glasses of water and fills the tub. Into the swirling eddy beneath the tap, she adds two drops of the lavender oil Ulysses gave her. Its fragrance suffuses the air. Gloria watches a few vaporous waves disappear through the open window. The room being purged of its demons.

She lowers herself into the cold water. Her sunburn stings then cools. "Judith," she whispers, and water rushes into her mouth as she speaks. Her chin is immersed, only her upper lip showing. Straddling two elements. "Did you suffer?" A tiny wavelet flows from her lips as though her voice has taken on liquid form. "I don't know if it hurts to drown." She coughs, sits up straight, and spits a stream of water into the tub. "Were you afraid?" Her feet slide along the cast-iron wall of the tub with a sonorous, underwater squeal. "Did you look him in the eye, the man who killed you? Did you fight back?" Her tears fall, their salt dissolving on contact with the bathwater. Gloria lets her head sink all the way back. Her hair fans out around her like so many plumes. In its opacity, she gives a moan that turns into a bubble, such a strange shape for affliction to take. Out of breath, she resurfaces, her face crimson. "I should have been here. Forgive me."

* * *

The field mouse is back. At first, it's the same faint sound of a nut cracking that alerts Gloria. Opening the pantry door, she sees the mouse huddled there as though braced for a blow while shielding a dust-covered almond with its body. In slow motion, Gloria takes a step back, grabs a wild cherry from the table and sets it down in front of the creature. The mouse considers the cherry, in shock, as though it's a live grenade. Gloria watches as it takes a few shaky steps forward, sniffs the fruit, then grabs it and beats a retreat to the darkest corner of the pantry. She shuts the door with a smile. The day is ending on a positive note.

However, by 2 a.m., she still hasn't slept. In a creaking crescendo, she walks down the stairs and curls up in an armchair, a cup of chicory tea in her hand. The seepage on the walls sketches a strange map devoid of topography or roads. Coupled with the cracks, it looks like directions to the dead, similar to the ones found deep inside pyramids. Instructions on how to go back in time. In a daze, Gloria gets to her feet, casts around for a piece of paper and a pencil, and carefully copies the drawing, which has almost pulled away from the wall's surface in its insistence. The minute she is done, she collapses into the chair and falls asleep. When she wakens, her first thought comes in the form of a question. Why is a sketch of the outline of Parc Rouge at her feet?

* * *

"Never forget we were two shakes away from becomin' American. The fact we didn't isn't thanks to the French. Or the English. But to the First Peoples."

This last pronouncement of Solomon's, delivered in a self-righteous tone, doesn't give rise to the epiphany he'd hoped for in his listeners. Barely sparing him a glance, his two helpers, here to plant tomatoes with him, stick to their task. Solomon doesn't lose his verve, however.

"If Pontiac hadna been such a great leader. If he hadna been the smart military strategist he was. If he hadna managed to win over Pierre-Joseph Neyon de Villiers of Fort de Chartres in Upper Louisiana. The uprising in Fort Détroit woulda fallen flat, and the Brits would've been sittin' pretty."

"Same as always," Ulysses whispers into Gloria's ear. "The minute he starts working, he's off on another history craze. Hey, Eunice's here now," he adds, glancing behind him. "This should be fun."

Gloria smiles. She waves at Eunice pushing a wheelbarrow full of rusty garden tools.

"Here's everything I had in the shed. I'm donating the whole lot to the 'IAO,'" she announces in a wry tone.

Then, turning to Gloria, she exclaims, "Not getting your hands dirty?"

Gloria brandishes two bottles of lemonade and a box of cookies. "I'm in charge of supplies."

"Or else," Solomon continues, raising his voice slightly, "the Treaty of Paris of 1783 would've looked a whole lot different. The Americans would've insisted like nobody's business on gettin' Fort Détroit. A stronghold on a river between two Great Lakes, you bet! But by then, the place had already carved out quite a reputation for itself. The British were given such a rough time for trying to hang on to it, no one else wanted to touch it."

Beneath the shovels, the earth is warm and ashen; it opens like a pair of jaws to clamp down on the plants' tiny roots.

"People thought Fort Détroit was protected by an alliance of demons: the Catholics' Satan, the Odawa's Wendigo, and Nain Rouge, or the Demon of the Strait. The Americans wanted nothin' to do with it."

Having listened without a word up to that point, Eunice suddenly looks up. "Come off it! As if the Americans would've given up Fort Détroit 'cause of some superstition! If I remember my history lessons rightly from school, it wasn't the Treaty of Paris that decided the city's fate, it was the Treaty of London. Everything revolved round business. My dad always said, 'They gambled the city away like a pile o' poker chips!'"

"But why Fort Détroit and not some other place, huh? There were a coupla tempting forts bordering the lakes back then. The way I see it, there's a spell been cast on the city, a kinda charm—"

"'Cause of where it's located! For the love of…Fort Détroit is *north* of Essex County! Hard not to see it as Canadian."

"How d'ya explain them leavin' the Francophones in peace for the next hundred years?"

"No one caught onto the fact that there was money to be made here! But as soon as industry started up, they saw the benefit of being on the lakeshores."

"Me, I still think it's the First Nations' resilience that allowed Fort Détroit to become a Francophone town—"

"British."

"—a site of resistance and liberty!"

"You kidding me? The city stands on land stolen from the First Peoples, plain and simple. Ya don't think it's a bit much lumping the Odawa, the French, and the English together on the same team?"

"But they were! From the get-go, Cadillac partnered with half a dozen nations—"

"And made them move to other territories. He cooked up an alliance that'd serve his own ends and did it all backward. When it started going sideways, he burned down his allies' camps."

"That wasn't him, it was Dubuisson."

"Same diff. It was his fault to begin with."

"I'm not denyin' it. But you've gotta give Caesar what is Caesar's!"

"I want no part of this," yells Caesar from the other end of the field.

"Having the First Peoples involved changed everything for our town."

"Involved, exploited . . ." mutters Eunice. "Seems to me what it comes down to is, if a city's founded on a crime—"

"Détroit is founded on a dream as much as a crime…"

Eunice snorts. Behind her, the two old fellows nod, applauding both Solomon's flights of oratory and Eunice's comebacks. Ulysses winks at Gloria, then he points to the sky where two hawks wheel overhead, tracing the symbol for infinity. Soon they'll return to their nesting boxes on the sides of the abandoned skyscrapers they've claimed as cliffs. On the ground, Eunice and Solomon continue debating while Caesar, slow but efficient, finishes a row of tomatoes and starts down a row of snap peas. Suddenly, as though in unspoken accord, the two history buffs fall silent. Solomon surveys the field.

"Raspberries'd be fun."

Eunice looks in the same direction, toward the imaginary bush full of berries. Like Solomon, she seems to have reached some abstract limit after her deep dive into the past. Beyond the urban grasslands, the Tour de Lys, crooked and eternal, seems to sway in the wind.

"Yeah, I'd like that."

Gloria pours them some lemonade. The bubbles in their glasses strive to spell out the rest of the story.

* * *

Their bags are strangely heavy given their meagre finds. The weight of Gloria's on her shoulder seems bent on dragging her to the ground, into the burrows of groundhogs that think they're invisible. As for Eunice, she curses the box whose edge keeps digging in to her back. Gloria has shifted the groceries around three times trying to remedy the situation, to no avail. Something is determined to prod her friend.

"At least we found bananas. I haven't had a banana since Papa turned sixty-eight. I remember, I'd wanted to make banana splits for everyone with homemade ice cream. But the power went out the night before. By morning, the cream had dripped all over my freezer. I ended up making milkshakes instead. I even gave some to your little girls, poor cuties, drooling as they watched us through the fence…"

As with any other time she mentions Gloria's family, Eunice breaks off, hesitant, not knowing whether her anecdotes help or hurt Gloria. As if the city wanted to join in the conversation, suddenly one of Francelin's *MISSING* posters appears on a fence post. Warped by rain, the two girls' faces are blurred, unreadable. Gloria takes a deep breath. The smell of ripe bananas makes her heart ache.

Their rounds of the grocery stores, more ambitious than usual, had led them to a grocer who sold them the last of his imported fruit, plus some flour, sugar, and other simple foodstuffs. The two women head home under the setting sun, their legs worn out from their day-long trek. Overhead, a railway bridge covered with colourful knit fabric vibrates, indicating either a train's approach or another's passing a few kilometres farther down. Unless it's telling a tale of stoic porters and hobos drunk on space. Wool tends to encourage sentimentality.

On Avenue Clyde, Eunice pulls something out of her pocket that Gloria takes for a ball at first. With a triumphant air, she holds it up to her friend's face. The orange is plump, pock-marked, luminous. As the peel tears off, it exudes a bright mist, an almost tart perfume.

"I didn't see any oranges there," Gloria mumbles round the pulp filling her mouth.

"They were hidden. Behind the counter."

Gloria chokes as she swallows, "You stole this from the grocer?"

Eunice dismisses her neighbour's scruples with a wave. "At the prices he charges for his 'grosseries,' he's the thief!"

Gloria is about to protest, but a cry interrupts her. It's coming from Eunice's backyard. Gloria follows her friend between the houses.

"Ugh, another brawl between malefactors!" Eunice exclaims.

Under her clothes horse, two scrawny figures are fighting over a pale, limp object that looks like the body of a ghost.

"They're after my threads—stealing 'em right off the clothesline, damn it all to hell!"

She races over, shouting and throwing orange peels, and the two intruders take off into the fields where their tattered shapes dissolve. As though to ensure their total evaporation, Eunice keeps up the chase. Gloria watches them for a little while. Gradually, another presence makes itself felt, warm and stocky. Eyes locked on her. She scans her surroundings then spots it. A dog, a massive pitbull, its right ear torn off. Gloria feels her heart skip a beat. The animal's powerful jaw is open, its muscles bulge. But it doesn't move, it just stares at her, all-knowing. Gloria raises an arm, takes a step in its direction. Immediately, the dog slips into the tall grasses. Just like the two thieves, its body vanishes; the grasses don't swish, no rustling is heard. The vacant field has swallowed the dog whole.

* * *

Tremors traverse the evening air. On the steps to the back porch, Gloria sets out the five green apples she unearthed at the grocery store. Their taut skin shines, turning them into five green lights burning in the twilight. When full darkness descends, Gloria hides behind the door. The moon illuminates the yard, the wilted tulip, the mound of ashes. Shards of broken bottles glisten like pearls on the bed of the sea.

Night stretches over Fort Détroit, and, seated in her small straight-backed chair, Gloria slips from awake to asleep, asleep to awake, without pause, as though the transition from one state to another were nothing but a single sustained breath. Around ten, she discovers there are just three apples left. The air thrums with silvery humidity. Bats fly into the void. An hour later, two apples remain. A fierce howling sounds—a dog hurling abuse at a coyote or vice versa—then a metallic din as of iron animals losing parts of themselves. By 5 a.m., there's nothing left but a single apple core nibbled in uniform wedges. Birds shower dawn with the juice of apples and with their song. Gloria stretches in the warmth of the rising sun. The children glimpsed at Solomon's have eaten her fruit and spat out their seeds under the light of the moon—she's sure of it. The sun's rays lay an egg in the middle of the fields. In June's early swelter, flowers open to summer.

* * *

Always straining in the fields, Solomon's broad hands transform when they touch a deck of cards. Knots disappear. Far from shoots and fruit, his skin gives off its own perfume of mint leaves and rainwater.

"The cards," he explains, "will hear your question, spoken out loud or not."

The backs of the cards are an oxblood red with gold illumination. The deck looks to be a thousand years old.

"They were my great-great-grandmother's," says Solomon. "She predicted the city's fate. The uprising, the epidemics, the damage, the austerity. The exodus, the children orphaned by drugs. Even the return of wildlife. My ancestor was a great fortune teller."

With his right hand, Solomon divides the deck in three. "Do you have your question ready?"

Gloria closes her eyes. She thinks of Judith and of her

killer still at large. Her forehead burns at the thought of Cassandra and Mathilda. They are the ones she must find first. She nods. In one move, Solomon fans out the cards. Outside, a cardinal brightens the grey of the sky as though its trill could lift up the horizon.

With great care, Solomon chooses a card, which he turns over and lays on the table. A youth, holding two disks. The second card reveals another young-looking figure, this one armed with a sword.

"Hey now, that didn't take long! Your granddaughters are here."

Her expression unguarded, Gloria peers at the two figures. Solomon's index finger drops onto a third card. Five men bearing staffs look to be confronting each other. The fourth card represents a moon above and dogs below, and the last shows a group of individuals surrounded by soaring circles.

Even though Solomon has not yet spoken, Gloria feels like crying, as if just looking for an answer has changed the course of events.

"The Knight of Pentacles and the Knight of Swords. Called 'princesses' or 'girls' in the Waite-Smith tradition. No doubt about it, these two are Mathilda and Cassandra. And they're shown upside-down. A sign of material and physical insecurity and uncertainty with respect to the future awaiting the Knight of Pentacles ... As for the other card, the Knight of Swords, it represents impatience, impulsiveness. An excess of poorly channelled energy. A good fit, don't you think?"

"I can't say. I don't know them that well."

Solomon turns back to the remaining cards. His chest expands with each breath, like shutters opening and closing.

"I think the Tarot wanted to show us the people first, next the situation. The Five of Wands'd be the past. Some kinda struggle in a just cause. The idea of a problem to be solved, a tough knot to unravel. Guilt too."

Next Solomon's hand stops above the Moon card. "The Moon is a Major Arcana. That means it's powerful, defining a whole period. In this case, it's about the present. About instability, isolation. Emotions have taken over. What we see is an illusion, and whatever we don't see is vast. The Moon tells us to follow our instincts and find ourselves again."

Gloria feels as though there's an eel spinning inside her head. Across from her, Solomon's solid, patient bulk still leans over the Tarot.

"The Ten of Cups is a great card to end with. It shows a positive force in the future, a collective force. The feeling of being at home with others and with one's self. This is all good. Very good."

He looks up at Gloria, who is anxiously fidgeting with her cup.

"It's hard to know if the cards are about you or your little ones," Solomon adds. "Probably all three of you. And maybe Judith too."

The fortune teller lays his broad hand over Gloria's.

"Something seems clear though. That they're alive. The way I see it, those little ones had a rough life, but they were survivors. You've got every reason to hope. Keep lookin' for 'em, Gloria."

Gloria takes a sip of tea, yet the lump in her throat remains. A blade has lodged itself where her voice quivers. Going slowly, Solomon picks up the cards. One escapes and briefly hovers above the table, levitating. It drops with something like a snap.

"Huh, the Tarot's got somethin' to add. What's this?"

Cautiously, he reveals the image of a man tiptoeing away, his arms loaded down with five swords, his head turned to look back at two more swords still planted in the ground.

"Hmm. The Seven of Swords. The card of thieves."

* * *

When she was two, Judith began to eat dirt.

This was well after the stage when babies tend to discover the world through their mouths, lovingly coating everything they touch in a film of saliva. At two, Judith already knew how to walk and could pronounce more or less distinctly a few dozen words. One of them was "dir."

The minute she was set outside, she'd trot toward the flowerbeds, singing to herself. Her chestnut locks bounced with each step, her hand-sewn dress waltzed round her plump calves. Then she'd plunge her hand into the earth and shove a big fistful of humus into her mouth. Rushing over, it would already be too late for Gloria to intervene.

Gloria monitored her closely. Their outings to the backyard resembled a strange shadow game. The second the small shadow bent over, the tall shadow with the same curly locks, the same long dress, followed suit. If one put a hand on the ground, the other did likewise to stop her.

But Judith was inventive, and it didn't take long before she discovered the potted plants inside. The minute her mother turned her back, she'd feast on the dry earth of the cacti and the root-veined dirt of the spider plants. She even stole spoons from the kitchen to better stuff herself. Gloria would find her hiding behind armchairs, her face smeared with mud, neither joyful nor guilty, just content, her strange hunger sated. It went on till Gloria no longer knew whether to laugh or to scold. She decided to ignore her. What would have happened had she insisted on keeping her daughter from eating dirt? Would Judith have better understood the limits to her desires? Gloria ponders the question under the harsh neon lights of Station 38.

After an endless wait, a drawn-looking sergeant comes over to greet her. Straight off, he announces there are no new leads in the investigation into her daughter's murder. He pronounces the word *investigation* hesitantly, as though the term doesn't exactly fit the work the police carried out after Judith's death.

"I'm here about my granddaughters," replies Gloria. "I want to know where the investigation is at into their disappearance."

The sergeant looks at her for a moment, of two minds. Then he leaves the room and returns with two skinny folders that he lays down silently. "No new leads there either."

"Could I see the files?"

"They're confidential."

Gloria would stake her life on the sergeant having brought out two empty file folders, just to make himself look good, and on no investigation having ever been launched into the girls' disappearance. And on the fact that they've either been forgotten, like Solomon's little gatherers, or simply ignored.

"They've been missing since the day their mother died," she nevertheless insists. "No one I've talked to has seen them. Can you really not tell me anything?"

The officer picks up the thicker file on Gloria's daughter and studies it more closely. Then his index finger drops onto the blue ink of a sentence.

"One thing. They're the ones who called for help. That means they were the first on the crime scene."

Gloria opens her mouth. She has to remember to breathe.

"When the officers arrived, the house was empty. Except, of course, for the victim."

Tears streak Gloria's cheeks. The mention of her granddaughters, alive and devastated, is shattering.

"If you like, you could try to track down the recording of their call. The emergency call centre is located at this address."

Gloria takes the card he holds out, as agitated as she is incredulous at such negligence. As though reading her thoughts, the sergeant resumes. "Listen, send me a picture, I'll circulate it among our fellows on the beat."

Gloria gives a curt nod and gets to her feet. She knows now that she will not be sending this man a picture and will never expect anything more from this place. On her way out, she finds herself face to face with a raven carrying something resembling a smooth stone in its beak. At the sight of her, it throws its head back, swallows, and flies off. Gloria could swear it has just ingested the philosopher's stone. She imagines tracking down the bird and killing it. She'd slit open its belly and clutch the warm stone in her hand. Then time would fold back in on itself, and the stone would return the missing to life.

* * *

Standing on the sidewalk, Gloria waits for her shadow to vanish from beneath her feet. Then she crosses the street to call on Jonah, the neighbour who, according to Eunice, hung out at Judith's house. The shutters are closed; the doorbell doesn't work. Gloria strikes the door softly with the flat of her hand. The lower portion is covered in scratch marks. Some animal's endless plea. The seconds trickle past. Gloria insists. She's made of the same fabric as whatever creature left the mark of its claws behind. Powerless but impatient. Inside, shapes move like ink flowing through water. Maybe someone's smoking, lying on the floor. Spirits dancing. Finally, she retraces her steps. In the yard, a pile of old tires devours all light.

Setting foot on the pavement, Gloria senses a rumbling, an echo of the morning's rain shower. Her feet tingle. The underground current makes her think of Mathilda and Cassandra. She's not even sure she would recognize them in person. She only saw the youngest once, and that was over seven years ago. But she is sure she would sense a vibration similar to this one, intensely familiar.

At the end of the street, she catches sight of Raquel, who's dragging a shopping cart, rings sparkling on her fingers like burning embers. Gloria lowers her gaze. Something inside her head is shining back.

* * *

Lac Sainte-Claire is itself a creature of the wild, a world where the synthetic and the organic commingle. At this early hour, it looks like a sheet of quicksilver being shaken by invisible hands. Then, as morning brings heat and light, plastic objects, immersed steel structures, and an oily sheen become visible on its surface. Large ships advance in cavernous silence, waterfowl rise above the horizon.

Mindful of what she learned as a child, Gloria is careful not to say a word. Nor does she watch Eunice and Francelin with their fishing rods as their eyes probe the lake. Sounds rise from its depths, submerged organ notes, giant drums tumbling in the currents along the lakebed.

Gloria can scarcely remember how they got here. Francelin showed up at dawn in his old Cadillac, and, the next thing she knew, the three of them were sitting together in this rowboat. Eunice, somewhere between drowsy and watchful, alternately yawns and clears her throat. Francelin puffs away on a cigarillo and surveys the surroundings as though they belong to him. His arm, on which his vitiligo forms a meandering map, trails in the cold water. Gloria didn't feel like fishing, but, like them, she waits for the fish. For mermaids and the bodies of the drowned too; she waits for them all to resurface and tell their tale.

Suddenly, Francelin's line goes taut. The two fishers busy themselves round the rod, exchanging brief, clipped words. Eunice grabs the landing net. A large soft-bellied fish emerges, looking furious and vanquished. It thrashes around inside the net, its spasms growing slower and slower. Through the grey mesh, Gloria contemplates the creature, the last in a long line of inhabitants of this lake whose ancestors both fed the first inhabitants of the region and feasted on those of their ancestors who drowned, two ancient families giving themselves to each other, for centuries trading lives. Gloria blinks, dazzled by the sun's reflection off the water and by the fish's death throes. The others start rowing, returning the boat to the shore whose contours waver in the humid air. A storm is brewing.

On the trip home, Francelin conveys the latest news.

Word is that the wind tore three trees from the ground on Boulevard Michel, one of which knocked out the mailman. Word is that Dan Dupuits is busy restoring the Shling's sound system for concerts. Word is that Alain's dog caught a small rattlesnake. Word is that workers were seen at the foot of the Tour de Lys. Gloria lets herself be rocked by the flood of rumours. Her gaze alights on the pike in the ice bucket. Like all dead things, it seems to breathe, still so near to life. Along the window battered by rain, drops follow twisting paths. One in particular, in a corner of the glass pane, slowly changes colour. It shines red, like a wound.

* * *

"I don't understand what you turned into, Judith. I never will. It doesn't matter."

Gloria dunks her head underwater. Cold and warm currents intermingle, displacing islands, sandbars. The air is bracing when she resurfaces. "I know I've come too late. But I'm here now. For what's to be. For the girls." The water swirls as if a monster lurks beneath the surface. Gloria feels her body give in as it is sucked downward. "I think they're afraid to come home 'cause the house is haunted. But not by evil ghosts. By you. I know you're here, Judith. I know you hear me. You've got to help me. If you guide me to your girls, I promise you I'll look after them for the rest of my life. Even when they're grown, even if they leave and want nothing to do with me. I'll watch over them all the same. I'll never abandon them. I promise you. I'll help them find what they need to live. Fort Détroit isn't a dead city, it's not true that it's in ruins. It's full of life. I beg you, Judith, let me make amends. Give me a sign."

Gloria falls silent. Little by little, the bathwater grows still till it is nothing but a sheet of glass. Then, from the tap, silent until then, three successive drops. Dot-dot-dot.

* * *

Eunice bends over the strawberries. They haven't stood up well to being transplanted in the field. Gloria joins her, considers the limp leaves, the anemic flowers.

"It's my fault. I think I watered them too much," she says.

"Not any more than the curly endive, and look how great it's doing."

As though hearing her, the frisée proudly waves its leaves. Beauty queens. From the row he's busy raking, Solomon shoots an approving glance.

"We could do with some help from the nuns," Eunice adds. "You should've seen the strawberries in their garden. Had us drooling with envy in the schoolyard. The charge we'd get from stealing a few when the wimple-wearers turned their backs."

"You went to school with the nuns?"

"Like most everyone hereabouts, at least in my generation."

"The generations before too!" Solomon chimes in from the end of the field.

"Funny, I never thought of Fort Détroit as a Catholic city," Gloria says absent-mindedly as Eunice gestures wildly to get her to stop talking.

But it's too late. Solomon has already straightened up to gaze out over the vegetable garden like an orator before a full house, holding his rake like a talking stick.

"Come off it! Didn't you notice all the churches? Almost

as many as stop signs! It's part of what drew so many immigrants here. There were other big industrial centres at the time, but what made the Poles, the Irish, the Italians—maybe even your ancestors, Gloria—wanna come here to work was they could keep practising their religion in Fort Détroit."

"My family's not from here," Gloria reminds him hesitantly.

"And it's the Catholic churches, schools, and hospitals," continues Solomon, ignoring her, "that urged 'em to learn French, not English. It was 'cause of religion that French survived. You can badmouth the parish priests and nuns all you want, at least they were good on that score."

Eunice bites her lip. Gloria leads her over to the tomatoes. The Mortgage Lifter, Better Boy, and Golden Jubilee seedlings have taken root. True to their name, the Early Girls are already showing promising fruit, while the other varieties are still devoid of flowers, offering nothing but the tantalizing perfume of their leaves. Gloria pulls a few weeds, Eunice bends tenderly over each seedling, removing suckers, and Solomon ploughs on.

"At first, there was the Saint-Ours seminary founded by Bishop De La Fresnière in 1838," he states, pointing east as though the institution could be seen from where they stand. "It gave generations of young Catholics an education, in French and in Latin I'll have you know! The college burned down in 1887, was rebuilt a few years later, then had to close its doors with the ban on French education in 1912. At that stage, the priests came into play again, fighting to reverse the federal decision. Not that that solved the whole anti-Francophone issue. In the twenties, the Ku Klux Klan tried to blow the seminary up with dynamite! After years of terrorizing the Blacks, the same bozos in hoods got all stirred up seeing their friends farther west set fire to the Collège de Saint-Boniface. But the Séminaire Saint-Ours didn't succumb! It stayed standing to welcome the sons—"

"No daughters, of course," Eunice hisses.

"—of the region's Catholic families. Same thing for the Hôpital Saint-Martin that cared for the ill and delivered babies free of charge, on top of welcoming Blacks fleeing slavery in the States. The nuns gave out fresh supplies and nursed 'em, a real haven at the end of the Underground Railroad. I'm sure they helped some of my ancestors along the way. Maybe one of yours woulda been through here, too, Eunice?"

Ripping out weeds with growing aggressiveness, Eunice has had enough. "First of all, my ancestors were already here as of 1730. French settlers mostly, but some Wendat and Africans forced to flee their homes. Second, 'haven' my ass! The only reason the nuns welcomed the Blacks was so they could convert 'em! My dad always told us how they threatened to throw his great-aunt out of the hospital a half-hour after she gave birth 'cause she didn't want the baby to be baptized Catholic."

"Well, she's got her revenge then. You're a bigger atheist than a stick of wood."

"Besides, before it turned, almost by sheer fluke, into a hub for the Underground Railroad," Eunice hammers on, "I'll have you know that Fort Détroit was sitting on close to two centuries of slavery. Then, as soon as the War of Secession was over, our fine citizens, Protestants and Catholics alike, lost no time telling Black people they had no business here anymore."

"I'm the one taught you that!" exclaims Solomon, indignant at having his own lessons trotted out to him. "When I showed you my ancestor Josiah's diary."

"And don't get me started on the priests' abuse," Eunice adds.

"Well, yeah, some sickenin' stuff went down. But, you know, I'd never have learned to play the piano if it wasn't for the nuns. That's somethin'."

"If memory serves me right, the nuns only helped you up to the day they found out your mother was Jewish."

"That's not how it happened."

Solomon drops his rake as though readying himself for a shouting match. He clenches then flexes his big hands. But it's with a gentle voice that he continues. "All kinds of stuff didn't turn out the way I'd've wanted, and that's not the nuns' fault. You know what it was like."

Eunice stares at the mud-spattered tips of her shoes. "Yeah, I know."

Eunice's contrite expression is met by a softening of Solomon's. Like two old adversaries, they know when to call it quits and when to drop their swords. Solomon lays a conciliatory hand on Eunice's arm, and a great wind tousles the grasslands.

* * *

At seven, Judith ran away from home for the first time. Her father had punished her for breaking a china cup he'd inherited, one she'd been explicitly told not to play with. Banished to her room, she escaped through the window. She made it to the ground thanks to the Virginia creeper that covered the front of the house. She ran to the road unseen by Gloria, busy sewing in the kitchen. Her absence lasted for over an hour and a half. Hearing nothing, Gloria assumed that her daughter had cried herself to sleep. She imagined wiping the damp strands of hair from her child's cheeks with a washcloth. She would offer to glue the pieces of the cup back together for Judith. Her husband had decreed it a waste of time, but Gloria was determined to try. With her daughter. Watch her small hands wield the glue and the china and reach out for help. Gloria would show her how it could be done, and together they would erase the accident.

Mid-afternoon, a farmer who lived three kilometres away brought home a tearful, red-faced Judith. He had found her on the road, singing at the top of her lungs, bent on making it as far as the village. What she meant to do once she got there remained vague. Gloria dragged her dehydrated daughter into the kitchen. Without a word, she gave her something to drink, then she wet a cloth and wiped her face clean of dust and tears. Erasing her bid to escape.

When he got home, her husband tore the creeper off the house.

"Good idea," Gloria said by way of thanks. "This way she won't be able to run off anymore."

Her husband shrugged. "Not through her window at least."

Gloria suppressed a sigh. He was right. There is no way to keep a child from fleeing.

* * *

Gloria hasn't yet ventured into downtown Fort Détroit. The idea of deserted monuments and empty buildings bothers her. But the address the sergeant gave her is to one of the rare office towers that is still occupied.

It wasn't easy to organize the trip. The main bus line

serving Chesnay, Gloria's district, has been suspended for the past five months. Cab companies went bankrupt a long time ago, and it would take hours to walk to the emergency call centre. Eventually, it was Olivar, Francelin's cousin, who came to her rescue. He's the owner of a converted electric car he often uses to shuttle people to and from downtown. In exchange for a few kilograms of scrap metal from the dryer lying dormant in the basement of the yellow house, he agrees to drive Gloria.

The trip takes close to three-quarters of an hour. Rain pours down, and the sewers have overflowed in several places, necessitating detours. Francelin is in the front passenger seat; after their rounds, he'll get off at the Shling hall where his talents and tools are needed to secure the stage that collapsed when an attempt was made to set speakers on it. Beside him, Olivar steers his car as though it were a space shuttle travelling along the belt of a black hole, tacking between crevices, potholes, and roadwork abandoned partway through. He's forever exclaiming, "What on earth is that? What've they gone and done here?" He stops twice, first to pick up an old man who sighs impatiently every time they slow down, then a young androgynous person whose ears are hidden by the headphones of an old Walkman. The whine of notes falls like seeds from a hole in a bag.

"What's that you're listenin' to?" Francelin shouts.

"Bouzouki," is the teen's only muttered response.

"You should drop by the Shling later. Gypsy guitar like you've never heard before!"

"Have they started giving shows again?" asks Gloria.

"No, it's just background music while we work. No amps."

Soon the skyscrapers appear, windowless for the most

71

part. The upper floors are surrounded by flocks of crows and smaller, pointier birds. Olivar drops the two other passengers off in front of a government building and pulls out again, grousing, "How can this be? Really!" Next, he comes to a stop in front of an elegant art deco building. As Gloria shuts the door, the structure's facade vibrates with the thrum of hundreds of pigeon wings. She looks again at the business card the officer gave her.

The elevator no longer works. Fortunately, the offices she's looking for are on the fifth, not the thirtieth, floor of the Godley Building. Patiently, Gloria climbs the stairs. On the steps, cigarette butts and bread crumbs speak of parallel lives, as frail as a body's last breath, that coexist with the lives of the staff still onsite.

The emergency call centre buzzes with a muffled ringing. The operators work in a closed room, but it's as though the calls for help well up from within the walls themselves. Gloria is greeted by a gravel-voiced receptionist. The skin of her face is so loose and wizened it looks like she's wearing a mask.

"I've come to listen to the recording of a call."

The woman hands her a form. Once Gloria has filled it out, the receptionist takes it back and disappears into another room, dragging her heels. It's hard to imagine her capable of managing five flights of stairs every day. Gloria envisages a small alcove fitted out between the warm bellies of the two photocopying machines, a filing cabinet-cum-bedside table, and a bed laid out on boxes of white bond paper. And a woman growing old between the walls of a building's gradual abandonment.

She returns with an ancient tape recorder and headphones.

Gloria sits in a doorless cubicle furnished with one straight-backed chair. Her hand trembling, she hits play. —*Hello?* The timbre of her granddaughter's voice shakes every fibre in her being. —*Yes, I'm listening,* answers an older woman's voice. —*It's our mother. She's drowning.* —*Where are you?* —*At home. Forty-five Clyde.* —*You say she's drowning? In a pool?* —*No. I think she's dead. I don't know what to do.* —*I'll send a team over. Meanwhile, I'll walk you through the steps to resuscitate her. Where is she right now?*

There's a click then a blast of white noise. Gloria startles at the clatter signalling the end of the recording. Looking up, she gives another start at the receptionist's penetrating stare.

"Tissues to your left," the woman says, and her voice grates like metal.

* * *

Gloria has no memory of the hour she spent in the pouring rain on the bench in a square in front of the Godley Building. She is equally unaware of the drive back, only of arriving home. Francelin guiding her to her room, the single mattress on which she stretches out. Eunice bringing her a cup of chicory root tea. Gloria lets them. She sleeps with her eyes wide open, then closed. Waking, she finds herself alone with a few cookies and an old cracked phone on the bedside table. Francelin wanted to be sure she could call for help. Even though, in bad weather, the cellphone network doesn't cover Chesnay. Gloria lifts the device to try to catch a stray radio wave. One of the push-buttons drops to the ground. Iggy, the field mouse, mistakes it for another of the seeds it now eats from Gloria's palm and grabs the piece of plastic and sniffs, trying to find some hidden meaning to this mysterious object.

Two days in bed get the better of the cold she has caught but not of her distress. Something deep inside plummeted when she heard the recording of what she assumes was Cassandra's voice. At each stage of her quest, with each new discovery, the dense and invisible mass lodged in her belly grows. When she tries to eat, food ends up trapped, obstructed by its bulk. Even air has trouble filling her lungs. There was something very dark in that recording, a shadow zone she can't seem to penetrate.

She steps onto Avenue Clyde without knowing what she's looking for. Jonah's house still looks deserted. In front of Theophilus's place, a woman and a small toddler with feverish red cheeks wait to see the nurse. She considers joining them. But what could Theo do? There is no bandage or remedy for a lump in the belly. She finds herself stopping in at Raquel's.

The old woman greets her as if she has been expecting her all along. Remembering what Eunice told her about their neighbour's former profession, Gloria assumes that her past may explain why she's ever-willing to open her door to others and to their ravaged bodies. Raquel leads her guest into a living room decorated like a colonial manor. She urges Gloria to remove her shoes and, without asking, begins palpating first her head, then her neck, her cheeks, her chest. At her stomach, she gives a triumphant "Ah!" like a prospector who has just struck gold in a depleted vein. With a commanding gesture, she motions for Gloria to lie down on the couch. The leather gives silently under her weight. With great difficulty, the old woman kneels in front of her patient and places her hands above her abdomen. Gloria stares at the misshapen fingers and the rings sparkling above her flowery blouse. Raquel orders her to close her eyes.

In the dark, Gloria can't tell whether the old woman's hands are touching her belly or not. She feels no pressure, only incredible heat, a burning breath flowing inside her that tracks like a dog in flames, searching for the bone, the growth, the meteor. Raquel utters a rasping sound somewhere between an exhalation and throat singing. Suddenly, the creature of fire collides with a weighty mass that begins to swell. Gloria trembles, the healer's rasp does nothing to reassure her. Finally, the mass bursts and unbearable heat floods everywhere, from the tip of her nose to the curve of her heel. Gloria cries out and opens her eyes.

Raquel gets to her feet with a self-satisfied air. Gloria jerks upright, burning as though she's been plunged into a metal in fusion. "My body's on fire!"

"Yes, that's quite possible…" Raquel mutters, massaging her knees.

"But will it go away?"

Her expression stern, the old woman leans in closer to Gloria. "You darn well needed to be lit! That's what'll get you moving. The point isn't to rid yourself of it, the point is for it to push you to go further."

She leaves her patient alone with a large glass of water and a small glass of cordial. The wind, the sun, and the trees create daubs of light that dapple Gloria's feet. Wisps of voices can be heard outside, voices of feather and pine cone. In her head, embers glow.

* * *

Amid the starving colours of Fort Détroit, Gloria finishes weeding a row of peppers. Solomon hums as he ties raspberries to their stakes.

"Thanks for comin'," he says. "With Caesar feelin' rough, I can't keep up."

Gloria notes the old man curled up on a bench, his skin pale. She reaches out to feel his forehead. "What's wrong with him?"

"Not sure. We think it's the water's fault. It comes in waves."

In the cool of evening, Gloria follows the path to her house. Her thick linen skirt soaks up the damp from the soil. On the trees, clocks painted on square boards show impossible times: 2:76, 30:22. A mobile made of vinyl discs bobs in the wind; walking beneath it, she hears a subtle blues melody play.

She reaches their own vegetable garden, impeccably maintained by both her and Eunice in the middle of the tangled grasslands. Along the trail, her steps create a living wave, dozens of grasshoppers jumping, hundreds of flies rising. From afar, her house looks different. Its white and yellow angles give off a soft glow. It's a lantern house, a cat's eye shedding light on the wild fields. Once there, she picks up the laundry basket. Francelin helped her install a clothes rack in the middle of the yard. Her blouses quiver in the wind, in the crickets' chorus of secrets. Voices echo all over Fort Détroit; everything whispers and speaks, everything sighs all the time. It took her a month and a half to begin to hear and assimilate what is neither a recital nor an incantation, more like a list whose words, lined up end to end, tear away the world's opacity. With her clothes now folded, Gloria looks up. The moon is almost round, almost singing; it feels as though it has revealed itself fully tonight, even its hidden face. She climbs the stairs to go to bed in her granddaughters' room, and, for a fleeting moment, on the verge of sleep, she has a vision of the two of them where they lie hidden, as different as the pit and the fruit. Wrapped in darkness and their sleeping bags, the adolescents close their eyes, yawn, first one then the other, and fall asleep, held tight in the web of Fort Détroit.

* * *

Her first thought is that Eunice's old Pontiac has grown legs. As she draws closer, she listens for the expected, the clinking and clanking of tools tackling the engine's flaws. In vain. Nothing moves under the old car.

"Eunice?"

Perpendicular to the vehicle's frame, the legs don't budge, but, soon enough, she hears an intake of breath.

"Come on out, I've brought you a mountain of cucumbers."

"Okay," Eunice's voice replies, echoing as if she has spoken into an oven.

The sun beats down on the wasp's nest–coloured car. Its paint seems about to crack and liberate a furious swarm of bees. Eunice still hasn't budged.

"Uh, are you okay under there?"

Gloria sets down her crate. Freed of their load, her arms have an urge to drift upward.

A zydeco tune tumbles toward them from the end of the street, yet is not enough to dislodge Eunice. Her voice comes again, choked with embarrassment.

"Could you help me out?"

Bent double to view the rest of her friend, Gloria spots Eunice's mortified expression.

"Did something fall on you?"

"No, I…I can't get moving."

Gloria pulls on Eunice's legs; fortunately, she's lying on a skateboard. She emerges from beneath the car, veins pulsing on either side of her forehead. Gloria takes her hand and helps her bend her wrists, her elbows.

"What happened?"

Eunice stands and wipes dirt off her overalls. Her fingertips are as dark as if they had brushed up against the night. Her eyes too.

"It happens every once in a while. I go stiff and lose all strength. Often waking up. Or thinking of my dad. I must have fallen asleep under Clothilde."

"Clothilde?"

"The jalopy."

"Ah."

"Maybe it's despair that paralyzed me. This car's a lost cause. It's not tools I need, it's the great Sainte Jalopette in person."

"So we'll pray."

A few seconds later, Eunice gives herself a shake, puts the crate of supplies under one arm, and heads for the house with a firm tread. Gloria follows, impressed at the return of Eunice's strength. Stunned that anything could have paralyzed her neighbour.

* * *

At fourteen, Judith went with Gloria to see a fortune teller. From one day to the next, the teenager had developed hips and breasts, light, wavy hair, velvety lips. She seemed utterly unaware of the transformation. She smiled little and spent her days in morose apathy. The only sign of any vitality was her love of singing, which grew as her voice reached a fuller octave.

Gloria had proposed the session on the pretext of exploring what professional future lay ahead for her. But somewhere deep inside, her greatest desire was to pierce the tough bark, the shell of this daughter who had become a mystery to her.

Madame Mireille greeted them like long-lost relatives in the basement of her bungalow. Judith asked where she kept the crystal ball. Gloria, meanwhile, expected the seer to examine the lines of her daughter's hand. But she did neither. Madame Mireille looked deep into Judith's eyes and, without preamble, began to speak. She didn't touch on either the past or the future, only focused on Judith herself.

Gloria's daughter listened stone-faced as though the woman was speaking of someone else. Madame Mireille evoked the forces battling it out inside Judith: a deep hunger and appetite for the world pitted against a desire to flee. To possess and to abandon. To devour and to reject.

A dozen minutes later, the adolescent broke in, "But what about my job, my studies in all that? My mum wanted to know what field—"

The clairvoyant interrupted Judith. "Your career, your health, your loves, all will be determined by one thing only: your ability to master those two forces. If you keep them on a short leash, you will thrive. If you let them run wild, you'll be torn between the two. Be careful. You won't be able to count on your mother for help. She doesn't have the grit."

Teeth clenched, Gloria paid the woman without a word of thanks. They drove home in the rain, Gloria dismayed, Judith impassive. Nothing emanated from her daughter, neither hot nor cold, nor fear or pluck or pride. She had thought her daughter was like her, a neutral presence in the world. That her child might harbour destructive forces was insane. Judith asked nothing of the world. Why on earth had Gloria taken her to see that woman?

* * *

"'French Canada's Tower of Pisa,' that's got a punch to it, doesn't it? You see how it leans? To the northeast. No coincidence that, you know. On a map, you can trace a line straight from the angle of the tower to Montreal and to Paris. At the time, people hereabouts'd say, 'The City's pointing to its sister, then its mother.'"

"Its mother? Really ..." mutters Eunice.

"Three great cities greeting each other," Solomon adds.

"Tell me, how many Ojibwe or Potawatomi villages could we have landed on using the same logic?" Eunice interjects.

Beside her, Gloria tries to recognize the angles and arches of the pale stone monument she's seen from a distance ever since she first arrived in Fort Détroit. Its base is fenced in, and large sections of its circumference are covered. All around, a crew is readying the grounds with dynamite, surrounded by some forty curious bystanders waving their phones to immortalize the fateful moment. Theo and Francelin try to estimate its height and width and the explosive charge required to bring it down. Marina clutches her daughter to her belly as though she were the one slated to be blown up. Ulysses sits smoking on a concrete block where the yellowing shreds of one of the more recent *MISSING* posters can still be seen. Raquel knits while shaking her head—hard to say if she disapproves of what's happening with the tower or with her handiwork.

"What's that written by the door?" asks Gloria, squinting.

"It's a plaque in memory of Antoine de La Mothe Cadillac," says Solomon. "This was his project. A monument to New France's glory, and to his own—apparently, he included a bas-relief of his own face in the original design. Our Tony thought he was pretty hot stuff! The guy actually invented a title of nobility for himself—how crass can a fella get? One of the many myths the city was built on."

"Where's the bas-relief?"

"Oh, it disappeared ages ago! The first tower was demolished in 1764 during Pontiac's Rebellion. The French Canadians were plenty mad! The Brits blamed the Odawa, but really, they were the ones who did it to pit their enemies against each other."

"Wasn't it a trapper who fell asleep in the tower while he was smoking his pipe?"

A dull thud sounds inside the building, and a flock of birds streams through the windows. Solomon ignores Eunice's comment.

"When peace returned, the Francos started rebuilding the tower. They had to be discreet about it since the Anglos wouldn't have appreciated it much. Every night, carpenters and masons added another metre or two. They built it tilted on purpose, leaning toward France to show everyone le fait français wouldn't die. By the time the Brits realized it had grown back, the tower was part of the landscape. An elegant but simple building, all in wood, with brick foundations."

"So, is that the one that burned down 'cause of the fellow with his pipe?"

"Those are just urban legends, Eunice!" Solomon says impatiently. "We don't know how it came to burn down."

"We don't know if they built it leaning either. The tower didn't even make it to its tenth year."

Workers come and go from inside like mice in a block of gruyère. Confused instructions leak from their devices. On the tower, Gloria makes out some worn fleurs-de-lys and a few illegible Latin phrases.

"What about this one, how far back does it go?" she continues.

"1922! Built by a noted philanthropist who'd decided to restore the city's Francophone heritage."

"A noted *Anglo* philanthropist," Eunice points out.

"David Redstitch was a francophile. He devoted his fortune, his connections, and his own engineering talents to rebuilding the monument—in stone this time, to be resistant to fires."

"His engineering talents didn't stop the tower from leaning again just like the others."

"He did it on purpose, obviously, as a tribute to the ones that came before!"

"Is that so? I've got a picture of my grandma in front of the tower in the forties. Let me tell you it was a heckuva lot straighter back then."

"Listen here, you gonna pick holes in every word I say?"

"You've got that right!" Eunice laughs.

"Crooked or not, it's still a site that, for decades, gave the city's population a place of refuge. The ones who survived police repression, fires—"

"I hid in there when the witch-hunt was on for communists," adds Theo.

"You were a communist?" Eunice asks, surprised.

"It's here, too, that the young women from the brothels

came to work when the raids started," Raquel points out.

"I did more bangin' here than in my own bed!" Ulysses exclaims, provoking stunned glances all around.

The demolition crew has started stepping away from the site. One worker asks the bystanders to fall back. In the mist, the tower looks like it's either shivering or stifling a laugh.

A countdown begins. All heads turn to the tower. All chins lift, all feet take a few steps back. Mouths murmur silent blessings, wishes, entreaties. A force field is about to give way. Gloria clenches her hands, as though this all had something to do with her, as though she, too, had grown up, fled to, and made love in this leaning tower. One of the workers triggers the process. There is no visible lever or detonator, his gesture is slight, almost impossible to detect. But a sudden roar erupts, and the moment it sounds, it's as though it has always been there, a rumbling beneath their voices from the very start. Although they all knew what to expect, the bystanders are taken aback both when the tower cracks and when it gradually plummets to the ground. Around them, nothing but one huge crash, a cloud of dust. In a matter of seconds, French Canada's Tower of Pisa is no more. Eunice bows her head. Solomon touches her shoulder.

"Don't be blue. It'll come back just like it did before. All it takes is time."

* * *

The house shakes every night. And every night, Gloria tells herself it's the wind or an airplane flying over Fort Détroit. Or the coyotes' howling that makes the air quiver like an old tablecloth. Each time, she gets up and peers into the bathroom to be sure no one's lying in the tub and no spirit has risen from the plumbing. She heads for the dormer window, checks that nothing is burning outside. The walls and beams keep on quaking. The house is like a soldier back from war. It startles at the faintest sound and cries in its sleep. But when a stranger enters, it freezes, paralyzed by its familiarity with violence.

And so, on this night of a full moon, Gloria understands that something unusual is happening. The air is petrified, the silence suddenly thick and loaded. Unexpectedly, a blade has penetrated her dwelling. Gloria tiptoes to the top of the stairs.

For what seems like an eternity, the intruder doesn't move. Moths flutter upstairs, the front door stands ajar. At last, without hurrying, he crosses the living room and steps into the kitchen. Judging by the length of his stride and his sweeping gestures, Gloria guesses this is no petty spoon thief.

The man methodically opens and closes cupboard doors, looking for some rare, precious lost object. Gloria thinks of Judith's urn foolishly left on the kitchen table like a forgotten plate. But the intruder doesn't seem to pay it any mind. After casing the ground floor, he heads for the stairs. He walks slowly as though giving Gloria time to find a fitting weapon to confront him with; using her eyes and heart, she does, in fact, cast around for something to defend herself with—she thinks of Eunice, *You should get yourself a weapon*. Gloria doesn't like guns, she hated her husband's and got rid of it the day after he died. Like her daughter three decades earlier, she could leave through the window and climb down the creeper. She visualizes the frail vines clinging to the west wall and imagines her fall. Better than dying at the hands of the very man who may have robbed Judith of her life.

Just as she's about to step forward, something erupts on the ground floor. It takes her a second to sort it all out. Barking. A scream of pain. Growls. A struggle between a dog and a man. Gloria can sense the latter's fear, his efforts to break free, and then, moments later, his panic-stricken escape. Her heart pounding, Gloria lingers in the aftershock of the showdown. She hears the dog sniffing, trotting toward the still-open door, stopping on the threshold. The second it leaves, she races over to the window, scarcely surprised to recognize the one-eared pitbull she had seen once before. Regal, it crosses the street to the ruins of the incinerated house, climbs on top of the rubble, and rules over the night.

* * *

The day after the intrusion, neighbours flock to her place. It took only a quick mention to Eunice for the whole community to show up. In the mangy flowerbed, a dozen people stand, including Theo; Marina, flanked by her daughter and her elderly mother; Alain and his dog Hugo; as well as the gruff woman everyone calls Block and her partner. Unwelcome late-night visits have been on the rise on the street over the past few months. Everyone thinks they have a piece of the puzzle.

"You really didn't see the guy?" Alain asks again.

"No."

"Not even his shadow? He didn't leave a single trace?"

"Drop the investigation, Columbo," Eunice interrupts him. "He can't be the same guy as before. Wasn't it a woman at your place, Marina?"

"Uh-huh, but there were two of 'em. I didn't see the other one."

"What'd they take from you?" asks a man wearing a toupée that clashes with the colour of his own hair.

"What silverware I had left," says Marina, while her mother, upset, clasps her hands together.

"We've gotta band together, get organized, I've been saying it for months," decrees Block. "Us residents, we're more isolated by the minute, that's why we're targets," she adds as several people nod vigorously. "We need to put some teeth in it."

"Teeth?" says Gloria.

"Yeah. Teeth. Sticks. Bullets."

"Maybe we could sign up the dog that saved Gloria," jokes Marina.

"We've already got Hugo," retorts Alain.

"Not to be insulting, but Hugo doesn't have what it takes to be a killer. That dog'd shake a paw with the thief even as he's pocketing your watch and loose change."

Everyone laughs except Gloria. Her body's still wobbly on its axis. She watches the charred ruins disintegrating in the wind across the street. She'd swear the pitbull doesn't have the makings of a killer any more than Hugo's dog does. It just looks that way. The canine's essence is not one of violence, but of heroism. Otherwise, how could it have known an attack was in the offing? Why did it tackle the intruder and not Gloria?

"I'm not sure arming ourselves is the solution," she ventures.

Eunice and Block roll their eyes, but Theo nods.

"Gloria's right. More often than not, any weapons're used against the people they belong to."

"Not having a weapon can be used against you too," retorts Block. "I say we need lookouts. We could spell each other off to keep watch and sound the alarm the minute a stranger shows up on the street. Sweetie's got a compressed air siren we could use, don't ya, Sweetie?"

Block's partner gives a solemn nod.

"What if the strangers're only passing through? Or lost?"

"We scare 'em off. No need to maim 'em to convince 'em not to come back," says the man with the toupée.

"That's not very kind."

Block stares at her in exasperation. "Well, no, Ms. Straight-off-the-Farm, it isn't kind. You know what else wasn't kind? Your damn daughter. Always half stoned, half crazy, always beatin' on her kids or tryin' to sell the clothes off their backs to buy more dope."

"No wonder they ran off," adds toupée guy.

"It's 'cause of her the street's ended up in such a fix," continues Block. "She attracted all Fort Détroit's crooks and malefactors here, and now we're stuck with 'em."

Gloria looks at Eunice, who, instinctively, has drawn closer, then at toupée guy.

"Come off it, Block," Eunice retorts, "there are looters on every street, in every neighbourhood. Judith had nothing to do with it."

"Maybe, but it makes me wanna puke to see your pal show up here flashin' peace signs where her eyes should be when her daughter's heart was where hens purge themselves of their eggs. I've got no lessons to take from someone who raised such a cruel mother."

With that, Block turns on her heel, trailed by Sweetie, leaving in her wake an uneasy pall. Marina lays an apologetic hand on Gloria's arm as she bids her goodbye. Alain and Hugo take their leave as well, quickly followed by the others. Theo offers to drop by later. Gloria nods distractedly. She stares at toupée guy.

"Why did you say my granddaughters ran off?" she asks as he's leaving.

"I swear I saw 'em," he says without stopping, "the day your daughter died. They were heading east, carrying big knapsacks."

"You saw them?" Gloria intercepts him. "How did they look?"

Clearly in a hurry to get away from the cruel mother's mother, the man quickens his pace without saying a word. Gloria turns abruptly to Eunice.

"Is it true my daughter abused her children?"

An uncomfortable Eunice looks around as though the right words were to be found somewhere, ready for the plucking.

"Listen, it's not false. I thought you knew."

"I knew nothing, Eunice! When will you all get it through those heads of yours that I knew *nothing*!"

Spinning on her heel, Gloria strides over the pineapple weed, the broken glass, the anthills, and the gaps in the porch, her skirt flapping like a flag announcing plague. She tries to slam the door, but it's too humid outside, the wood is warped. She forces it shut with her shoulder, avenged by the click of the lock.

* * *

The bathwater is scalding and refuses to run any cooler no matter how hard Gloria tries. So, fine, she immerses herself in one go, something she usually reserves for the frigid waters of a lake. Immediately, her skin smarts. Just what she wanted. To plunge inside the violence she has remained blind to for so long.

Up to her neck in water, her face criss-crossed with tears, a moan escapes her in a never-before-heard octave. Molten lead tumbles inside. "Judith!"

The ceramic tiles both absorb and disgorge her cry. The minuscule syllables she had once detected deep in the tub remain still now as though the lingering presence of her daughter has opted for silence. "How could you treat your children that way? Why? I'm beginning to think nothing can redeem you, no excuse, no explanation. You weren't raised like that. You didn't grow up with cruelty. What changed you? I don't believe in your destructive impulse anymore. I think what it comes down to is there was nothing inside you. Nothing solid. When ugliness wanted in, there was nothing to block its way. It took hold of you."

Gloria plunges her head underwater where not even the burn penetrating her ears and her nostrils is enough to chase away the images that papered the house when she arrived. The broken furniture, the absence of everyday objects. One twin bed for two adolescents. Their stripped-down room. It was writ everywhere: a dark, all-consuming hunger. The mother who swallowed her children's lives whole. Gloria had simply lacked the resolve to decode it, the clairvoyance to distinguish between the deterioration of the house and that of her daughter.

Her head is underwater still. Gloria keeps it there. Her throat cries out to open, urgent, her lungs insist on expanding, but she holds on to the little air they still contain. Behind her eyelids, colours go from the black of a confined chamber to the blue of a vein, to the purple of a bruise, then to the red of an open wound. Everything hurts, inside, outside; her body and her mind, nothing but pain. Her granddaughters appear, running through the fields, huge backpacks bouncing on their shoulders, then Judith, as a child, traipsing through the yard, her eyes riveted to the ground. Gloria's mind balks at a question taking shape, the thought that she herself has failed, that she was unable to fill her daughter's needs, to shape her properly, but her thoughts scatter in the bathwater like shotgun pellets.

She doesn't know what brings her up for air. Her conscious self was on the verge of abdicating, something else has taken over. Gasping for breath, she opens her eyes to plumes of steam. Everything around her is red. The image of her two granddaughters resurfaces. They vanish into the woods against a backdrop of red tiles, red water like diluted wine, the ceiling forming droplets, the red of blood, the red of survival.

* * *

That evening, she waits for dusk. She waits for the cool and the crickets. Her skin is still crimson as though it had been repeatedly slapped. Rummaging through the bag of groceries Francelin delivered, she unearths a box of Algerian dates. At her right heel, Iggy trains imploring eyes on her. Gloria snaps a plump, sticky fruit off its stem and holds it out. The date is almost as big as the mouse, who eyes it like someone who has just won a new car. "Careful, there's a pit inside," warns Gloria. Iggy starts nibbling greedily. Gloria can still hear Eunice's voice. *A field mouse isn't meant to be tamed. It's a wild animal.* She gets to her feet and grabs her purse.

Night has fallen. Gloria steps outside onto the porch and takes a few breaths. Across the street, the ruins of the charred house don't seem as high as the day before, as though they have dwindled in the interval. A bright light shines below, smothered by collapsed debris. The minute she squints, the light disappears.

Her friend opens her door, and, without a word, the two women take their places at the table. Shortly, Eunice makes her way to the large cupboard and brings out an unlabelled bottle. She fills two small glasses. The women drink, clear their throats.

"I should have told you," Eunice says finally.

"It's not your fault."

"I wanted to protect you. Maybe myself too. The truth is, I was relieved at first to have the house empty and to see an end to all the goings-on. It was heartless of me. I'm sorry."

"You shouldn't be. It's only normal. Anyway, I think when I got here, I didn't want to know. That's changing. Changing faster than I can keep up with. That's always been the way. Everything changes too fast for me."

They drain their glasses. Eunice pours another round and studies Gloria's face.

"Why're you so red? Did you get another sunburn?"

"Something like that."

Gloria fidgets with her glass. A drop remains on the bottom, unattainable.

"Is it true she sold their clothes?"

"Their clothes, their shoes, even their school stuff," Eunice replies. "Plus a good part of what was in the kitchen cupboards. I think the malefactors brought in more than they took."

Gloria sighs and shakes her head.

"But don't think she didn't try," Eunice adds. "I remember, when the girls were little, she signed up for a group. She wanted to turn herself around. She was clean for a few months, but life caught up with her. Her boyfriend's death…"

"Yes."

* * *

Gloria stares at the bottle. Looking for a blurring, a wavering. Eunice gets to her feet, this time rummaging through a drawer, producing a vague rustling sound. She pulls out a small plastic box like the ones Gloria uses for storing her needles and thimbles. But rather than some sewing accessory, Eunice brandishes a deformed cigarette.

"You ever smoked pot?"

"No!" exclaims Gloria, scandalized.

Eunice looks at her amused. "You're over sixty. Seems to me you're entitled to give it a try."

Gloria gives a pinched snort, but the minute her neighbour lights up, the smell of weed goes right to her head. She accepts the joint and contemplates the way her mind fills with fog. Eunice chuckles. She coughs. Then emits a small "ha."

"Voices are funny," she notes.

A moth flits round the lamp, trying to find a gateway to the bulb.

"My father's voice just kept going deeper. It dug him out like a cave the older he got. A grotto to hide his memories in. His ideas just fell further and further. He got hollower and hollower. Near the end, when I spoke to him, it felt like my words got lost somewhere inside him. He wound up with a labyrinth there. And his voice was an echo."

"That's kinda like with my daughter. Except she was born that way. Do you know, she had a fabulous voice."

"Uh-huh, I remember."

"That's what stays with me the most. Judith singing. I think, for a while, it's what kept her alive. But it wasn't enough." Gloria sniffs, gives a sad smile. "She ate dirt when she was two. Trying to fill herself up."

The joint has gone out, having given enough. With a crinkling of dead leaves, Eunice lays it down in her glass.

"Can I ask how come you never came to visit?"

Gloria sighs. "I dunno . . . I wanted to. But Judith never reached out to me. When she moved here, it was up to me to run after her. She never called, never invited me. I didn't want to push. She had her own life. I missed her so much. I loved her more than anything, more than my husband. Till Cassandra came into the world. Then that love multiplied, grew so much I didn't know what to do with it all. But I could never see them often enough. There's something awful about occasional visits. They make the way time passes even more jarring. I've always had a hard time accepting the fact that things change, that my daughter was growing up. I wanted to be able to lock in place every moment with her. But her life ran through my fingers. After she had Cassandra, I spent three months with her: I slept in the pink room, woke up in the middle of the night, listened to the two of them asleep. The baby's breath was quick and faint, as though air barely entered her body. She almost never cried. I gave her her bottle at 3 a.m., stroked her hair. Her tiny fingers. At first, they couldn't even make it round one of mine. But at some point, her whole hand circled my thumb. She was growing too; she wasn't some enchanted infant, she

93

wouldn't be a baby forever. It gave me this unbearable long-ing. After I left, for months I couldn't stand the thought of going back. I was paralyzed. When I got over it, Judith had a new boyfriend. She didn't answer the phone, didn't want to see me anymore. I spent the next fourteen years playing catch-up with her. I only learned about a second child the year after the baby was born. They came for my husband's funeral; the girls were five and seven. The little one looked to be sulking. The eldest watched me with eyes like saucers. That's when I learned that Mathilda's father had killed him-self. They stayed for two days. Judith didn't cry. She was skinny, pale as a sheet. I thought it was grief's doing, I never imagined that drugs were involved. I didn't even want to think it. I should've done something, made them stay on, gone to see them, but I was dead beat after looking after my husband for so long. I never saw them again."

Her eyes shimmering, Eunice listens, her chest broader than usual as though her heart has expanded.

"If only I'd've known, I'd've called you. I…I figgered she had no family."

"Don't worry. In a way, she didn't."

Eunice fetches a loaf of bread from the pantry, sets it down on the table, and starts tearing off small chunks.

"Did you hear what Clarence said?"

"Who?"

"The guy with the toupée."

"Oh! Yeah…"

"They're alive."

"They're alive."

Eunice looks over at Gloria and holds a chunk of bread out like a question.

94

"I'll start looking. In Parc Rouge. I've got a feeling that's where it's all going down."

"Makes sense. We've heard tell of children hiding out there for years now. But it could be dangerous."

"I'm going anyway. That's all I can do."

As night advances through space, and as the hours inexorably weave time's thread in one direction only, the two women drink and toke some more, until despondency transforms into something like joy, and joy starts them crying from laughing so hard; while outside coyotes prowl, children keep watch, and, farther still, from the roof of a shed, a pitbull makes sure the world turns as it should.

* * *

Her backpack is full to bursting. Besides a flashlight and a first-aid kit, Gloria has stuffed in biscuits, jams, and a Thermos full of tea. Eunice insisted on accompanying her to the edge of the Rouge's woods, uttering endless words of caution. The park, she insists, is a haunt for maniacs of all sorts. Its hollows are full of poison ivy, and the river of murder victims. The coyotes, actually coywolves, are masters over it all. Plus, dusk is falling; soon there'll be no seeing a thing. But Gloria doesn't back down. There's no better time to make her move.

The two women head out along Avenue Fieldvale, which leads into the park. Clearings give way to wooded areas and to patches of forest where branches and trunks form a complicated tangle of sinuous lines, like the mesh of netting. Through the dense foliage, the light takes on underwater tones. The trees and tall grasses swish and toss in the evening air. Shadows quiver, always hidden, always behind something else. Gloria and Eunice reach the river, a twisted arm screened by lush vegetation. Its lapping can be heard, the thread of its thoughts unknown. Something echoes overhead, like a great opening rocking the dome of the sky. Gloria stops. Eunice holds out her right hand. Gloria squeezes it. Her friend tries to slide a cold object into her grip. A gun. Gloria pushes the pistol away. Just as she knows that she has to look for her granddaughters here, this evening, she also intuits it is better to approach without a weapon. With open palms.

Just as she's about to set out, a sturdy body emerges from the bushes. Resolute, the one-eared pitbull has come to join her. Eunice looks at the dog, then stares at Gloria. Without fear, Gloria caresses its head. Then, to the accompaniment of the river's stifled laughter, she plunges into the woods, the animal on her heels. A giant compass clasps them in its deliberate embrace, in its invisible certainties.

II

My eyes are made of dungeons and rubies,
of blustering insults, slumber and pacts
of blood, of babble and tranquil lakes, of spilt milk.
Nothing approaches me, books tell lies.
I come from the dark of the air, I carry fear, revelation.
I belong to the children.

BENOÎT JUTRAS

s the dealers watch the young girl sidle up, a darkness grows inside the cruel and elastic part of their being that expands in moments such as this and contracts at others—when someone sings, when there's hot food to eat, when the stars befriend their fatigue. But now, a drum beats in their sinews as Rasca's little fingers slide a few muddy bills into the paw of the taller dealer who hands over a baggie, a few pebbles weighing next to nothing even as they weigh tons. Rasca doesn't bother putting the baggie in her pocket; she has no pockets in her dress that's grown too short over the spring that spurs everything to sprout; there is no place where she can hide things on her person because she is five and a half. All her secrets are exposed.

As she drifts away, the two dealers stay standing, arms hanging at their sides, sullen, at loose ends.

"We're always the bad guys," the shorter of the two fumes.

"Not true," whispers Pretty from her hiding place.

Rasca lets herself drop at the foot of the tree where her pipe waits, then she puts one of the pebbles inside, waiting for a go-ahead from the others who stick resolutely to their roles. With a shrug, she sticks the pipe in her mouth, and, with a less than assured hand, makes as though she's heating it up with a silver lighter that Wolfpup found in what used to be an old snack bar that has been taken over by a colony of marmalade cats no one pats because they're covered in mange.

"Crack!" she cries in her dusky voice.

She inhales, once, twice, three times, throwing her head back. When her face reappears, it shows no ecstasy; it is contorted, as ugly as a wound. She coughs, mutters, then convulsions seize her body. She collapses to the ground, her tiny feet jiggling, her body goes rigid, then, suddenly, nothing—she emits one final gurgle and dies.

"Come off it, there's no way an overdose looks like that," hisses Method.

"Shh," Lego cuts in. "That was our cue!"

In one bound, the two small figures leap up from behind the old canoe and the dealers give a start.

"You killed our sister!"

"It's not our fault!"

"It'd so be your fault. You cut other crap into your batches!"

Weapons appear and blows rain down. Yatim aims for the two truants' kneecaps, Pretty tries to scalp one of them with her pocket knife, Adidas pierces an eye with a nail, Method shoves the barrel of her gun into the older pusher's mouth while Lego empties the boy's pockets and throws the drugs into the fire. Lastly, long blades are thrust into the hearts of the merchants of death who breathe their last together, their fake blood mingling with real mud. In the ensuing silence, a rasping makes itself heard.

"It's Rasca! She didn't die!"

Immediately, Lego races over to the young, still-barely-conscious-looking girl at the foot of the tree and launches into a frenzied cardiac massage, which sets her little body to bouncing like a ball. For the first few seconds, Rasca remains utterly limp, but soon hysterical laughter crosses the seal of her lips.

"She's alive! We saved her!"

This is when she should be picked up, held high above their heads like a banner, and thrown into the arms of the trees, but Rasca remains lying on the ground, laughing and shooting sidelong glances at her playmates, who eventually figure out what it is she wants.

"One! Two! Three! *Go!*"

The children, half a dozen of them including the pseudo-dealers, rush over to tickle her, sliding their fingers into the tenderest and most hidden spots, attacking her from all sides, and she immediately begs for mercy, but none of them has learned to respect the others' boundaries, in such a way that "yes" and "no" are used interchangeably to say the opposite of what one wants or to give and take back things that either don't belong to them or that they don't know they have. So the group torture continues, twisted birds flitting round Rasca's armpits, her knees, her neck, and maybe she truly would have died—of laughter—if Wolfpup's authoritative voice hadn't cut through the shouting and the tree trunks.

"Lego, we'd be needing you! We've got a newbie," Wolfpup cries.

Straddling his little sister, Lego straightens, something foundering inside.

"I'm coming," he replies.

* * *

As expected, the new kid wants no part of it. Lego places the object on the big rock and covers it with his hand to quiet his racing pulse and the ticking of the watch; he'd like to do the same for the kid with the elephant ears who's screaming as though one of his own knuckles had been laid out on the log, but Fiji gets to her feet, about to recite the regulation. Lego can hear her already in his head—*Objects not allowed in the Ravine are . . .*—and decides he doesn't want to listen, that the litany of ever-changing laws is just as bad as the things they forbid, so he raises his baseball bat high and before Fiji can open her mouth or the boy protest one last time, he swings and the watch explodes. Its face is instantly disfigured, its needles scatter, and hundreds of microscopic pieces of glass fly to the four corners of the camp.

"The Kingdom of Rouge has spoken!" decrees Fiji, determined to place a lofty phrase somewhere.

"It's the only thing of my dad's I had left," the newbie moans.

"If a arm-clock's all your dad's left you, you're better off forgetting him," declares Wolfpup, lobbing a pine cone into the trees.

She walks away followed by Fiji, who spares an indulgent and magnanimous glance for the boy who has collapsed onto the boulder, sobbing. Adidas lays a hand on his shoulder.

"It was only a watch. You got a place to stay here. That's better, wouldn't you think?"

The boy waves him away, and Adidas thinks back to his first time in the Ravine; he's not the only one—everyone remembers. He showed up dressed in tatters like a dead tree and wearing a brand new pair of running shoes he'd ripped off the day before at risk of life and limb. They were whiter than both freshly fallen snow and his mother's breasts; they practically radiated their own light, so much so that all he could look at was his feet and all he could talk about was his shoes. The others eventually threw them into the fire. Adidas had howled, punched Lego, and laid waste to two huts.

"If you wouldn't stop bawling, we're gonna call you Watchface," Adidas said to the still-crying boy.

"Yeah, or Rolex," adds Lego.

"It wasn't even a Rolex." The boy sighs.

Lego tosses the baseball bat which starts spinning like a boomerang and, as with every other time he has to wield the long arm of justice, for a second he's afraid it might swing back in his direction and crush his skull. But the bat drops at the end of its trajectory. Lego turns on his heel.

* * *

Back from their expedition, Magic and Stutt lay a blanket full of provisions down by the old canoe. Stutt's puny arms tremble from carrying his burden over several kilometres, but he doesn't complain.

"We found Captain Ratface's cache!" Magic shouts. "His treasures'd be ours!"

A clamour greets the news. The other children crowd round.

"Did ya slay him?"

"Whattaya got?"

"What's 'slay' mean?"

"Lotsa grub!"

They dump out cans, rice, nuts, crackers, soap, gauze, and a book whose cover shows a half-naked man embracing a woman in a torn blouse. Lego grabs and leafs through it, then throws it away as admiring exclamations ring out at the loot gleaming in the shadow of the woods, setting hearts to pounding above empty bellies. As a jumbled mass of kids hug Magic in thanks, Pow-Pow shakes a bag full of small pale pellets, making a sound like a rattlesnake.

"What's that?"

"Chickpeas, you idjut," retorts Magic.

Pow-Pow opens the bag, grabs a pea, bites down, and spits it out indignantly. "No good to eat! Our teeth'll break."

Everyone stares uncertainly at the bag of legumes. Stutt's voice cuts through the silence. "Th-they're n-not c-cooked! G-gotta s-soak 'em in water all n-night, th-then b-boil 'em f-for an hour."

Everyone stares at the boy who smiles timidly, but not for long since Pow-Pow throws a chickpea at his face. Stutt tries to retaliate, but the projectile misses his opponent and hits Lego in the eye, and Lego responds by levelling a kick at a huge box of crackers that explodes like dirt on a battlefield, like the kid's watch earlier, like smoking frogs and haunted houses on fire.

"Stop, you jackass!" yells Magic, as three kids throw themselves onto the supplies to protect them with their bodies.

Magic stations herself in front of Lego, but it's too late. Lego has reached his rage zone, the real one, the one that incites blindness and shifts tectonic plates. He pushes Stutt who falls over the canoe, and the others step out of reach immediately, knowing full well that the only way to put out a Lego blaze is to remove any fuel—in other words, to vanish from sight.

Back in his hut, Lego is still fuming, dying to destroy more than a watch and a pack of soda crackers, to destroy something that would bleed, a deer or a fox with an arrow to the heart, to lop off a malefactor's head, anything to still the thing thrumming in his head like bees in a sarcophagus.

He grabs his pillow and punches it, kicks wildly at his ever-damp mattress. Rasca shows up mid-tantrum and scans the scene, taking it all in stride.

"Wanna come fishing?"

The little girl holds a stick out to her brother; she's tied a slowly wriggling and dying worm to the other end of the string that dangles from its tip. Lego looks at her, looks at the worm, and drops his pillow. They strike out from the camp to find the barracuda and narwhals waiting for them hidden deep below the surface of the Rivière Rouge, beneath its iridescent grins and inscrutable promises.

* * *

Perched on the large boulder, Fiji watches evening close round the camp. Humid air rises from the river, the sky transforms into shredded indigo and pink ribbons, faces take on superhuman hues round the fires: at this time, every child looks like a hero, and every tree like the pillar of a palace. No one would imagine that a city of steel and fear surrounds them, just as no city dweller imagines this nest of freedom in the heart of the Rouge's huge park. They are safe, Fiji tells herself over and over, they are invisible.

She closes her eyes, the sounds in the background like the loops in knitting, stitches that hold fast, hanging on to each other to create the fabric of habit, something predictable in the randomness of life in the woods. The fire that crackles, the girls who sputter in laughter as they trade potty humour, the creaking that tumbles from the treetops, her belly that gurgles and will only be indulged once everyone else has eaten. She opens her eyes. In the mauve light, the cloak of darkness has fanned out, shrouding the battered canoe that marks the centre of camp, its hull dented as though it had fallen from the sky; night settles in. Magic and Adidas stir the contents of a pot, its aroma far-reaching, and the starving youngsters squirm as they hold out their bowls, their eyes beseeching, but the minute they catch sight of the fricot, they'll start whining that they don't like sweet potatoes, beans, canned meat, stew. In his spot, Pow-Pow keeps watch over a bowl of immersed chickpeas as though some supernatural force were about to snatch it up, then he jumps to his feet crying "pee-pee!" and Adidas and Pretty race over and yank down their pants to urinate on the fire; the girl's aim as good as any boy's, which is what earned her her name, Pretty-Stands-to-Pee, and she gives a sardonic laugh, watching the smoke rise from the hot stones.

Farther along, a mini, a boy, cries from exhaustion as does an older girl with a nosebleed—a rule of thumb in the Ravine is that there are always one or two children crying, two or three laughing and fighting, half a dozen who are sleeping, a few emptying their intestines after having ingested unripe fruit or stagnant water, and one caught up in the throes of death. Their lives are short and magical, hard and full, and all are governed by Fiji. She repeats her mantra—*they are safe, they are invisible*—clings to it, actually, because after all this time as the camp's leader, there are two things that still keep her standing as tall as her spine will allow: omnipotence and responsibility. The greater the latter weighs on her, the more the former grows, like two loads that balance each other out to prevent a boat from capsizing.

In the evening's first chill, she glides toward her hut where Yatim has left maps of the city discovered in the library's trash cans, ones she'd started looking at earlier.

One of them seems to represent the park, oily concentric ripples, which she can't quite figure out but will examine further to unearth their secret.

Just as she's about to step inside, Magic hails her. "I'm keeping a plateful for you, Fij."

"Serve the others first."

The jute partition drops behind her, a sound like running water; the pleasure, for the briefest of moments, of being shielded from sight.

* * *

With evening come the detonations; Pow-Pow prepares to shoot holes in the dark with his black powder, and through the gaps dreams will enter to lead the children to slumber. Wolfpup would love to bed down for the night, but she has to keep watch: spring has brought back wolves, shadows, child-eaters while, still entangled in winter's tatters, the sentinels have yet to fully regain summer's maximum vigilance when days last forever and nights never sleep. Entering her hut, she grabs her weapon, shakes it, pleased to note it is loaded, and hurries back outside.

Without a sound, she heads for the camp's periphery. That is her great talent, the ability to move silently, to remove herself from the kingdom of the audible, something learned very early in her life in a world that now weighs no more than the crater left by a bomb in her memory. The first two she comes across are Method and Terror. As always, their eyes are peeled: no chatting, no nodding off for them, as stiff and mute as javelins.

Yatim and Pretty are another story: the former has one hand jammed deep in his armpit and is flapping his arm up and down like a one-winged hen while Pretty doubles up in laughter at every eruption created by her partner's antics. A fireball could be racing toward the pair, and they wouldn't see a thing. A predatory smile on her lips, Wolfpup kneels, takes aim, pumps her weapon to the max, then pulls the trigger. Two screams resound. Wolfpup snickers soundlessly. Her victims, their backs soaked in a wet bull's eye, turn round.

"Wolfpup?"

"That's *Colonel* to you!"

"How come you sprayed us at work?"

"If you was working, you'd have heard her coming with her watershooter, lazy bums!" says Terror from farther away.

"Not even true, fat tool!" Yatim blows up. "We were real focused."

"On your underarm farts," retorts Wolfpup, her hand pressed against the boy's chest to stop him from throwing himself at his sworn enemy.

"We're sorry, Colonel," says Pretty, "we'll—"

"Shh!"

A far-off noise. Steady but slow. The sad, weary footsteps of a grown-up.

"Sound the alarm."

Without hesitation, Pretty-Stands-to-Pee grabs the ocarina hanging round her neck and raises it to her lips. With nimble fingers, she produces an airy call reminiscent of a turtledove's. In the camp, Adidas gathers up the minis and the others race to the armoury; in under thirty seconds, all campfires are out, the youngest are hidden away, and the big kids join the sentinels to form a fiery circle round the camp.

The intruder's silhouette appears, heading straight for

Wolfpup who, through the darkness, notes the heavy tread, the long hair, the weighted bag, and even the dread seeping from the intruder's chest like a swarm of flies. Terror joins them, and Yatim gives him a little push.

"Would I shoot, Colonel?"

The Ravine's best marksman holds a slingshot in his right hand, and in his left, a gun.

"Start with a stone; we'll save the bullets."

Frowning, Terror slips the pistol into his back pocket and raises the slingshot, which groans as he pulls back on the elastic and hisses like a witch when he lets go. The projectile grazes the intruder's shoulder, and the ensuing cry sets the undergrowth to trembling. Wolfpup doesn't waste a second, she picks up a big rock, her eyes narrowing till she has a clear picture of her target: the slack mouth; the snub nose; the frown line between the eyebrows, that's where she'll aim. With one clean shot, she hits the stranger mid-forehead. Her target falls back and doesn't move. Yatim rushes over to the victim.

"Out cold. Transport!"

Wolfpup joins him and peers at the individual, an old drunk who'd have passed out from a lot less than a rock to the head.

"Grab his backpack."

Yatim pulls from the pack a bottle of vodka and a fetid blanket. Three big kids come running, and in no time flat the drunkard and his hooch are carried away in a tarp, his five porters escorted by Method, Terror, and their guns.

"Where they taking him?"

Wolfpup turns. The newbie stands there looking stunned, his eyelids swollen.

"Outta the park."

"They gonna kill him?"

"No, just dump him. He's gonna wake up tomorrow morning, start drinking again, and won't remember a thing."

"How come they got guns anyways?"

Wolfpup squints, takes in the kid's tuber-like head and protruding ears, and walks off without a word. Back in the camp, the fire has already been rekindled, the minis have fallen asleep, piled on top of each other like one big ball of stuffies and halitosis, and, in his corner, Pow-Pow has gone back to his black powder and lighter, ready to blow something else up. Wolfpup swoops in with a pail of water that she pours onto his arsenal.

"Hey!" he protests.

"Silence," retorts Wolfpup, throwing the pail at his feet.

* * *

The newbie wakes just as sad as the day before. It started to rain overnight, his clothes are wet, the other kids aren't nice, he wants to poo but there's no toilet, he wants his dad's watch back, he regrets handing it over to that half-mad girl, he's hungry, he's got gum stuck in his hair, coming here was a mistake, he should have stayed home—having André around might not be as bad as this place after all. A few children drag their feet on their way into or out of their huts, scratching their butts, others sleep all over the place, heads on logs, feet in the mud, and he can still hear Pow-Pow, who let him share his hut with him, his ridiculous snoring, something between a bear's growl and an industrial fan.

He finds the boulder he collapsed onto the day before. His body assumes the same position and tears well up in his eyes—or have they risen from the stone? With the tip of his tongue, he confirms that a salty liquid has indeed formed there—even rocks are unhappy here, everything cries, everything rains. At his feet, a small pile of onion peels covers the shards of his shattered watch, and the new kid wonders if he could find some still intact part, maybe the second hand, a fragment to slip into his pocket or slide under his tongue to keep hidden from Wolfpup, something to stroke each time he's overcome by the strangest form of homesickness that exists, the kind you feel living where you've always lived. That's how he kept going when his sister fell for that big jerk André, and when that big jerk André moved into their place, took over his dad's chair and robe and bedroom, and when he started whaling on him for the slightest thing, eroding the fragile balance he and his sister had managed to strike before the thrashing that put an end to it all. Back then, he'd stroke the watch's face, think about how time takes care of everything, that this, too, shall pass, this, too, even big jerks, and, leaning back against the reassuring warmth of the fridge, he'd grow calm. In the end, he was the one who'd been made to pass, to move along to something else.

A sound not of this earth pulls him from his musings. He looks up, to the centre of camp, where the fires still give off the smell of reddened palms and melted potatoes. There's a girl with translucent skin and stark white hair twisted into a bushy crown. She's singing. He doesn't recognize the melody or the words, or even the language, and assumes it's an invention, a language created for this air, this morning in this flat light, beneath this mist. The song encircles his waist, lifts him a metre above the ground, keeps him hovering there for a few seconds, then sets him down, right next to the singer. He looks at her, her long, frail limbs, her movements like a grasshopper's—or more like a spider's, the ones that big jerk André called daddy long legs and liked to swallow to shock him—and the sheer white girl keeps on singing, eyes shut, and when she finally opens them, her irises are as red as glowing embers.

Slowly, the children rekindle the fires, conjure up water, provisions, and blessed life-giving aromas; others group together in twos or threes to carry those sleeping to beds out of the way, the heaviest are rolled over to the foot of trees and covered with waterproof tarps. Tears still run down the boy's cheeks, but now he doesn't know why, he no longer remembers what weighed him down so on waking, he knows nothing other than the melody and made-up words that open whole countries inside his head; he watches the most beautiful girl in the world singing the most beautiful song he has ever heard, and no one asks questions, no one interrupts the least little thing. Not until, after an indefinite length of time, he realizes the song is over, the white-haired child has disappeared, and another girl, the one he heard being called Magic, is tapping him on the shoulder.

"Here, Tick-Tock, have your breakfast. After, we'll show you how to Dumpster dive."

Tick-Tock stares at her, his mouth hanging open.

"Who is that?" he finally utters.

"Who's who?"

"Who was singing."

"Your oatmeal's gonna colden."

"Okay."

"That'd be Bleach."

"Bleach."

"Yup."

* * *

Wings always hurt a bit as they unfurl, like when you've slept all bent out of shape, sort of like rusted metal unbuckling. Bleach can't let the others in the Ravine see her wings; they'd be jealous, they'd try to take them for themselves, even though everyone knows a fairy's wings can only be used by her—they'd wilt on someone else's shoulder blades. So she waits to be alone before spreading them wide, far from the camp, in Chesnay, the neighbourhood she always returns to, never finding the home she grew up in because she has forgotten, perhaps, or the house no longer exists, or her body refuses to take her there, or it never existed. It doesn't matter because Bleach has chosen another house, or rather the house chose her, an old building as yellow as a canary's heart, one she first entered with Magic to steal cutlery, then on her own, to bathe in the warmth that reigned within its walls and to observe the wide-hipped woman who moves so little. Once, she even drew near to flood an ants' nest while the woman slept on her porch. Fairies don't like ants.

They do, however, like butterflies, and the second her wings open, Bleach ascends to follow their fluttering, speaking to them in their language. She asks them about the house.

"Why didn't it burn down?" she whispers.

"Because it's protected," the silvery blues among them reply.

"Who by?"

The ochre cloud blurs the air around Bleach and disappears—butterflies know many things but are very secretive.

Bleach shrugs, which toggles her large white wings and makes them miss a beat; she just about plummets but manages to catch herself, her heart pounding.

A small voice sounds next to her ear, orange and mocking. "I know something you don't know!"

Butterflies are also very mean-spirited. Bleach turns to the painted lady snickering as it whirls round her and decides to fly away without responding; in a few wing strokes, she's overlooking the moss-covered roof, a living tundra she'd love to lie down on and bask in the whispering of the microscopic insects sheltered there. But the painted lady keeps circling her.

"Okay, I'll give you a clue. It's linked to what's in Paradise."

Still annoyed, Bleach pulls away from the butterfly without a word and continues to glide toward the backyard; she contemplates the field in the distance, yawning like a great tawny mouth, but the orange-hued butterfly interrupts her again. "The woman living there is called Gloria. She knows the girls gone to Paradise."

Bleach turns to the butterfly hovering there as though there was nothing to it, as though the painted lady had no mass, while Bleach's own weight is a constant encumbrance as she flies.

"I knew that already!" she retorts before squashing the insect between the palms of her hands.

She touches down at the foot of the yellow house, her heart heavy and unsettled with everything she knows but doesn't disclose. Sometimes it feels to her as though she has lived a thousand years and seen the whole of what there is to see, that she holds all secrets, all fables, all magic formulae of the world. She heaves a sigh that lands a few metres away, wilting a white tulip. At that precise moment, through the upstairs window, a mattress takes flight and lands smack in the middle of the yard. Immediately, Bleach jumps to her feet, her wings well hidden beneath her shoulder blades. This she must tell the others. A mattress is not something that can be allowed to go to waste.

* * *

There are two of them, minis, more fearless than fearful, too little to realize the danger; all they care about is showing they're worthy of the Ravine. Pow-Pow doesn't seem aware of the risks, either, even though the tower leans like a tooth ready to fall out, even though it's missing half its steps and the spiral staircase makes heads spin just setting foot on it, as though entering an optical illusion. Lego, however, remembers the climb there when he first arrived: Rasca was too young to make it up, so he took her on his back, and, despite the cool of October, he was sweating so much she kept sliding through his arms as he carried her through the stairway's loops, following the spiral that kept bringing them back to the same spot even as it bore them higher. At the top, Rasca cried out with joy—she didn't have words back then, just cries—and Lego felt like throwing up but didn't. Winter was approaching, they had nowhere to go, and they had to pass this test, every test, do whatever was asked of them, even the impossible. At the time, Vishnu was the one who supervised the trials; once they returned to the foot of the precarious old tower, he confirmed their admission into the Ravine and it was as though Lego were witnessing the beginning of the world. As for Pow-Pow, he doesn't remember his initiation…or anything, for that matter; life begins afresh for him every morning; the only thing that stays with him is the recipe for concocting explosives, out of nowhere making fireworks fly.

"You'd be putting on a display tonight?" Lego asks, keeping an eye on the two small silhouettes as they pass in front of the narrow windows.

"Nah. That nutcase soaked my powder."

"Nutcase?"

"Your pal Wolfpup."

"She's not my pal."

"You're both in the boss club."

"It's not a club."

Having no reply to this, Pow-Pow spits on the ground. A beetle struggles in the sticky mucus.

"For real, I've had it with Fiji 'n Wolfpup," Lego continues.

Pulling his lighter from his left pocket and a cigarette stub from the right, Pow-Pow lights up, almost disappointed to see nothing explode, and inhales so deeply he has to spit again before holding the butt out to Lego who shakes his head.

"Least you're on the leaders' side," remarks Pow-Pow.

"Yoohoo! We almost being there?" cries one of the minis through a narrow slit not far from the top.

"Keep climbing 'n you'll find out," retorts Pow-Pow.

The two of them showed up one day with a third mini, all three complaining of tummy aches and a need to pee—God knows how lost children always end up in Parc Rouge, there must be some sort of special compass that cares nothing for north but shows children with no family the way to the Ravine—they had ticks burrowed all the way round their ankles and a greenish tinge from drinking river water. The third mini died that first night. They buried his body on the

116

opposite bank of the Rouge with the others. His companions recovered, then looked to be settling in, so they were told of the test; Pow-Pow wanted firecrackers to be part of the trial, but Fiji wouldn't hear of it.

"Fiji, she always ruins everything," he adds, throwing his butt onto the trapped beetle.

"I know. She figgers she's growed-up."

"She *is* growed-up."

Rummaging through a third pocket inside his jacket, Pow-Pow pulls out a silver ribbon.

"Look on this: magnesium. Light it, and it'd explode whiter'n Bleach's face."

"Cool."

"Come find me tonight. We'll burn it. That'd bug the nutcase."

Another cry echoes from the tower: the minis have made it to the top and are waving like passengers on a cruise ship. "Yoohoo, we did it!"

"Great! Now throw yerselves off!"

The kids' faces crumple, pride giving way to stupefaction; for a second, they actually consider jumping since they don't yet get Pow-Pow's jokes, but mostly because they're willing to do anything and are filled with renewed faith. If they did jump, maybe they'd float instead of breaking bones. Maybe arms would finally reach out to catch them.

* * *

Summer has barrelled in, burning stages and skins, and the Ravine is blistering, its ground heaving, underground springs seeking the light; Fiji senses them there like secrets burning the lips of the forest and the thought reminds her

117

of Paradise. She looks for Bleach, and as though even just the thought served as a summons, Bleach emerges from the undergrowth, flanked by Yatim and Magic returning from a mission.

"Success, your majesty," Yatim declares proudly, brandishing in one hand a bundle of creased posters showing children's faces and, in the other, a half-dozen seedlings.

"Nice reddies!" adds Magic.

Fiji examines the limp sprouts sporting strawberry buds.

"The Old Man didn't see you?"

"Negative, he weren't there but two spies just 'bout nailed us."

"Lucky thing those dames're too fat to run after us!"

"Water 'em before they dry out. We'd plant 'em tomorrow."

Yatim and Magic run toward the creek, and Bleach makes as though to follow, but Fiji motions discreetly to her. The two separate, Bleach heading to the left, Fiji taking a wide detour to the right, only to meet up behind a resin-spattered tent. Fiji coughs three times behind the mosquito netting deliberately orientated toward a dark corner of the camp, and Bleach's milky features appear like a pale body surfacing in a lake.

"Did you go see the sisters in Paradise this morning?" Fiji asks.

"They still be there."

"Did they ask to come here?"

"They'd be too scared. The Big One snivelled the whole time. The Little One barely says nothing."

"They still sick?"

"Not as much. They don't stagger or sweat no more."

"Whattaya think's wrong with 'em?"

"Would've been the water, like usual. Or in their heads."

Fiji shoots her a questioning look.

"Grief sick," Bleach explains.

"I dunno."

"Anyways, I'm back tomorrow. Magic got vitamins."

"No one'd better follow you."

"No one can follow me," Bleach retorts with a wink.

When Fiji gets up again, the moon's chalky face hits her like fruit from a tree. The coyotes are close at hand tonight, she can hear them howling as though she were inside their bellies. At times like this, she feels like the world has come unanchored, that her efforts to hold everything together are in vain, and she wishes someone would tie her to the dead canoe like the man in Stutt's big book, a sailor who asked to be tied to the front of his boat to hear the sirens' song without falling into the water.

* * *

The world belongs to them. It breathes like a big soft belly into which they plunge their sabres and throw their bombs. The world, and the creatures who struggle there—to eat grow win take find—is easy prey, or it is when your name is Terror and when you handle weapons the way a juggler would and when your voice drowns out all others.

"Let loose the last one! Show no mercy."

His troops activate the catapult, and a huge explosive rock soars through the air and crashes onto the enemy fort, releasing on impact both a multitude of small projectiles bristling with blades and a platoon of rats that infiltrates armour, provoking horrified screams among the Flamers. Their rearguard loses no time in retaliating. Method gives the order, and flaming arrows rain down on Terror's troops who can only hope the arrow tips haven't been soaked in venom; but before Terror can grab one to examine it, three of his Cutters fall, bodies hurtled backward like a spray of life, and two others catch on fire. They're left to burn, no time to extinguish the flames; the survivors unsheathe their sabres, scimitars capturing the sun's rays and flinging them into the enemies' eyes: the sun is a bullet they propel at will. Their name should be Death Suns.

"Our name'd be Death Suns!" decrees Terror.

Cheers greet the new moniker.

"Doesn't rhyme with Flamers, couldn't work," Method protests.

"No way a numnah like you's gonna decide for our lot!"

"We got a new name, too, so there. We'd be Dragons of Destruction."

Forced to acknowledge the excellence of their choice, Terror regrets somewhat the change he's brought about. With his Cutters, he had one up on the Flamers, but now the scales have been tipped in the opposing clan's favour, and God knows that names count, he saw it himself when he took up Terror and dropped Kitten. When the cat that used to follow him everywhere went and died, he ripped up his sailor suits, lost his dimples, and acquired sharp incisors as well as a poker face when confronted with blood; the time for change had come. Now, to regain the upper hand, he decides to invoke the divinities.

"O immortals," he roars, lifting his eyes to the canopy, "let your power rain it down on the infidels!"

Seconds pass, Terror feels his army's skepticism growing and amusement spreading through Method's ranks, but, at last, the gods heed his call: a shower of broken glass, nails, and other celestial scraps of metal crashes down on the Dragons of Destruction (hitting a few Suns in passing, who don't dare rail too loudly at the divine intervention). The enemies cower, taking refuge under their thin shields, muttering curses while, arms raised, Terror roars in laughter. The opposing army has been routed. Method has no way of stopping the hemorrhaging; his mercenaries bleed and cry, they're hot and want a taste of some of Magic's bannock that smells so good, it's a stampede, and Terror rejoices even louder, victory like the taste of raw meat in his mouth. The upper hand is always his, and he laughs and cries in the same breath because this life that he holds in his hand like a beating heart is too easy, something he can squander without it ever running out; he doesn't understand this abundance, this ease in a place where everything is hard, but guesses it must emanate from him, from that part of his being that protects him from loss and amputations. A gift bestowed without his having sought it out—perhaps, when all is said and done, the gods really do exist and watch over him, gird him, sharpen his teeth.

* * *

Whale watches the scene from on high, the only possible viewpoint. From the ground doesn't work. Not with a body that has always been too heavy, too cumbersome, for as far back as Whale can remember. But all creatures experience grace in their element, and Whale has found it in the trees. The ground is an unstable place, especially with summer's approach when heat causes the red of the river to rise and the camp turns into a wasp's nest where blows rain down and teeth bite out of the blue. Whale is afraid of fights, of hurting others, afraid of sweating, crying, getting mired in the spongy earth, and seeing folds of flesh invaded by dark humours. So the treetops have become home: a hammock, ropes, a platform, and pulleys; a spyglass so keeping watch warrants the height, though its lens mostly picks up the parade of caterpillars, the complicated choreography of birds, the smoke from fires that twines round branches. Also, inevitably: the to-ing and fro-ing inside the camp, Fiji's iron-fisted reign, Tick-Tock's shuffling feet, Rasca's teddy bear, Pretty's creations, Stutt's library, the animals Method talks to as though to confidants; and, off in the distance, downstream along the Rouge, other children like them out near Île Gus and beyond; on Rivière Détroit, cargo boats disappearing down the elbows of a river as leaden as a dead snake, as deep as the tomb of a cyclops.

Below, the clamour of battle rises, but amid the cool of the branches and the shimmering of leaves, Whale hears nothing, the silence of the sapwood like a cloister. Reflecting on war, on peace, on what both threatens and protects; imagining what it would be to take flight, to be reincarnated, to be free of gender or to harbour a novel organ between one's legs, a fig, a chanterelle, a star; reflecting on how to make this life last forever, to never have to come down from the trees, how to halt the city's encroachment and pull off the feat of never growing up, this is what Whale ponders from above. The platform creaks under Whale's weight, the bark quivers, Whale can hear the murmur of its sap. It's Simon, the maple, insisting that immortality is not for humans, telling of the life eternal shared by trees through their roots, and Simon's words flow into Whale's heart—words spoken by trees both distress and illuminate.

Amid all the babble, one voice stands out, more incantatory than plant-born; it takes Whale a second to realize the words from below are meant for above. "Let your power rain it down on the infidels!" That's Whale's signal to dump out the bag's contents, just as Terror had instructed. Without further ado, Whale unleashes a shower of glittering objects onto the combatants, only grasping too late that the bag's contents are broken glass and rusty nails, not the confetti promised by Terror. Kids scream and cry and run every which way, some bleeding; Yatim pounces on Terror, but he dodges the blow with a laugh, and Whale, with a head shake of sorrow, wonders how it is that, even living fifteen metres above the ground, one still ends up hurting others. Terror gives an insolent wink, irresistible all the same; the fragrance of bread cloaks the camp, and Stutt appears, shouting in Whale's direction, "I've b-brought you s-some b-bread!" and suddenly, Whale can think of nothing but the bounty of the bannock, which, like anything that alters life, must surely come from above.

* * *

He enters a square, light-filled space in the centre of which a dark shape lies. It's a dog, he discovers, dead in the middle of a room that is white from floor to ceiling. Drawing closer, he sees that the one body hides another, smaller, darker, even more immobile still. Then a shadowy mass draws his gaze to a corner, and, approaching, he's surprised to come upon another lifeless dog. He turns back to the first two, but there are no longer just two, but four, and others are revealed across the square of the floor and he stops trying to count them. He feels tears rolling down his cheeks as he leans over each creature, finding infinite tenderness in the paws folded into bellies, the ears drooped limply alongside heads, the soft lashes, the snouts straining forward. He lays his hands on their flanks and is gripped by the cold, by the stillness; one by one he caresses them, unable to anticipate anything other than warmth and movement, and each time, he is shattered by the absence of life. He hugs them, crying, these dogs that are so much more than dogs; they are his brothers, he can tell, something profound binds him to them, and he stands, overcome with tears, seeking in this death chamber one lone survivor, one soul to be revived. In vain. Suddenly, two powerful arms grab him from behind. He recognizes the arms, recognizes the acts that prevent him from struggling, that cover his mouth, muzzle his voice, his breath, he knows exactly what the fingers will do as they inch toward his throat, squeeze harder and harder, hands that want to annihilate him as they did his brothers the dogs and, with every muscle in his body, he pushes away, pushes against the force of this huge adversary, but his efforts weaken him and he feels himself falter, fail …

In the dark of the hut, Adidas wakens; the half-light flashes off and on in his eyes as though he's been deprived of air, a whistling resounds in his ears. He turns his head. It's Lego, fast asleep, his breathing buried so deep in his chest that it has been altered. Adidas never sleeps that deeply, he is always wound tight, which he knows because of the leg cramps he wakes up to every morning. He resumes breathing. Nothing moves, the objects in the hut remain unchanged. The sounds of the forest wend their way to him: the rustling of birds of the night, the weightless footsteps of nocturnal mammals, the snoring of those asleep, the crackling of the fire someone watches over. Everything in its place. Adidas lies back, closes his eyes, not waiting to free himself of angst first, there's no point. He knows how to drop off despite fear. Gradually, sleep returns, a small dot leading him away, he advances toward it, steps into the world of the invisible, then the dot expands, takes on the definite shape of a square, and, slowly, the boy enters a room, all white from floor to ceiling, in the middle of which a dark shape lies.

* * *

It rained overnight in the camp, and this morning the sun thunders through the wet, the sparkle of water clinging to branches like the chiming of a new bell. From the ridge, Pretty watches, her head filled with the scent of the damp forest, the mud, the earth, and the wood filtering time, sap surging, and a ferrous perfume biting into her bones, climbing to the knots in her hair. It's this fragrance that drew her from her sleeping bag and led her outside so early, despite a night spent standing guard. Seen from the ridge, the minutiae of the Ravine become a landscape worth drawing—the confusion of the camp, the glory of the trees, the tangle of the bushes, the columns of light bombarding the ground. As always, Pretty sees both big and small, the expanse of the sky and the exact nature of the stones; treasures both immeasurable and infinitesimal.

But it's on her return to camp that the true finds take place: shards of broken glass, lugs, bits of scrap iron fallen from the sky—Pretty exults. She crams her pockets and the flaps of her jacket full, bundle-like, then fetches her secret box that contains the fruits of her last trip into the city's most sublime horn of plenty—the car cemetery.

She has never understood why none of the others are interested in it since, on top of all the pickings—sheet metal, headlights, knobs, coloured wires—that she uses as raw material, she often comes across the kinds of objects her pals have such trouble unearthing in deserted homes and stores that have already been looted a hundred times over. Bottles of water, cigarettes, toys; perfume, clothes, jewellery, phones, coins . . . It seems that certain grown-ups live as much in their cars as in their houses, and so their vehicles are themselves given over to essential articles. And that's not counting the one substance that's missing every time they try to light a fire under the camp's invariably damp logs: gasoline. Pow-Pow did tag along with her once or twice—Pretty is incapable of siphoning gas without choking whereas Pow-Pow has no problem whatsoever, it's like there's tempered steel where his throat should be— but the rest of the time no one wants to come along on her expeditions, which, actually, is for the best. The cemetery is a boundless treasure trove; as far as the eye can see lie wrecks in varying stages of dismemberment and corrosion, antennae, eviscerated engines—the exact opposite of the huge car factories she imagines as the city's womb, a uterus that makes automobiles the way others make promises or laws.

The junkyard manager's shack sits smack in the middle of the ocean of scrap metal, which Pretty, although she doubts a human being still resides at the centre of it all, steers clear of because of the dogs, mad beasts foaming at the mouth, each likely endowed with more than one head. So she stays on the periphery, working in concentric fashion, sometimes climbing onto the roof of a car to scan the horizon.

In the still-sleeping camp, she peers into her box and contemplates her raw material, a collection of gems and bits of glass, fragments and cast-offs whose shapes attracted her for reasons unknown, and which will be transformed into something new. It has little to do with her; sometimes, it's as though she has only to hold the objects before her eyes for them to reveal their true nature and the fate they awaited as they served another purpose in the entrails of some other structure. Figurines, toys, masks, garlands, mobiles, charms take shape from the nails, springs, and chains, the forest of an electronic panel, a badge from a part torn from the hood of a car. Spreading out the contents of her pockets and jacket on the ground, she admires the pieces, unable to grasp how others can be blind to their beauty, to their will to exist, which strikes the world like a tiny bell. Pretty thrills. Her gaze returns to the bottom of the box, then to her finds fanned out around her. Tiny bells. Something that jingles. That's it. She smiles, grabs a spool pin, and sets to work.

* * *

"You were my mommy."
"No, I was your daddy."
"Okay, you were my daddy."
"You called me Papito."
"Papito, I'm tired."
Rasca strikes a match and lights the lantern. The reassuring smell of smoke makes Wolfpup drowsy, the red phosphorus loosening her limbs. Slowly, the little girl takes the other girl by the hand and leads her to her mat laid out on a wooden pallet. The sides of the tent flap in the wind; Rasca

punches at them as though to subdue them, then folds the blankets down in an invitation to her child—a good two heads taller than she—to lie down.

"You'd want Papito to tell a story?"

"Yes!" Wolfpup exclaims.

Rasca sits sideways on the bed the way parents do—torso turned toward their child, legs turned toward the door, ready to plant a kiss then hightail it out—and runs her hand over her brow as Wolfpup watches wide-eyed.

"Once on a time, a little girl with gold locks walks down the street. She seed a abandoned house. She goes inside, seed some chairs, but when she sits, they're broke."

"Just one was broke."

"Just one. But after, she seed the oatmeal. She took a little taste, but it was poisoned and her tummy hurted, so she goes to lie down on a bed too high for her—"

"The oatmeal wasn't poisoned, just no good."

"If you don't stop talking, you're gonna get a slap! Okay. In bed there's a wolf dressed like a granny who wanted to make her get naked. The little girl cut his head off and throwed it out the window. After, she sleeps for a hunnerd years, and when she wakes up, all of it's covered in leaves, and trees grow in buildings and up chimneys, all of it's abandoned for a hunnerd years. But with her magic, the little girl got ridded of the plants and made the trees go back underground. She fixed her kingdom, killed off all the wolves, and there was a big party. That's it."

Wolfpup smiles, she doesn't know why, but every time Rasca tucks her in she feels a swelling in her chest, a delicious tickling sensation that makes her want to roll around on the ground like a mad dog.

"Gimme my kiss, Papito."

Rasca leans over and kisses her daughter's forehead, then her cheeks, then her mouth, at length, and Wolfpup giggles and squirms till Rasca pulls the covers up and bids her good night, sweet dreams, no bedbugs, no rainstorms or wetting the bed, no mosquitoes, only owls to watch over her sleep.

"Rasca! I mean, Papito."

"What?"

"You wouldn't tell Fiji, right?"

The little one makes like she's sewing up her lips, and Wolfpup closes her eyes. Rasca watches her for a bit to make sure she's not cheating, and soon muffled snoring confirms her child is asleep, so she tiptoes out into the night that smells of earth and hard-won fires and follows the music of the scrap-metal garlands Pretty has hung from the bushes. Up above, an owl hoots; happy, the mini heads for her hut while, poised a few metres overhead, Whale smiles.

* * *

Tick-Tock still doesn't understand how it works. He's okay with playing hide-and-seek, but if the play area is the whole city, he doesn't see how Pretty and Pow-Pow will ever find them or how anyone will know who's won. The absence of boundaries and the baffling rules make his head spin; it's only when he glues his wrist to his big ear that he grows calm: the sound of the watch continues there as though its workings have found their way into the bone of his arm, and the soft ticking reminds him of both who he is now and who he is no longer. Of course, it's impossible for him to know the time or how long he and Method have been hiding in this shed that reeks of motor oil, but the rhythm remains and, if he wanted to, he could count the seconds, number off the minutes, and calculate what, since his arrival in the Ravine, has seemed undefined and elastic.

As for Method, she can tell the time is nearing for them to get a move-on; the ambient energy is in flux, threads of darkness spin round them like birds of the night, and the wind clatters; their adversaries are close. She drags Tick-Tock outside the shed into a yard peopled with metal figures that look like zombies made of scrap material. The two are exposed now, so Method drops to the ground to crawl toward a house whose peeling walls look goosebumped. Tick-Tock follows suit.

"Method? What're we doing?"

"Shh."

Tick-Tock stops talking for a second.

"Method? How come Fiji's not here too?"

"Fiji did never play with us."

"How come?"

She opens her mouth to tell him to shut up, but a sinister noise sounds behind a gossamer hedge, like some big lug cracking his knuckles; to Method it sounds more like a monster chomping on a kneecap; she feels a trickle of urine run down her leg, a phenomenon she no longer pays attention to—she has never managed to fully control this bodily function, there must be something that isn't working between her legs. The noise continues, more muffled but omnipresent, a constant gnawing. Tick-Tock peers closely at the feathered hedge and suddenly, throwing caution to the wind, cries out, "Bleach!"

A white face appears between the branches, soon joined by a black one; Bleach and Stutt look at them with round eyes.

"What's that you're eating? I thought you was ogres!" Method says.

Laughing, the two children show them shiny, half-eaten green apples.

"Have you s-seen P-Pow-Pow and P-Pretty?" Stutt asks.

"I think they're keeping close to the park to nab us."

"Where'd you find those apples?"

"You gotta filch 'em on the quiet."

"At the yellow house, thattaway. There'd be some left. But you gotta wait for the mauve."

"On the q-quiet?"

Tick-Tock echoes, "The mauve?"

"By surprise," Method clarifies.

"C'mon, I'll show you," Bleach says.

As the two friends plan their attack, Bleach holds her hand out to Tick-Tock; the contact of her opaline palm is like the touch of water when you let your arm dangle from a boat. Bleach advances quickly, yet without running; she knows her way through the vacant lots, past the empty doghouses and the few houses that throw squares of light onto vegetable gardens. In backyards, garbage bags and piles of rotting boards glisten, the world is wildly beautiful when Bleach leads you somewhere in secret.

They skirt a fence, off which Bleach tears a poster that she rolls up and stuffs into her pocket—Tick-tock has barely enough time to decipher the letters *m-i-s-s-i-n-g*.

"If you'd see others like this, with pictures, you gotta rip 'em down," Bleach says in an even voice.

At last, they come up on the yellow house. Tick-Tock can't say why it looks so friendly exactly—maybe because of the windows like two eyes edged with lace lashes . . . On the back porch, three green apples shine like billiard balls. Tick-Tock lunges forward, but Bleach holds him back, her hand hollowing out a wild nest in the boy's chest.

"You gotta wait for the mauve, I said."

Had Bleach looked closer, she would have seen in his eyes her friend's boundless love for her, but all she notes is the surface—his stunned confusion—to which she responds with a knowing smile. "Look on the window. The lady waked. It's blue. She'd be watching."

In the ground floor window, he does indeed catch a glimpse of a blue-tinged glimmer that seems to expand and contract, like a torso breathing.

"She'll sleep again soon."

The minutes, possibly even hours, that pass outside the ticking of seconds are the fullest of all, more alive than Tick-Tock has ever known; the simple fact of lying there on his belly next to Bleach plunges him into an inexpressible state of bliss—his heart pounding like a bass drum, his cheeks burning with the desire to laugh and cry at the same time. As for Bleach, her mind is a blank, she is nothing but patience, a string drawn between the window and her eyes, between the woman and herself. Finally, the colour shifts, the indigo warms to become, as announced: "Mauve!"

The children penetrate the bubble of the woman's snoring and, slowly, Tick-Tock reaches for an apple, a green so green it hurts, like freedom, he closes his fingers round the taut surface, a nerve of peel, but before he can bite into it, an anarchical clamour explodes, a confusion of human voices and a metallic ringing. Bleach takes Tick-Tock's hand into her own again, but this time the touch is limp, she could just as easily be holding a banana peel or a dogless leash. They run to the street flooded by other kids Tick-Tock recognizes from the Ravine, but they've undergone a metamorphosis, sporting makeshift armour, equipped with rusted stakes, bits of Frost fence, car spoilers and scorched metal scraps, they scream and roar like barbarians bent on tearing a country apart. Once again, the game has shifted, and, for a second, Tick-Tock fears he'll be trampled, then Bleach drags them, him and his apple, through the dark streets and the fires galvanizing the night; they run madly, their cries exploding as naturally as though they had always been this red horde unleashed on a city so empty it is full, so broken it blossoms.

* * *

Rasca doesn't wait for the weather to improve or the water to be warm; she doesn't wait for the big kids' permission. On the flats used by otters to enter the river, she sits down to pull out her vials, her eyedropper, and her solutions. Under Cocotte's attentive gaze, she advances along the bank, startling frogs and salamanders; she draws a small quantity of water for the tube then pours it into each of her three vials. Next, she opens her bottles with their different solutions, adds three drops from the one stinking of vinegar into the first sample, repeats the operation for the second with the bright red mixture smelling of cherries, then seasons the last vial with a combination of the two. "Now, I gotta do wait a bit," she tells Cocotte, the trees, the plants foaming along the turbid river Rasca loves like a best friend, like a grandmother, like a fairy godmother. She lets a few seconds go by, lifts up her vials, shakes them to examine their contents, then delivers her verdict. "Water did be good. We coulda go in."

She throws Cocotte into a pool formed by a large boulder and a tree that has fallen across the river and joins her friend, who has begun to sink but is soon fished out by Rasca who throws and spins her in the air. Cocotte is dizzy, she doesn't know how to swim, she snivels. Annoyed, Rasca holds her underwater to shut her up, for an hour, almost a minute, till she's learned her lesson, then pulls her out of the Rouge's froth and lays her down on the bank where Cocotte collaps-es like a disappointed smile. A tireless Rasca dives under-water again, she thinks she hears voices, knowing murmurs following the current that she wants to decipher, but she doesn't know the words, and the river speaks too quickly, too loudly, in several languages at once. Holding her nose, she dives again and again, letting herself be rocked by the chattering of the waves, opening her eyes to watch the sun's rays separate underwater like so many fingers; she resur-faces slowly and floats there, becomes a water lily and lets herself drift, her back cold, her belly warm.

Out of the blue, she is lightning-struck. She jerks upright, her feet slipping on the muddy rocks, and scans first the water for an electric eel, then the sky, imagining a storm or one of Terror's mean tricks, but there's nothing, no one. She dashes out of the water, her body still electric, grabs Cocotte, and casts one last glance at the Rouge, which has what looks like a long shiver running up it from downstream. Abandon-ing her vials, Rasca bounds through the woods, the distance still to be covered suddenly seeming insurmountable. She starts to cry, she wants to find her brother; or even Wolfpup, who knows how to order sadness around; she wants a big kid to take her by the hand and guide her to the fire, rid her skin of the stinking water and her body of the shock that ran through it. Just then, a large, familiar figure appears. It's Priscilla, the one-eared beauty, trotting toward Rasca for some of the clumsy, unrestrained caresses that only young children know how to give. "Can I climbed onto you?" The dog lets the little girl try a straddle at first before she opts for a prone position, her trunk dangling off one side, her legs off the other. "Okay, go," the child orders, but the mutt doesn't budge, its ear twitching forward and back, back and forth like a watchful bird. "I was too heavy." The minute she slides off, Priscilla starts to trot, guiding the drenched girl through the trees, and soon the contours of the camp surface from the undergrowth and the crackling of a fire reaches them. When she sees her brother, Rasca throws herself into his arms.

"Pee-yoo! You swimmed in toilet water again!"

Rasca keeps hugging him fiercely. "The river electercuted me."

"You don't even know what electrocuted means."

"A stinging wave did be in the water. Coming from thataway, going thataway," Rasca explains pointing south then north.

Lego notices the dripping stuffed toy. "You dunked your stuffy? Tarnation Rasca, you knowed it'll take a hundred years to dry!"

An annoyed Lego grabs Rasca by the wrist and drags her over to the rainwater tank where, under Priscilla's attentive gaze, he washes his sister, dries her off, then gives her a warm drink and hangs her stuffed bear over the fire. Later, when she's asleep, it's his turn to sob into the pitbull's neck, and the darkest regions of his soul will open up for the space of a heartbeat, of a shot being fired.

* * *

The animals know the camp's boundaries better than the children. They perceive its invisible borders and walk like tightrope artists along its periphery in such a way that shallow ruts have been traced round the Ravine with the passing of deer, foxes, snakes, and coyotes, tracks that no one but Method notices, and which make her feel better protected than by the sentries. Over time, she has learned how to approach animals, how to understand them; now she has her crow, her raccoon, her chipmunk, and even her beaver, all of whom she considers friends. She was there when the mother raccoon gave birth to her first litter and cried with her when five of the six offspring died one after the other from hunger or cold or prey to the great horned owls' appetite—some lives are only granted a few days to unfold, and some sibships are destined to concentrate all their good fortune in just one of their own. Method is well placed to know it and, like the animals, has accepted the state of affairs for what it is; she doesn't grieve the dead for long, and she celebrates the ones who remain.

Just as Bleach reports to Fiji in secret, the animals keep Method informed of the goings-on along the Rouge— malefactor orgies, logjams, fish heads floating after the passing of packs, babies drowned in mud. She shares the strict minimum of this intelligence with the other children; she follows the wildlife's movements and only sounds the alarm should something out-of-the-ordinary occur. This morning, the ordinary has been overturned.

The lifelines that cross the sector, usually straightfor- ward and distinct, go every which way now: deer have left behind their yards, beavers have turned their backs on their territory, and hares leap through the centre of camp in huge frantic bounds. In the ardent dawn, early now with the approaching solstice, Method slips outside the encampment and studies the tracks left by this strange migration. The first animal she encounters is a lone coyote that seems totally indifferent to the easy prey she would be. It drags its hindquarters as it walks; she can hear the weak groans deep beneath its panting and immediately grasps that for this creature nothing exists anymore, not hunger, not instinct; it is nothing but pain. In the trees, the morning's jabberers squawk in terror, Method is unable to pick out even one clear message from the cacophony. She makes a chattering noise with her cheeks, hoping to summon the chipmunk, but assumes it must be in its nest in the heart of some tree trunk, staying close to its provisions. She advances through the scattered trees, the rays of the nascent sun making this most beautiful of woods weep, a bow of light poised to touch a violin, then suddenly, she catches sight of them: a family of deer she has never before encountered. They come from the south with faltering steps, fluttering ears—five females, three young stags, eight fawns, and, a rarity, a buck following them at a distance. They seem lost, collide with fallen logs, become tangled in the underbrush; some forge straight ahead but startle at the slightest sound as though none of their reference points make any sense, as though they have been stripped of all certainty. The older ones try to find their way, the little ones want their mother, but can't reach her.

As they draw closer, Method sees the red: their muzzles carry the stain to varying degrees, as though from crushed berries, and she wonders whether maybe they ate inedible fruit, which has disorientated them. But soon, she can no longer deny what is right before her: the animals are bleeding, not only from their nostrils but some from their mouths, others from their eyes even; they can no longer see where they're going, and, without their sense of smell, they no longer know who they are. A fireball rises in her throat when the deer pass right by without seeing or fearing her, these creatures like earthbound fairies that something is destroying from within. "What has happened to you?" she asks, reaching out to caress the last one, an old female with dull fur. As though her touch were enough to awaken something in the deer, the animal turns her majestic head toward Method. Birds fall silent, insects fold their wings, and Method sees, in the deer's eyes, the catastrophe: water become death, the damaged corpses, the venomous river. Then, like the last compartment of a train containing everything of worth, the last deer disappears in the wake of her herd, and the rustling of the crow's wings enfolds the child.

* * *

Yatim had forgotten it was possible to move this fast. Everything in the Ravine is slow: the river's current, the impossible-to-resolve squabbles, the pace of the minis' steps that one has to abide by, water that takes forever to boil, meals that take even longer to cook, sleep that doesn't come and hasn't come since the accident, the accident that seems to have happened at the beginning of Yatim's life, before the Ravine and the hair on his legs, before the infinite period of freedom. Now, pursued by Captain Ratface, Yatim is jubilant. Upright on the pedals of the BMX, he races ahead with Adidas straddling the seat, laughing and crying out that his balls hurt, dragging the huge plastic garbage can like a trailer full of that night's haul: a deck of cards (with two aces of spades), a hunting knife (smeared with blood—bear's blood, according to Adidas), three woollen toques (hand-knitted), cans of food (tuna beans pears corn meat lentils tomatoes), a butterfly net (for Bleach), a sleeping bag (that smells like pee but still zips up), and a baseball trophy (of which there can never be too many). As for the bike, it was in a house whose ground floor and all the rooms on the second floor had been emptied except for one bedroom that remained intact: the single bed, the desk, the dried-out felt pens, the phosphorescent stars on the ceiling, and, leaning up against a wall, this brightly shining bicycle that looked as though it had never been used. The minute Yatim dragged it out of the house, Captain Ratface roused his army of demons and the Thirty Evildoers launched in pursuit of the two boys.

The garbage can weighs them down, but Yatim's legs have found strength he never dreamed he had, it's as though he's been in training in another life to flee from diabolical platoons by bicycle; he doesn't remember ever having learned how to pedal—he doesn't remember much other than the accident that gave him his name—but in this moment, the bicycle is like an extension of his body, a strength that is shared between the metal frame and his sinew. The demons persist in their pursuit of the pair, but as long as they can keep moving, no one will be able to catch them.

They reach the outskirts of the park; the neighbourhood, with its parade of houses abandoned yet as erect as a smile full of rotting teeth, is still dark as the sleepless night comes to an end. Yatim and Adidas slow down; they have shaken off their pursuers. They jump off the bike and untie the trash can; its bottom has been mangled by the ride. Yatim grabs the BMX and holds it up high so it won't get caught in the bushes while Adidas, grousing, drags the rest behind him.

"If it'd be too heavy, drop the sleeping bag here, we'll come back for it," Yatim suggests.

"I don't want no malefactor to come piss on it again."

The two boys plunge into the woods. The approach to the camp is dense and thorny as though, years ago, someone had planted bushes to protect the ones who would settle here someday, but once past the barrier of vegetation, an area of mature, well-spaced trees opens up, criss-crossed by a dithering pond in the shape of a glove—Whale was the first to catch sight of it from among the branches. For Yatim, there is no more beautiful place on earth; to defend it, he would kill, descend to the depths of hell, brave a giant snake.

The fire has been rekindled by the time they get there, heating the already warm air. Yatim brandishes the bicycle even higher, ready for cheers to greet his find, while Adidas drums on the trash can to attract the attention of the small group crowded round the glowing embers, but the others show no reaction, not even a greedy smile at the spoils.

"Lick poo then, ungrateful bums," a furious Adidas shouts, dropping the trash can.

As his friend disappears into his tent, Yatim carefully sets the bike down and approaches the small gathering. Fiji faces Method and Wolfpup, and Terror, Bleach, Lego, and Pow-Pow stand between them.

"What'd happen?" Yatim asks.

"The river," Bleach whispers.

Method is crying, seemingly in despair, Fiji is wearing

her cheeks-of-marble empress look, but beneath the marble, Yatim can tell her thoughts are spinning.

"They been escaping north?"

"Where's north?" Pow-Pow asks.

"They're not the only ones took off. Look on the herons flying past every coupla minutes," Method insists, "look on the hare tracks on the ground."

"Same as always," is all Lego says, observing the prints in the mud.

Method shoots him an exasperated glance.

"Normalwise, there'd be no tracks. They'd circle round the camp, not go right through it."

"If Method says something's up, then it is," Terror declares. "We'd need an expedition is all."

"To the south—"

"Where's south?" Pow-Pow moans.

"—there's factories and policers that way and the river's dangerous," Wolfpup objects. "We'd not go looking for trouble on accounta some girl thinking she talked to the animals."

An outraged Method spits; her saliva lands on the tip of Wolfpup's shoe, who lashes out with her fists.

"Stop it," Fiji orders.

"Wacko!" Method hisses at her assailant.

"Liaress!" the latter retorts.

"Method's right," a voice from the sky interrupts.

Everyone looks up to the supple branch on which a large figure, hard to see through the foliage, sways.

"How come you say that, Whale?" Bleach inquires.

"Me, too, I heard a problem happened down the river."

"Who told you?" Lego asks.

"Cybele."

"Who's Cybele?"

"The weeping willow."

This is too much for Wolfpup, who aims a kick at the bike and storms off. Fiji ignores her, still turned toward Whale.

"Cybele says we're gonna see lotsa sick animals. The trees know 'cause of their roots. There was poison in the river."

Method casts a triumphant gaze all around. Fiji bows her head, takes a moment to think: everyone stares at her, some with respect, others with impatience, envy, hostility, admiration, she who has reigned without contest for so long, for no reason other than her conviction in her own authority. Yatim waits with bated breath for Fiji to speak.

"We got no choice. We do gotta go see if the kids in the other camp are okay. We'll have an expedition. We'll build a raft. We'll find volunteers."

"Rafting down the Rouge'd take at least two days," Lego points out.

"We'll get food ready."

"We gotted a sleeping bag!" Yatim says.

"Great, Yatim, you'll go with your sleeping bag. Method, you'll go with him."

"Me too!" Terror declares, and Yatim just about changes his mind, but he's too glad to see his sleeping bag being put to good use.

"We'd need a fourth," Method announces.

"Me!" says a small voice. "Me—I love the river."

Everyone turns to look at Rasca, who has crept up unnoticed.

"Okay, but your damned stuffed bear stays behind," Terror decrees.

To think he just about missed the whole thing, the *pow* of the century, the high mass of pyrotechnics, the most important thing to have happened in the city since his first Devil's Night, when he grasped, dazzled, the difference between a fire and an explosion. If Tick-Tock hadn't knocked over his pyramid of canned food in their shelter (Pow-Pow likes to call it a shelter instead of a tent, it sounds more nuclear and is a more fitting tribute to the large canvas structure that overhangs their mats), he would never have woken up on time. Pow-Pow cursed his friend at first, then hugged him with all his might; thanks to Tick-Tock's deafening blunder, he'd been given time to make it to the tower. He shrugged on his special shirt, all white except for the left sleeve that was burnt last fall, and a mauve string for his tie. Tick-Tock called it a "bolo" and told him all he needed now was a cowboy hat, and Pow-Pow ploughed him one, which didn't stop Tick-Tock from whistling a country-and-western tune as he watched his sheltermate disappear down the trail.

Pretty insisted on coming too; Pow-Pow grumbled at her get-up, a fleece outfit that gave off a rank odour and was so filthy it could have walked on its own, but he let her tag along because of the great charms and medal she'd made for them to take turns wearing after the explosion.

As they wended their way through the tangled grasslands, Pow-Pow wondered if he should feel sad and turn on the waterworks—like at funerals when you don't really feel tears coming but make yourself cry because *after all, he is your father*—then decides not to; the Tour de Lys won't be gone forever, everyone knows that, and anyway, if he himself were a tower, that's the way he'd like to make his exit, with three hundred pounds of nitroglycerine. Pretty's jewellery makes a pleasant clinking sound that adds a spring to their step, making it jingle even more and firing their steps further so that, by the time they arrive at the tower, the two children are jumping like caracals in the fields.

Once there, they spot Fiji and Bleach, crouched beneath a cedar tree, carrying binoculars, and Pretty makes as though to join them, but Pow-Pow sits off at a distance, resolved not to ruin the moment by spending it with the queen. Pretty hesitates, then plops down between the two behind a bush full of red berries. The tower, too, is done up in its Sunday best, with sheets of canvas covering almost the entirety of its expanse; the trucks belonging to the demolition company are parked at a remove. Pow-Pow recognizes the logo from beside the park; if he'd known that drab warehouse hid a goldmine of explosives, he'd have broken in by now. He promises himself to swing by there really soon, then turns his attention back to the tower, at the foot of which the explosives have already been set up. He's dying to get closer, but there are too many grown-ups; and the blasters are an imposing lot: with their orange helmets and resistant clothing they look capable of blowing a fellow up just by pointing at him. He hears Fiji and Bleach comment on the scene in knowing tones, and he rolls his eyes. No one other than him grasps the complexity of the set-up, no one else could identify the i-kon III electronic firing system and the PETN-based detonating fuses. The scene unfolds in a language he speaks, one that could have been his mother tongue; he alone can decipher all the subtleties and intricacies, and the peremptory attitude of the two big girls exasperates him, to the point where he actually prefers Pretty's blissful ignorance.

The final preparations take forever, and the presence of grown-ups makes him nervous; still, none of them thinks to scan the periphery, turned as they all are toward the tower. Pow-Pow affectionately studies the old arcades, the chipped window frames, and remembers how the first time he caught sight of the monument, he thought it was a church, an arrow climbing to the sky. Back at the camp, everyone thinks he has no memories, but that's wrong, it's just that he can't choose or call them up at will; they appear without warning and leave without explanation, as fleeting and intense as bombs.

The blasters take their positions, the grown-ups back up, their voices subdued. An all-consuming silence expands then retracts and, finally, a velvety din fills the sky. The detonation itself, its burning breath, lasts only a second, but in Pow-Pow's eyes, that second goes on and on, crushing everything. Afterward comes the collapse, dry and gravelly; a spectacular but too-grey cloud, disappointing after the red exuberance of the explosion; and, in a matter of seconds, the tower is no more.

Dust still fringes the epicentre as Pow-Pow spins on his heel with Pretty close behind complaining "it was too loud, my ears hurt, the tower gone disappeared," but Pow-Pow doesn't answer. He's aware of something choking him, a strap tightening inside his throat—and now, finally, he wants to cry. Seeing him, Pretty hurries to slip the medal round his neck saying, "Don't be sad, it'd be back," but Pow-Pow shakes his head.

"I'm not crying 'bout the tower. I'm crying that it's over."

* * *

145

They're seated in what is more of a heap than a circle, but that's the way they like it, especially the minis, lying on the bones of others like they are pillows. Rasca, in particular, has assumed the pose of a pasha—she's exhausted from building the raft, which siphons off her days as well as those of half a dozen other brave kids. Stutt is sprawled next to the nucleus of little ones and could easily be one of them; he's the same size, and it's only the fact that he can read and write that differentiates him from the others, so much so that no one can ever figure out if he's a big kid in a mini's body or a mini with a big kid's brain. Magic is slumped on one side, Yatim on the other, both acting as dikes and cushions for the minis.

"Tonight," Adidas announces, "I'll tell you Prince Darling's story."

"Yaay!"

"Oh no, not a prince."

"I know it!"

"I don't!"

"Silence," Magic barks.

Heads lean together, bodies wriggle, and when the squirming mass finally achieves relative immobility, Adidas begins.

"Once on a time, there was a king with a really, really nice little boy, and so everyone called him Prince Darling. One day out hunting, the king meets a pretty white rabbit and, 'stead of killing it, he put it in a cage. At night, the rabbit did turn into a white lady. She tells him she coulda give him a wish. So the king maked a wish for his little boy to always be as nice as nice and turn into a good as good king. The fairy said okay, she got something perfect for that: a ring, and if you put it on, it stings you if you be mean, but if you be nice, it won't sting none. The king said thanks and gived the ring to his little kid the next day."

"Wh-why d-didn't he w-wear it himself?"

"I dunno, 'cause he was king."

"B-but even k-kings c-can be m-mean s-sometimes."

"Well, not him. Anyways, not much after, the king got sick and died. The prince was so mad that his dad did die, he went out hunting and killed all the animals."

"Oh, no!" Rasca exclaims.

"Uh-huh. But then, when he did that, the ring stinged him, and the more the ring stinged him, the madder he got and killed more animals and the ring stinged him more."

"A v-vicious c-circle."

The others don't even bother shooting a confused glance at Stutt.

"Keep going, Didas!"

"After that, he gone and met a girl he wants to marry. But she sees he's gotten mean, so she said no. The prince got so mad, he locked the girl up in a room, then got drunk and went for to rape her. But just before, the white lady did showed herself."

"What'd she do? What'd she do?"

"She morphded the mean Prince Darling into a fierce beast, with a lion's body, a monkey's head, and a snake's tail, then she says, 'I promised your father to watch you and make you stay nice, but you're awful mean. You're gonna be a beast so long as you don't be nice again.'"

"Good punishment!" says Yatim with a yawn.

"So anyway, the prince stayed inside the beast's body for lotsa years. At first, he was real fierce and wants to eat everybody. Then he got tamed, didn't bite no more, so the white lady turns him into a dog. Being a dog, he gets even a bit nicer, he gone decided to share his meat with the others, so the white lady makes him into a dove. Once he's a dove, he gotted as nice as could be, and so the girl from before adopted him for a pet bird. That's when the white lady comes back and turns him to human again, then says, 'Bravo, now you're just like you should be.' Then the girl seed he was like before, the real Prince Darling, and wanted to marry him. The prince put the ring back on and never did take it off again, and it never stinged him again 'cause he kept being a good boy."

Adidas delivers the last words in a whisper because all the children are asleep, even Magic, flattened by the weight of the minis, even Stutt who'd stopped making comments, even Whale above, whose hammock expands and contracts with each breath. Adidas wonders when they all slipped off to the land of nod and what was the last thing they heard. He likes telling tales to the little ones to put them to sleep, but sometimes he wonders whether, by systematically failing to hear the happy ending, they aren't missing the point and if dozing off in the middle of an attempted rape or a human turning into a fiendish beast isn't a sure recipe for nightmares.

Quietly, he gets up, contemplates the piled lives inhaling and exhaling with one single breath, like some chimerical creature, tender and covered in bruises, and slowly nestles up against his kin and their collective slumber.

* * *

Terror keeps nodding off. He hasn't slept for two days, or maybe it's been ten, there's too much work to do building the raft. Plus, it's summer, and all the heat and light make him never want to go to bed again; he's constantly on the move, but the second he stops, sleep comes for him. When it's his turn to stand guard, his attention wanders, the rustling and creaking he's supposed to be alert to meld with the whispering of his nascent dreams, the slingshot in his palm goes limp, taking on the texture of a blankie, and he gives a start at discovering his thumb in his mouth. Pretty makes fun of him, humming lullabies he has to bat away like spiderwebs so as not to end up trapped inside.

"*Sleep, baby, sleep...*"

An annoyed Terror twirls his nunchakus, which Pretty evades with a laugh.

"*Your father's watching his sheep...*"

"Shh!"

"*...sleep, baby, sleep...*"

"SHH!"

Separate from the song, Terror has picked out the sound of footsteps. Two sets. The first one doesn't worry him, he recognizes the trot of a tame animal and, in fact, a few seconds later, the bulky silhouette of the pitbull that Rasca has baptized Priscilla extricates itself from the vegetation. The animal wags its tail, begs to be petted, but Pretty can't stand the smell of dogs and so only scratches its head with her fingertips. Meanwhile, the other creature keeps advancing, its step weary but distinct, neither the tread of a malefactor or a wolf—this person, a grown-up, is cautious but determined, and sober, which means it will take longer to bring them down. Pretty listens, frowns, exchanges a glance with her partner. She has never heard anything quite like it either: a voluntary, non-predatory intrusion. Terror strokes his slingshot, and Pretty tightens her grip on the ocarina, but neither can decide what to do.

As though sensing their confusion, Wolfpup appears out of the bushes.

"No, I don't think it's a policer," she whispers over her shoulder.

"You don't think so, or you're sure it's not?" retorts Fiji from right behind her.

"I'm sure."

"Will I fire?" murmurs Terror.

"The pitbull's here," Wolfpup adds.

Beneath the stranger's footfall, leaves crackle like mist dispersing, and the glow from a flashlight sweeps the tree trunks. This person is organized. Knows what they're looking for. The row of sentries stiffens. In the dark, a woman's voice sounds.

"Hello? Anyone there? I've come to ask for your help."

Wolfpup lays her hand on Terror's forearm as he keeps the intruder in his sights.

"Wait."

It's the first time they've ever been addressed this way.

"Children?" the voice resumes, sonorous and gentle. "I know you're there. I don't mean to bother you. I'm looking for two girls. Their names are Mathilda and Cassandra."

Fiji gives a start. Without consulting her colonel, she orders, "Knock her out. Now."

Stunned, Wolfpup stares at her leader, who nudges her with her shoulder to get her to stand between Pretty and Terror. With one blow of the whistle, Fiji summons Lego; slingshots and guns are trained on the woman, and Fiji follows each micromovement, intent on the space between her line of defence and the intruder, watching it charge itself like an electric field, feeling the activation of the Ravine's force of repulsion, ready to send this stranger back to where she came from. Terror lets his rock fly and doesn't miss; the woman is struck between the eyes and falls back, her flashlight, which drops by her head, revealing blood trickling down her face. The dog gives a whimper of dismay.

Bleach has witnessed the whole scene from the sky, only realizing too late what is happening. As Lego rushes over to the inert body, she flits down to a branch to stop and think, but, the moment she lands, she realizes everything has already been thought out, she knows what she must do. Resuming her flight, she soars up high, joins her hands, closes her eyes, then opens her arms in one swift motion. Her gesture embraces the entire scene, enveloping Fiji, still stationed between Wolfpup and Terror; and Pretty, unable to stand still; and Lego, having trouble finding the victim's pulse; even Tick-Tock, watching from the shadow of a brushpile; and with this one sweeping gesture, Bleach plunges everyone into the honey of her spell. Lego straightens like an automaton, backs away from the victim, and returns to his station; the stone returns to Terror's slingshot, and the woman jumps to her feet as though her body is on a spring; Fiji swallows her words and backs into the bushes, slowly joined by Wolfpup. Once she has brought everyone back to the right moment, Bleach relinquishes her hold over time. She folds her long, diaphonous wings together to float to the ground and lands between Fiji and Wolfpup.

"No, I don't think it's a policer," says Wolfpup.

"You don't think so, or you're sure it's not?"

Bleach draws closer. The beam of the flashlight sweeps across their feet, and Terror raises his slingshot.

"Hello? Anyone there? I've come to ask for your help."

Bleach can feel Fiji stiffen beside her and takes her hand to calm her.

"Children? I know you're there. I don't mean to bother you. I'm looking for two girls. Their names are Mathilda and Cassandra."

"I know her," Bleach says in a hurried whisper. "Fiji, she's the grandmother of the two girls in Paradise."

"We've gotta stop her right now."

"Okay, but no doing her any harm."

"We won't have no choice, Bleach."

"She won't do a thing to us, she won't say a word. She was a friend of the Old Man's. She'd not be dangerous."

"She'll be even less dangerous knocked out."

"No. She'll just wanna talk; after, she'll go back to the other side."

"We couldn't let her come into the camp."

"So go see her before she gets too close."

Fiji stares at Bleach, unsure, and Bleach's ruby eyes hold the most confident expression she's capable of.

"If that don't work, we can always knock her out after."

"That's true," Fiji concedes.

In the beam of blue light, three shadows escorted by a one-eared pitbull make their way toward the woman who waits deferentially. Lego holds his baseball bat; Fiji, her imaginary crown; and Wolfpup has a gun hidden in her pants. Tick-Tock, still stationed in the brush, has no weapon but is ready to pounce if need be, to impress Bleach.

Once they draw near, the dog sits between the two camps as though to prevent a confrontation. The woman turns her flashlight up to show her face, then, likely realizing it must make her look like she's about to tell a horror story, points it down at the ground. On further reflection, she turns it off and lets the moonlight adhere to their faces before speaking.

"My name is Gloria. My granddaughters, Cassandra and Mathilda, disappeared after the death of their mother. I thought you might have seen them."

Arms crossed, the children stare at the placid-looking grandmother. There is no doubt that, between the adult and the three children, the latter are the ones in charge; they know it, and the woman knows it. After a moment's hesitation, during which Wolfpup and Lego wonder whether they're supposed to speak on behalf of their leader, Fiji finally opens her mouth.

"We don't know 'em. We're here playing hide-seek. Our parents been waiting for us. We'd not be s'posed to speak to strangers."

Gloria crouches as though talking to young children, making herself smaller than they are; uncomfortable, she half-straightens, her back bowed, trying to find a way to make herself seem both less threatening and respectful.

"I see. But maybe you came across them playing hide-and-seek?"

From her backpack, she pulls out a picture of two little girls whose smiles reveal a few missing teeth.

"This photo isn't too recent…they're older today. Twelve and fifteen. But it gives you an idea. Have you seen them before?"

Lego shakes his head firmly; after a slight hesitation, Wolfpup follows suit and Fiji brusquely pushes the photo away.

"No. They'd be too old for the hiding game."

"If you come across them, could you give them a message? That their grandmother is living in their house. That there's nothing left to fear there. That I'd love to see them again. To look after them. Can you tell them that?"

Fiji's only response is to turn on her heel, followed by her two sidekicks. Priscilla heads for the river, and the grandmother starts rifling through her backpack.

"Get outta here! And don't come back, crazy old bat!" yells Terror, who feels obliged to at least hurl an insult if not a stone.

As Wolfpup whacks him across the back of the head, the intruder lays down on a stump a package of cookies and three tins of food that Tick-Tock hurries to gather up, not even bothering to stay hidden. Slowly, the grandmother sets off toward the east, and Fiji and Bleach, one worried, the other relieved, watch her walk away at her slow pace as though even the night, the forest, the proximity of armed children, and the city of Fort Détroit itself were not enough to alarm a woman such as she.

* * *

The sunlight clings to her face like a mask—down, way down the tunnels of her memory, she sees a woman half reclining, her face coated with a creamy paste, her body both expectant and relaxed, and Fiji tries to assume the same posture, as though the pose holds the key to a certain serenity. Because everything weighs on her today—the secrets, the fatigue, the pictures of missing children posted throughout the city, the poison in the river, her unstoppable growth, the decisions, Bleach, authority, and that damn woman who snuck into their camp. She feels like her body is made of fine glass and that mere air pressure could shatter it.

It was during the winter that she discovered how to arrest the sapping of her internal resources—she had never had to before, it seems to her that her head didn't used to be as full, but last winter, at the height of the gastro epidemic, she felt herself suffocating. So she found this pine tree, its branches forming a natural roof, its trunk like the pole of a marquee tent, and took refuge there; she positioned herself at exactly the right angle so the sun would caress her, then closed her eyes saying, *I'll stay put just till the sun's ray leaves my face,* and for that instant, she stopped thinking. Little by little, movement replaced the absence of images, something abstract and shining, the play of colours and light through her eyelids. Soon, nothing existed save for the pink and orange wisps dancing against her eyes and sparkling deep in her heart.

Today is like that but different, it's hot out and spruce gum melts in her hair, the wind is gentler, but the sunlight is the same, trickling over her like syrup. The sounds are many, they enter her skull through small hidden doorways— ants marching, petals rustling, twigs snapping—she even thinks she hears her nails growing, her bones creaking as they lengthen, and, high above, stars colliding.

Peace moves in, and Fiji feels deep inside that everything is where it should be, she finally belongs to another, she is a baby the forest rocks in its boughs of wood, she has nothing left to do, no choices to make, nothing to win. Everything is so forgotten that she thinks she might have dozed off; the shapes sailing across her closed eyelids slow, the pink is now almost motionless between the fingers of orange, but she isn't asleep. In the eye of the cyclone, queens keep watch.

* * *

There is always something burning. When it isn't a log, it's a hut; when it isn't a hut, it's a car; when it isn't a car, it's a house; when it isn't a house, it's an entire street. No one but Stutt seems to fear the flames—everyone lives with the perpetual stench of smoke glued to the soles of their shoes, to their eyelashes, to their lips. As for Stutt, he wakes at night to make sure nothing is burning; the only thing that worries him as much as fire is his library, and the more his collection of books grows, the more afraid he is of seeing it go up in flames.

It began with a looting run. Like the others, Stutt couldn't read or write; back then, he barely knew how to speak and his only thought was for food. He was going through a growth spurt; a devouring hunger ran non-stop through his body, he could feel the bones in his legs, the muscles in his arms, even his hair begging him to feed their urgent lengthening. Yet the rule had always been the same in the Ravine: if you want to eat more than the others, you have got to look harder than they do. Stutt spent his days criss-crossing the neighbouring districts, crying, all the while aware the endless walking was aggravating his hunger. No one gave him a hand because he couldn't express himself normally, his words tripped over each other, the collision of consonants and ideas giving him headaches and mouth cramps and earning him "talk normal!" remarks from the big kids. By the time he discovered the greenhouse, Stutt had reached the point of eating the plants' roots, newspaper, mud pies, dead crickets, candle wax, and bulrushes.

That first time, the Old Man wasn't around, and, afterward, he didn't seem to notice Stutt's presence. Thinking he'd been so careful, it took a while for Stutt to figure out that the man was just pretending not to see him; now he suspects the gardener of putting in conspicuous places the ripest fruit, the crunchiest vegetables, food Stutt had never seen before but that a dim part of his mind recognized as edible. As well as the vegetables, the old man sometimes left behind a chicken leg, bread, cookies that Stutt swallowed whole at first, then in a more measured way, tasting the bitter and the sweet, calmer about letting the nutrients help his body grow. Then the Old Man started leaving behind other objects—clothes, boots, and, one day, books.

They were only simple picture books and basic readers, but Stutt took possession of them without hesitation, even before he understood what they were. He spent long hours staring at the pages and, little by little, the symbols became familiar, then intelligible. In utter secrecy and with infinite patience, he learned of a detour between the world and his thoughts that didn't involve faltering speech or truncated words.

Of course, the others ended up finding the Old Man and his greenhouse too; Magic even thought to follow the gardener, discovering other supply points where, if they were parsimonious in helping themselves, they could return again and again. As for Stutt, he had come across another sort of horn of plenty: abandoned libraries. Rich people had cleared out of the chic districts as though the city were being bombed, leaving behind furniture, knick-knacks, cigars, stamp collections—and books. Piles and piles of books: some short, some long, some illuminated in gold, some hiding dirty pictures from the old days, all of them waiting in the bellies of the manors of St. Peter or Perlemère, and no one interested in rescuing them. Except Stutt.

Today, he owns books in nine different languages, some written in unfamiliar characters he likes to stroke with the tip of his index finger; beneath his touch, the curved and pointed letters murmur and sigh. Others have pages so thin they seem to evaporate when pinched; still others offer staggering illustrations and drawings showing the insides of things—bodies, planets, machines—most with way too many words. But Stutt reads faster and faster, sometimes too fast: given the trouble he has enunciating, he'd need four lifetimes to recite just one of the novels, some of which frighten him at times with their stories that dive too deep, revealing shocking things, worlds identical to the ones that buzz in his head, ones he could never name but had vaguely intuited, like the aftertaste of a fruit that has yet to exist.

Thanks to the greenhouse's ABC books, Stutt has converted half a dozen other kids to reading and writing. Some preferred learning on their own, in secret, without anyone else watching them muddle through and witnessing their crazy spelling. But Stutt is the one most attached to the mooring that paper represents: fragile, combustible, vulnerable to rain, frost, dirty hands, harrowing tantrums, and nose-pickings; he spends half his life deciphering volumes too advanced for him and the other half fearing they'll disappear; yet despite the precarity of what keeps him going, he owns something no one else does: answers. Because there is a book for everything, a chapter to shed light on each impasse, and now as the four amateur adventurers ready themselves to push off on their makeshift raft, Stutt has precisely the tomes they need: *Fort Détroit under Renaud Dubuisson*, *The Rouge River from 1701 to 1950*, and *Adventures of Huckleberry Finn*.

* * *

They tore logs out of the earth, which had already begun eating away at them, found muddy planks they secured to the logs using nails from the last battle between Terror and Method, lashed it all together with lengths of rope, then jumped wildly up and down on their barge to test its solidity. Rasca would have wanted them to install a mast and a sail and a cabin to shelter from bad weather, but she was made to understand it was impossible, useless, and ridiculous, childish concerns of the kind she'd have to suck up if she wanted to be a crew member. There was no time for finer points; their raft would be rudimentary, light enough to pull over logjams, and, above all, heroic. With both feet planted on the watercraft, Rasca can gauge the urgency with which it was built—planks shake, nails poke up, the wood smells of worms; it is barely big enough for the four of them seated, but one will always be standing to manoeuvre the pole that will help them follow the current and avoid any perils. Yatim has a waterproof tarp and a sleeping bag, Method has her collection of whistles and bird calls, Terror has a gun, and Rasca is in charge of provisions; to keep hunger at bay, Magic helped her make a hard, compact bread that settles in a lump in their stomachs.

When they woke, fog had conjured away the forest, but now the weather is so fine it's as though the sky has delivered on a promise, a guarantee that they will return safe and sound. Fiji and Lego and Wolfpup and Stutt and Adidas and Pretty gather on the bank; they dish out goodbye hugs, some with tears in their eyes, and Rasca has the sudden feeling that they are off to a rendezvous with death, but her brother slaps her bum hard, and she feels reassured. Stutt begs the big kids to let him bring his books along, but they refuse, claiming the raft is too top-heavy as it is. Rasca doesn't know how to read, but she agrees to carry one on in secret and hides it tucked in the waist of her shorts, like Terror carries his gun. Pretty has made them necklaces as talismans, Rasca's turns out to be smaller than the others; she's about to complain but bites her tongue, knowing they're waiting for just such a wrong move to call her a baby and stop her from being part of the mission, and instead she ties the string round her neck and, looking at the locket on her chest, recognizes the star symbol she's seen on cars, unsure it will actually bring her any luck. Fiji reminds them to be extra careful crossing the barriers formed by branches and trash and to head for the riverbank in the event of a downpour since some of the city's sewers spill into the river, which can rise by several metres in the space of a few minutes, but they already know all that—everyone remembers Murmur's death.

They climb onto the raft and their weight sets it to swaying in an alarming way, and Rasca wonders one last time whether they shouldn't have fixed up the old canoe instead. She has been told again and again that it is beyond repair, its frame shattered and the hull rotted from one end to the other; nevertheless, every night in her dreams, Rasca has seen them swiftly travelling up the Rouge, floating and flying, and she's certain the vision counts for something. Yatim sits beside her, irritated by his necklace that chimes with every move, he'll throw it into the water later on, or maybe offer it to Rasca—she wouldn't mind making a jingling sound.

Method is the first to manoeuvre, she pushes hard on the bank with a pole, the raft shudders and is snatched up by the current, and the explorers sail off to shouts of encouragement. Rasca is disorientated by the sensation of being *on* the river rather than *in* the river; her eyes scan the waves, looking for a point of reference, but the water is opaque, a stranger for the first time. During that first minute on the raft, she understands how much the Rouge has been transformed since the shock wave that hit her. She looks up at Method, who, for her part, is examining the forest canopy with the same worried expression: the emptiness Rasca has detected beneath the water is what Method sees in the trees. The voice of the river has been drowned, and those of the birds have taken flight.

* * *

Fiji arrives and, as though even nature is at her command, the wind picks up, as blue as a punch to the gut, shaking the foliage and sounding like a roar of applause. Immediately, Wolfpup feels the same wound opening in her chest, as with every other time the queen approaches her these days. For a while now, it has been as though Fiji speaks to her in another language, a language they both master, but from a distance, stuck on the end of a stick, with words that are always used against Wolfpup.

"Who've you got on the perimeter?" Fiji begins, her question already sounding like reproach.

"Pretty, Tick-Tock, and Pow-Pow."

"Tick-Tock? He couldn't hit a cow in a hallway."

"He'll not be so bad."

"You're missing one."

"We did it lots with three of us."

"It's gotten dangerous. We'll not be running any risks. Go with 'em—you be the fourth."

161

"It's getting dark out. I'll nod off, Fiji. You know I got no sleep yesterday."

"You're going, and that's that!"

Wolfpup studies her leader, searching her face to see where the order originated, that place where suspicion and reproach are born, then turns her gaze on herself, her body hiding so many knots, she who disappoints her superior in spite of her best efforts and discipline, despite a lifetime of obedience. Like a door slamming shut, her anger explodes.

"How come you're such a jerk?" she cries.

Fiji looks at her second-in-command as though she's just received a ball to the stomach. She takes the hit, then, in a honeyed voice, retorts, "Go do your beddie-bye, Wolfpup, and if someone'd come and demolish our camp in the night and kidnap a mini, it'll be your fault."

"Hey! Who's it bent on rescuing kids we don't even know down the river?" Wolfpup shouts. "All you'd need do is not send our best defence on an expedition if you don't wanna end up low on soldiers! You're going bonkers! Leave me be! Leave me be and go hide out in your palace you didn't wanna share with no one."

"My 'palace'?"

"That abaddoned building, locked with the key from your pillowcase! Don't think I wouldna seed you go there in secret, like it's too nice for us others."

Fiji drops her gaze to her ankle boots full of holes—even though her big feet peek through, she refuses to part with them—and then, so naturally the gesture seems to come of its own accord, her hand flies out to slap Wolfpup's cheek.

The two girls stare at each other, the same stinging pain pulsing in one's hand and the other's cheek; they are, for an instant, united by that burn, one and the same in violence's embrace, then Fiji spins on her heel and walks off, just in time, as tears begin to trickle down Wolfpup's cheeks. As though wakened by the smack of the slap, bats criss-cross the sky like a famished platoon, and an intense whistling pierces Wolfpup's ears; she can't hear a thing anymore, nothing but her anger and the terror of no longer being Fiji's second, no longer living under her authority and clinging to her certainties. In the deafening noise, she doesn't hear Lego's approach.

"You okay?"

Feeling both humiliated and liberated by the appearance of a witness, Wolfpup bursts into uncontrollable sobs that hit Lego like so many baseballs smashing into a glove. He hugs the colonel.

"A real pain in the ass Fiji's turned into," he mutters.

Wolfpup's only reply is a strangled gurgle.

"Is it true what you said?" continues Lego. "She's got a secret palace?"

Wolfpup steps back, wiping snot away with the back of her hand. "I seed her go there. Outside the wood, thattaway."

"The old pavilion?"

"I dunno. I tried to get inside lotsa times. It's locked. I don't even know how she got herself the key."

"Guess she's got her connections."

"It'd be real great to hibernate in. Way better'n our hut. But she won't want us going there."

Calm by now, Wolfpup examines her friend, the enforcer, the arm of justice as decreed by Fiji; Lego also has the worried brow of someone living under the boot of an unpredictable force. He, too, shoulders a burden that no one, not even the queen, can understand, that of being dominant and submissive at one and the same time, master and enslaved— caught between a too-reckless flock and an authority too transcendent to understand what enforcement of the law entails and what it costs in terms of joy and an untroubled outlook.

"You ever done wondered how old Fiji'd be?"

"No," says Lego. "Do you know?"

"Not outright," says Wolfpup. "But she's got more years'n a lotta kids who got theyselves banished."

"Not that many more."

"You seen her buds?"

"No!" cries Lego, scandalized.

"I think she bleeds 'tween her legs even. For sure, she's got the hormones."

Lego's features crumple as though his mind has just shrunk inside his skull, disgusted at the thought of the eternal leader's pubescence.

"Who knows, could be she's already a teen and we don't know it. She's been round forever!" he thinks out loud.

"It's not like she's gonna banish herself."

"No way she'll go and change the rules!" Lego objects.

"She's already started! You know the love rule?"

"No…?"

"Before, if someone got in love, they hadda go," Wolfpup sums it up.

"And?"

"And now, everyone knows Tick-Tock's in love with Bleach—"

"That crybaby's nothing but trouble."

"—and Fiji didn't do nothing."

164

"'Cause she's best friends with Bleach," adds Lego.

"'Sides, soon as someone's got the hormones, they flip-flop 'bout stuff like that."

"Teens like that love stuff."

"Arggh. Arggggh."

"I know."

"We lost Bluejean, Mayo, Nori, Vishnu, but none of 'em had the hormones as bad as Fiji," Wolfpup lists them off. "Bluejean's voice didn't even get to changing."

"She's cheating."

"Cheating and lying."

Lego and Wolfpup exchange a look. For the first time in their second life, the seed of rebellion enters their heads. They don't have the words yet, or the exact means or a plan, but a landscape has opened up inside, a breach in the established order.

Without drawing attention to itself, a small garter snake slithers between their feet, wriggles under dead leaves, around young sprouts, and penetrates the shadows leading to a tent forever smelling sweetly of milk; here two other children are deep in conversation, one crying, the second, on the other side of the mosquito netting, speaking words of wisdom and encouragement.

"We got no choice, Fiji. We gotta go 'n tell 'em."

Fiji takes a deep breath, her eyes turned to the sky crimped with new stars like the world beginning. Bleach is right, and Fiji knows it: she has just slapped Wolfpup; Paradise is about to be uncovered; she has lost control.

"Not tonight," she whispers. "Tomorrow."

"Tomorrow," says Bleach.

She rests a palm whiter than silence on the netting, and

Fiji lays her hand there, too, the gesture one of such total intimacy that Whale, observing the scene from high in the branches, looks away.

* * *

At night all cats are grey is what Tante Rosalind used to say in another lifetime. Magic would add: all houses, cars, telephone poles, churches, garden sheds, factories, everything is grey at night except the Old Man's treasures. His intergalactic vessel is anthracite grey; but, inside, dots of green, pink, yellow, and red stand out in such a way that Magic knows immediately where to go and where to send her companions. The latter seem blind to the colours that slash through the darkness, they need her to see. She can't explain it—all she knows is she could find these gems with her eyes closed, just from the scent of sugar and sap, their shape, their unique vibration, a configuration of cells in infinite variations. In the dark, she advances toward the Juicy Hearts, lays her fingertips on their ruby flesh and a shiver runs through her—all that life trembling in the hollow of her hand, an external organ offered up to the gaze and appetite of all. As she takes it, Magic feels tears well up, part regret, part delight, halfway between guilt and cruelty. The others, the kids she wrests from death day in and day out thanks to her finds, do not have the same response; they're content to ingest everything she gives them without realizing that their energy comes from somewhere, that their life has been stolen from the plants and the earth; they don't weep at the paradox. With a twist of the wrist, she picks the gleaming fruit and places it in her basket.

"Stutt, come help with the Juicy Hearts. Then go for the

Sweet Balloons. Adidas, there'll be Green Clubs over there. Pick some Mini UFOs too."

"Some what?"

The dark of the greenhouse comes to life, swirling with silvery wavelets, and baskets fill. They don't hurry. At night, there's less risk, the only true danger is sleep: early that summer, Rasca fell fast asleep harvesting Prickly Reds, and they had to abandon their loot to carry her back to the Ravine.

But tonight, everyone is wide awake: Magic gave each kid a square of chocolate so bitter that Adidas balked at swallowing it. The harvesting advances at a good clip, the baskets have almost reached their maximum weight and Magic is about to announce it's time to go when a deep voice is heard from the back of the greenhouse.

"Did those strawberry plants work out for you after all?"

The children freeze; Magic lets fall a Heart that bursts open on the ground with a wet thud.

"Did you plant 'em in the sun? If not, you would'n'a got much."

Slowly, Magic turns; the Old Man is sitting at the far end of the vessel, so motionless he could be mistaken for a huge worn-out puppet. In the darkness, his beard seems even longer and his hair thicker; his voice is cavernous.

"You don't hafta come at night, you know," he continues. "Or pick the garden goods in secret. I've got enough for everyone. Especially for those who help out."

Behind Magic, the boys have started to back away toward the exit; Stutt trips and falls spread-eagled into the Green Clubs whose stems prick him, causing him to cry out, startling Adidas. As for Magic, she doesn't budge, paralyzed by the words spoken by the Old Man who, although he has

167

often come across them helping themselves in his greenhouse, has always pretended not to see them—that's the tacit understanding they have: the children destroy nothing, always leaving behind more than they take, and the Old Man makes as though he is unaware of their existence.

"If you want, I could show you how. Strawberry plants need sunlight and well-drained soil. The carrot seeds you took last year can't be sown too deep or they won't sprout. Wouldn't it be better to know how to grow vegetables instead of just taking a few so it doesn't show?"

Caught up in his speech, Magic hasn't noticed the others taking off; when she turns, they're already long gone, she can see their dark shapes leaping across the horizon. She starts to hurry after them.

"Don't forget your tomatoes, Magic," the Old Man interrupts her.

Magic stops, looks again at this man who hasn't budged from his chair but whose stature seems to grow with each word he speaks. Her basket is within arm's reach; she hesitates, torn between the desire to turn down anything coming from this man who knows her name and the desire not to leave empty-handed.

"Don't be talking to me!" she yells finally before grabbing her provisions and hightailing it out of there.

* * *

The rain carves channels through the soil and the snarls in their locks; it's been so long since their hair was wet, and it feels so good, untangles their thoughts. In front of the girls, the pavilion looms, its old stones, from the rain shower, dark and shiny like a black gem; behind them, the soccer field unfurls thousands of tiny green hands, everywhere water scrapes and rakes and brings ideas to life. As always, true to form, Bleach, being Bleach, hums absent-mindedly while Fiji stares apprehensively at the entrance. The key, big and rusty like a dog's chain, is hard to turn in the lock; the door resists, and Bleach has to push it open with her shoulder.

The place still has a sickly dampness to it even though the sisters have gotten over the ailment that saw them isolated from the others soon after their arrival. It's dark inside, the shutters are closed, and the girls seem not to want to waste any candles, or maybe their matches have taken on the damp—or perhaps they like the dark, who knows where those two taciturn adolescents are concerned. Their bodies face each other in the half-light, bent over a game of checkers, but, with the sound of the door, the youngest turns to the two visitors, her coppery face framed by a starburst of hair; the eldest, tall with hunched shoulders, sinks further into her chair.

"Hi, Cassandra! Hi, Mathilda!" Bleach sings.

Without hesitation, she heads over to the tiny fridge, ready to fill it with supplies.

"Yuck. Mould. Into the trash," she decrees joyfully as she eliminates anything rotten, substituting apples, milk, biscuits.

Cassandra comes over to help, and Mathilda stares solemnly at Fiji, who surveys the impeccably kept room—floor swept, clothes folded, even the campcots made neat, not a wrinkle in sight.

"You can't be staying here no more," the leader states point-blank.

"Why not?" asks Cassandra, her cheeks immediately flushing.

"A woman come looking for you. Said she's your grand-mother."

"We got no grandmother," Mathilda retorts.

"We do so," Cassandra says.

"We didn't tell her nothing," Bleach assures them.

"But this place won't be safe for you no more," Fiji says.

"Got it. We're off," Mathilda says without the slightest trace of emotion, and begins stuffing clothes into her bag that fills too quickly; it's as though, in a matter of seconds, her life has been compressed into a canvas cube. As for Cassandra, she doesn't move, intuiting that the conversation is not yet over.

"Not right now!" Bleach exclaims. "You'll stay a coupla days more; we'd find you another place."

"What place?" Mathilda asks.

"I dunno yet," replies Fiji. "Probably deeper in the woods somewhere. Not too far from camp so's we can bring you food."

"We'll get you settled good," adds Bleach.

"Just one more thing," says the queen. "You said the police was after you. Before we move you outta here, you'd gotta tell us why. Elsewise there'd be no letting you into our Ravine."

The sisters say nothing for a while, Mathilda staring at the wall ahead, Cassandra's gaze intent on her younger sister. Watching them, no one could tell if the eldest's eyes are on the youngest to make her hold her tongue or in the hope she will say something. Seconds pass, and it's as though a steel plate has been lowered from the ceiling. Finally, Mathilda returns the gaze, and her sister bows her head, giving up the way someone lets go of a rope after hanging on for too long.

Outside, rain dribbles onto their kingdom and, beneath

a cracked windowpane, a dripping Tick-Tock listens—he hadn't meant to spy on them, he just wanted to follow in Bleach's wake, but now he pricks up his ears at the two runaways' tale and the queen's and the fairy's silence; he listens to the sound of the secret being laid down in Paradise.

He is still hidden behind a corner of the wall when Fiji carefully locks the door behind her, her voice slicing through the rain shower like a golden knife.

"We gotta look quick. If they come to smash in the place, Paradise has gotta be empty."

"We could settle here come winter," Bleach suggests.

"Maybe."

"Where'd we be putting the two of 'em?"

"Not too far from camp. Not too close."

"We'll find a place."

"I'm next."

"Next what?"

"To leave."

"Don't say that."

Fiji squeezes her eyes shut and shakes her head. "I'm getting too big, Bleach. The others can tell."

Bleach lays a hand on her friend's cheek. "You're never too big for me."

She locks her mouth onto Fiji's, and in the ease of that gesture, Tick-Tock understands this is not the first time, that the kiss has been ongoing; even when they're apart, their lips, his beloved's and the queen's, are joined, their tongues dancing, always, and no one, no one, he realizes with an aching heart, will ever be able to undo that eternal embrace.

He spits, his heart sinking low.

* * *

Rafting down the river took two days longer than expected, more food than anticipated, more scratches, bruises,
blisters, bites, more thirst and hours of sleep, more tears
and sunburns, more lives and flesh. The afternoon's heat
weighs on them like a large foot bent on trampling the raft,
they no longer have the canopy of trees to protect them,
they've reached the spot where the Rouge slows and wid-
ens, bordered by factories that appear deserted but still spill
their magma into the water all the same. The three children
are so thirsty they feel sick, but all they have left are a few
mouthfuls of water, and even that, the sun looks about to
take; fortunately, Method had the presence of mind to fill
the bottles the night of the downpour as, on the riverbank,
they looked for shelter and their raft drifted off—it took
them two hours to track it down the next day. Now they
would give anything for rain, to see the Rouge take one great
big watery breath, swell up, then spit out what the river has
stolen from them.

Earlier that day, they floated by the Old Mosque where,
according to Yatim, the other group of children used to
live, but they were too exhausted to venture onshore to
look around; the current was swift at that spot, and landing would have required energy they were no longer able
to summon. They simply called out "Ahoy!" like people on
a foundering ship, and their cries flew through the gaping
doors like pigeons, swirling beneath the building's vaulted
ceiling before making a grand exit. The building was empty.
They carried on.

Free of logs now, the river allows for an easy descent. Here
and there, rust-eaten tugboats and freighters with white-

hot hulls cling to the banks, emitting a painful creaking sound; the children shudder as they pass. The water is now a milky turquoise, a sublime and synthetic colour that burns the retina after too much exposure, provoking visions: That final image of Terror standing on the logjam, trying to dislodge the trunk holding back the mound of floating lumber. Once again, they see him lose his footing, fall through a gap between the branches, his body disappearing, unable to find the surface again for all the debris, the long minutes spent waiting for him to emerge, hoping in vain for a miraculous cry, cough, gasping intake of air from their friend.

Now the raft seems too big for them. The planks no longer carry the smell of earth or algae but of piss and poison, their legs are crusted in mud, their hair teems with lice, but at last they arrive at their destination—Fiji had said there would be two drawbridges, which they have just passed. The jutting shelf of Île Gus appears.

This is the epicentre of it all, just the sight of the facilities' pharaonic structure, its ashen colour, and the vertiginous silhouettes of the tall furnaces makes it clear that the river's fate is determined by what happens on this island. The closer they get, the more certain they are that the force that propelled the deadly wave upriver originated here, and the less they understand how any other children could have chosen to live so close to a site such as this. The din of the furnaces is infernal, a roar borne on implacable hatred. The water's surface sizzles in the sun as though to fry anything afloat there. The children huddle together in the middle of the raft for fear of being spattered. Despite the limpid blue of the sky, it's as though the world has gone dark and is covered in soot. Farther down, the river forms an elbow, which they slowly follow, no longer controlling their trajectory; like a sick yet benevolent hand, it guides them far from the island toward the opposite shore. The stench pursues them, metamorphizing from one second to the next, sometimes chemical, sometimes burnt, sometimes organic, rotten.

Rasca is the one who first spots the wharf, a long structure of old wood, almost anachronistic in this setting. Yatim is the one who makes out the jumbled heap there. He grabs the pole and finds the river bottom, close but invisible, it's too late to change direction, they are headed straight for it. Weeping tears of salt more than water, they run aground on a floating pile of bodies, some tall and frail, others short and round. Amid the tangle of hair and arms, they also distinguish fur and paws, a ferret head adorned with a small pearl necklace; there are toys, life preservers, sopping wool blankets, faces drained of all colour, eyes open to the horror.

With halting steps, Method, Rasca, and Yatim disembark and step over the floating grave, from which they cannot tear their eyes, to stand on the wharf and survey the scene. There are at least fifteen children there, some beached, others dangling in stagnant waters, with four times the number of animals, otters, ducks, raccoons, but no fish—maybe they're farther downstream, maybe they have sunk to the bottom. Still discernible in the air, under the intense stench of death, is the charge remaining from the shock that killed them all.

Method opens her mouth to speak—there's little to be said—"Quick, let's go"—and her two companions follow her along the dock that threatens to buckle beneath their feet. Just as they step onto terra firma, leaving behind the raft, the bottles, the book, the sleeping bag, a sudden snort is heard nearby. They turn as one. A tall black horse emerges from a row of bulk containers. It's the first healthy animal they have encountered in days.

The creature takes a step toward the children. Rasca and Yatim shuffle away while Method advances to caress its shiny, steaming hide. She leads it with ease over to a large rock onto which she climbs in order to lean into its ear and whisper a few words, then she signals for Rasca and Yatim to approach.

"He wants to," she announces.

She helps the little girl up, then the big boy, and jumps on herself, the animal barely seeming to register the riders' weight on its back. But the minute it feels them hanging on, the black horse dashes off through the woods, toward the cool and fiery north, toward home.

"D'ya think…they're all…all dead?" Yatim asks.

The horse's gallop joggles them, chopping up their sentences.

"Uh-huh," Method says. "Everyone'd be dead . . . back there."

"Their animals…too."

"Who…who is it…killed 'em?" Rasca asks through tears.

"The island."

"It's a death island."

"Uh-huh."

"We gotta do something."

"Uh-huh."

"We gotta take revenge."

"We gotta destroy it."

"We gotta talk to Pow-Pow."

They stop speaking, but for the first time in days, smiles

split their faces—not of joy but of something else, the underside of rage, the tipping point of powerlessness. The horse runs, a mirage of muscle and certainty that mutates at times, taking on the shape of a boat, a canoe flying between the trees, between Method's breath and Terror's ghost, and the other two wonder if Method called the creature up to save them or whether, from the great beyond, Terror has sent them a lifeline.

I will climb up on my kite again
Leaving you to your hundred thousand children
Left to their own devices
To cast the die in the hands of time

GILLES VIGNEAULT

Gloria emerges from the woods at dawn. The night was short, yet she feels as though an entire lifetime has passed since she took her leave of Eunice on Avenue Fieldvale. Pain throbs in the middle of her forehead, but she has no memory of bumping it. Perhaps it's her third eye burning. It has seen too much.

She starts down streets bursting with sunshine. A shower of birdsong accompanies her steps. She can't rid her mind of the images from last night. Before, there was nothing but her two granddaughters, almost abstractions. Now that she has had a glimpse of the children, they, too, reign over her thoughts—dirty, skinny, superb, with their village of mud and cardboard.

Once she'd been dismissed by the tall girl in ankle boots full of holes, once a prickly voice shouted after her to never return, once a boy with protruding ears had pounced on the provisions she left behind, Gloria strode away. She found herself on a promontory overlooking the small ravine. From there, she watched all night long, at first in the hope of catching sight of Cassandra and Mathilda—she didn't believe for a second the tall girl's words—then out of sheer fascination. Tents, treehuts, short legs in tattered clothing, bodies lying round bonfires made of trash. Shouts, weapons, hugs and not an adult in sight.

The shooting pain is still there between her eyes as she reaches Chesnay. Something rumbles beneath her feet; the sky snaps its fingers. She cuts through the grassland to make it home sooner. Gloria misses the pitbull's company; it stayed behind with the children. In the dark by the Rouge, it became apparent that the dog belongs to them much more than to her.

Solomon is already in the vegetable garden. He's busy fighting the rampaging weeds that seem to come alive the minute he grabs hold of them. From afar, it looks like he's struggling with a giant squid. Catching sight of Gloria, he lets go of his adversaries and straightens up.

"Did you find 'em?"

"No, but I did find some others. A whole gang. The littlest can't be more than five. They live in a kind of camp on the north side of the park."

"Ah, *that's* where they live."

"You know them?"

"From a distance. Kids from rough families that ran away or that social services lost track of. Orphans of overdoses, daughters of parents in prison. How many are there?"

"Around twenty."

"They stock up in my greenhouses. I even built one just for them, farther to the west. I suspected their squat was somewhere nearby."

"It isn't a squat. It's a shantytown."

"Aren't your granddaughters with 'em?"

Gloria rubs her forehead. "I'm not sure. I didn't see them, but I feel like they can't be far. The ones I talked to didn't want to tell me a thing."

"No surprise there. Those kids really stick together. They protect each other. And they don't trust adults at all."

"I saw that."

"But you can take comfort knowin' their lack of trust keeps Cassandra and Mathilda safe."

"Yes, but in what conditions?"

Without answering, Solomon pulls off his gloves and Gloria follows his gaze to the far end of the field quivering against the sky. Like some creature emerging from the soil, a body appears in the fields. Haggard and thinner, Caesar joins them, then kneels next to a row of vegetables. Gloria and Solomon watch, astonished. Caesar digs a hole with his left thumb; behind him with his right hand, he scoops up a clump of dirt and stuffs it into the hole as though it were a bulb. He is busy planting earth in earth.

"Caesar! What're you up to?"

The old man waves his hand to silence Solomon then heads for a crate of zucchini that he carries over to the plants, returning the vegetables to their stalks. The effort brings sour sweat to his skin.

"Caesar," Solomon says again, only louder this time. "Caesar, stop!"

But his friend keeps going, desperately trying to give the fruits of the plants' labour back to them, to cultivate the other way round. All of a sudden, he stops short, struck by some immobilizing force; his body sways like a rope dangling in the wind. He looks like he's about to collapse.

"Come," Solomon says gently, grabbing him by the waist. "You need water, old fella. Let's go see Theo."

Gloria watches them walk off, two pillars of a lopsided house, before she, too, leaves the field. In front of her home, her gaze is drawn to the charred ruins of the house across the way. Something has changed again, at the level of the ground, it's as though tree trunks have pierced through the soil from below. She shakes her head, and her aching brow protests, like an idea trapped beneath a flat rock.

*　*　*

Eunice's father always had a song on his lips. Even old, even senile, morning to night, he'd sing softly, often unwittingly; if he had had to make a conscious effort to remember the lyrics to "Jean Petit qui danse" or "Au chant de l'alouette," he'd have remained silent, paralyzed inside a web of elusive words. But the old melodies were buried deep in a part of him that dated back to before his own birth, lodged beneath his tongue and in his sinew for generations, resistant to forgetting and dementia.

After his death, Eunice felt her existence open wide. The perpetual stress and hard labour of every moment gave way to stretches of boundless time. That space eased everything: her body, the walls of her house, her thoughts…She'd been annoyed when Raquel had said she could finally breathe now—she didn't want to admit just how much her father's passing had freed her. Of course, she was as busy as before, addicted to ways of doing shaped by duress. But in truth, she lived and slept better than ever, at peace now that she no longer needed to keep watch over anyone else's slumber.

But eventually all the silence got to her. The soft hum of her father's presence had been as vital as water, air, intermittent electricity, and the smell of fires burning. Eunice would have liked to fill the emptiness with his songs, but the melodies eluded her, as though there had been a scission of some kind, as though she and her father spoke different languages. The hush weighed on her house like an anvil. She couldn't understand; after weeks of peaceful mourning, what was this thing sprung from nowhere, bubbling beneath the surface? Eventually, Eunice found the courage to look closer. And to recognize, with the weariness of those who, no matter what they seek, forever come up against the same thing—veiled anger. But something else as well; fury that has given birth, its offspring a haunting imperative, a wound to the spirit. *To see justice served.*

With the wind, the curtains billow and fly into her face. Eunice realizes her hands are still immersed in the dishwater, now cold, and still wringing the washcloth mercilessly. She lets it drop, listens. Gloria is back from her expedition. Safe and sound. Eunice steps out onto her back porch. She hears the kettle whistling, Gloria is making herself some chicory tea, perhaps a can of soup, too, judging by the sour smell wafting her way. She hasn't found the little ones. Otherwise, she wouldn't be in her kitchen making some pathetic meal, slowly and alone. But maybe she has stumbled across something. As has become customary over the past few months, Eunice leaves the green house for the yellow one to trade questions with her neighbour. It's so easy to drown one's worries in those of others.

* * *

The pitbull trots down the middle of the street. Her right ear hurts, the bite that tore it off still burning these many years later. Over time, she has come to understand that the pain will never end. It is part of her, has taken over where the ear and the fights left off, like a new organ replacing the old. A heart, a liver, two eyes, one ache.

She usually prefers the forest, its little humans and their

undisguised scent, but for several days now, the site no longer meets her needs. So she has returned to paved ground, to the smell of burning, to lovelorn plots of land. In the forest, evil lurks. The water is undrinkable. And the dog is thirsty—a great hunger and thirst run through her, but the dead crows and otters washed up by the river reek and are inedible. By the time she reaches the field where small rodents scurry, ones she easily catches, she has eaten nothing for days. Her hunger lessens slightly. A basinful of rainwater offers itself to her like a treasure. She drinks till her stomach grows taut; beyond, deep in her belly, small beings wriggle happily, nourished by her blood, tickled by the cold water.

Night is already falling. The dog isn't yet ready for sleep. She continues to wend her way through the neighbourhood. An old woman with crooked fingers keeps watch in her garden; armed with a rifle, she is on guard for any creature that would dare nibble on her plants. Sensing the proximity of bullets, the dog crosses the street. Behind a wall smelling sweetly of mould, two women laugh softly together, as though joy is to be kept secret. In the neighbouring yard, a man, exhausted from looking after others, lights a cigarette. Farther down, another man, unusually pale, walks into his house, a chemical odour trailing him like a shadow about to erase who he is. Next door, the skeleton of a building grows in the night. Across the street, the yellow house and the green house keep breathing side by side. In the first house, the soft woman paces back and forth; in the second, the hard woman tries to fall asleep on her grief as though on a too-rough carpet. The dog listens to their troubled breathing, then lies down between the two. It feels good to sleep close to wounded human beings.

* * *

Although she'd been told that work bees are a kind of cele-bration, Gloria wasn't expecting the scouring of Theophi-lus's community clinic to be quite this joyous. The house is full of people, some from Avenue Clyde and others Gloria doesn't know. Fort Détroitians come from near and far to be nursed by Theophilus, thus avoiding the city's only emer-gency room where patients, both the wounded and those with hacking coughs, can wait for up to two days before even getting to speak to a caregiver of any kind. When Theophilus asked for help, his patients rallied. The exam cot, door handles, walls, and even the magazines in the wait-ing room—nothing escapes them. The umpteenth wave of dysentery to hit the district is probably the result of poorly treated drinking water, but Theophilus believes the infec-tion can also be transmitted from one person to another. So he has orchestrated a vigorous disinfection of his facilities.

While a dozen people scrub the main floor exchanging call-and-response songs, Gloria helps Francelin set up a bedroom on the second floor. Theo usually doesn't house patients, but he believes that, by keeping Caesar close at hand, it will be easier to care for him. From time to time, Sweetie, Block's partner, appears bearing pillows or linens she drops onto a chair trumpeting, "Sterile! Sterile!" before turning on her heel and leaving it up to Gloria to interpret her announcement as either a statement or an order. Eunice left fifteen minutes after arriving when she slipped on a soapy ceramic floor, causing Theo to exclaim, "I don't need any more patients! Go home if you can't stand on your own two feet." As for a sprightly Francelin, taking his own strength for granted, he moves furniture and buckets of water around as though they were nothing more than beach balls. At any given moment, bursts of laughter rise from the foot of the stairs. The smell of coffee and bleach coils round Francelin's chatter as he delivers the latest gossip. Word is that Marina has moved to La Traverse, south of Fort Détroit, with her daughter and mother. Word is that the City is bent on demolishing the Shling even before it reopens. Word is that tourists come on photo safari tours to Fort Détroit to capture images of the ruins. Word is that there's been a spill on Île Gus. Word is that Solomon has a scheme to help the children from Parc Rouge. Gloria gives a start at this last bit of news, the way a lover startles at any mention of their loved one.

The room is ready in no time: a single bed with an adjustable head thanks to a mechanism designed by Francelin; a bedside table, a basin, a flat pillow, sterile blankets; light from the end of the world pouring through the east-facing window. Once their work is done, Gloria and Francelin return to the ground floor where their friends have gathered round a huge platter. The fries it holds are still fuming, smearing grease everywhere. A little girl and a teenage boy rush over to help themselves. Watching them stuff their faces under their parents' amused gaze, Gloria can't help but think again of the children of the Rouge, their hard faces and their skin-and-bone bodies. And of Mathilda and Cassandra, starving somewhere, so near and so desperately unreachable.

A man carefully removes a guitar from a canvas bag, then a woman pulls out a clarinet. Without looking at each other, as though not even noticing the presence of another musician, they launch into a tune one would think they had created together. Smooth and staccato, running and leaping from south to north, a melody to help survive exile and occupation, winter and heat waves, fatigue and nothingness. The tempo continues; then, in a crescendo, as though the words have gradually come back to them, those gathered begin to sing: *Here comes the new dawn / on the heels of defeat, / while on the shore yonder / rise bulrushes and reeds. / Though at times we must suffer / trying to find our way, / we will still laugh together / and advance toward each day* ... and Gloria sheds silent tears, struck suddenly by the sensation that she is not alone, she is not the only one.

* * *

Eunice notes the way Gloria moves in slow motion. Or maybe she herself has sped up, the desperation of doubt, the torment of helplessness having accelerated her presence in the world. A law of relativity stemming from the heart. At the counter, Gloria pours two glasses of lemonade with geological slowness.

Eunice sits on a straight-backed chair that seems a bit wobbly. She stands to examine the legs and notes that all four sit squarely on the floor, yet as soon as she sits down again, the feeling of instability returns; she never manages to truly *sit*. Annoyed, she gets to her feet and opens the pantry. "I've got spicy peanuts, you want some?"

In her hands, the bag seems possessed; its contents scatter outside the bowl. Gloria comes to her friend's rescue, picking up the nuts one by one, then returns to her spot— they each have their own place now, their habits together. As they bite into peanuts so spicy their eyes fill with tears, a creaking resounds outside like a wooden man stretching his limbs across the street. Eunice gives a start.

"It's just the ruins you hear," Gloria reassures her. "Actually, who knows? In any case, something must be settling inside the debris left from the house that burned down."

"Hmm."

"Eunice, are you okay?"

"I'm a bundle o' nerves. Too much coffee, I think. So, what's your idea for the two little ones?"

"Letters. I'll plant them all round the city. It's not as intrusive as going to the camp. Even if the girls don't find 'em themselves, eventually the letters'll get to them, don't you think?"

Having registered not a single syllable of Gloria's speech, Eunice gets to her feet a second time for no reason.

"Eunice, where is your head at?"

As suddenly as she got up from her chair, words leave her lips. An utterance fully formed with no forethought on her part. "I'm ready. I want us to try to find the a-hole who ran over my father."

Gloria looks calmly at her friend, seemingly little troubled by the abrupt switch in topics.

"All right."

"I dunno where to start."

"We'll help you. I'll help you."

"I dunno what I'll do when I get my hands on him."

"You don't know?" Gloria retorts. "This from the woman who totes a gun in her purse?"

Eunice pounds on the table. "They're cutters in my purse. My *gun's* in my night table drawer, I'll have you know."

Gloria bursts out laughing then lays a hand on her friend's wrist. Her fingers are covered in cayenne. Eunice clasps them all the same.

"I'm not planning on killing him, y'know."

"I know."

188

"But there's no one else to punish him."

"I know."

"I can't stand the way folks get off scot-free in this city anymore. I thought I'd gotten used to it. I haven't."

"Let's start by finding him. Then we'll see."

A shape stirs in the shadows of the empty room, gets to its feet, moans. Gloria narrows her eyes as though a dragon has surfaced while they were talking. Two black eyes shine in the dark.

"That the pitbull?"

"She invited herself in the other morning and doesn't seem to wanna clear out. Always plopped on my dad's bed."

"Looks like she's put on weight."

"No wonder, she eats like a sow."

"She's gotta be the only one who managed to fatten up in those woods…"

The dog approaches, lays her head on Eunice's lap, and gives a sad whine as though those were her thoughts exactly.

"I still can't get my head round it," says Eunice, patting the dog. "A band of young'uns living in the woods, not a parent in sight."

"I know."

"We've gotta do something about that too."

"Solomon says they've gone over to the wild side."

"He says he's figgered out how to tame 'em, too."

In one gulp, Eunice downs the last of the spicy peanuts, groans in pain, then heaves a sigh of satisfaction. The dog scratches an ear, making a sound like a bird taking off.

"Read me my horoscope, Glo. I've got a feeling it's time to get moving."

* * *

A deserted city in the light of day is one thing. At night, the emptiness is unstoppable. In the dark, Solomon contemplates the tomatoes, the pattypan squash, the raspberries. In a thousand different ways, they represent his salvation, a guarantee he'll never have an empty belly or hands. A way of holding on to what crumbles away.

The little ones are a long time coming, and for a second he's afraid his presence has turned them off the greenhouse. "They can't see into the future," he reassures himself. "They can't know I'm here." His thoughts switch to Caesar, sweating buckets over at Theo's. Fort Détroit hasn't finished hemorrhaging. The city continues to empty.

Solomon's patience turns into somnolence; his head bobs as, somewhere between wakefulness and being out for the count, his mind drifts. He dreams of travelling back in time. Fort Détroit full of people, full of music, full of words again, as full as full can ever be. He dreams of going even further back, past his childhood; of returning to the city that existed before the uprisings and the relocations, before industry, wars, and treaties; of seeing it as Cadillac did when he stepped out of one of his expedition's twenty-five canoes, the first colonists sullying their breeches at the sight of the approaching Iroquois; he would have loved to have seen the French get their come-uppance, engage in infighting, Cadillac being punched in the face. He dreams of gaining access, before the folly, to the territory teeming with an abundance of life and speaking a language at once slow, refined, and eternal. He dreams of the words uttered by glaciers and lakes.

A bossy whispering draws him from his torpor. Magic has just entered the greenhouse, accompanied by two other kids on tiptoes. For the first time, Solomon discovers the fabulous vocabulary they've invented for the vegetables: *Juicy Hearts, Green Clubs, Mini UFOs*. In his corner, he stays silent and still. He wants to observe the wildlings' doings, anarchic and efficient. The boy with the stutter is here. Solomon hasn't seen him since last fall; he thought he had died. Over the winter, the little ones must drop like flies. It's the first time he has imagined their existence outside their incursions into his universe. His mind never used to venture there. Gloria's foray has changed all that. He read it in the cards the day she arrived at Judith's place: this passive woman would stir things up.

The children's containers, fashioned out of oil cans and fridge drawers, have begun to fill. Solomon watches little Magic attentively as she touches the beefsteak tomatoes with reverence. So intent is she, she hasn't sensed his presence.

"Did those strawberry plants work out for you after all?"

It's as though he's dropped a seed into an anthill. The children's containers clatter to the ground, vegetables rolling at their feet, and the boy with the stutter tumbles into the zucchini patch. As Solomon continues speaking calmly, Magic stares at him as though at an apparition. Finally, he utters the most important sentence of all, the one he's been waiting half the night for: "If you want, I could show you how."

* * *

Like a visitor in a hurry to be off, grief has lost no time slipping away, only to be replaced by anger as white and colossal as explosive muscle. At the time, Tick-Tock envisaged denouncing Fiji, Bleach, and the two fugitives to the other kids of the Ravine, but that wasn't enough. He wanted to mow them down, tear them apart; he was willing to lash out at

191

anything to destroy their impenetrable world, to burst every abscess, to make words cry. He longed to set fire to time.

His clothes are still drenched from the downpour—they stick to his skin like an unwanted caress—rage throbs in his temples, and the farther he gets from the Ravine, the more it deafens him. From spying, he knows where the grandmother of the two hidden girls lives; he knows she's by the field, in the yellow house, where he and Bleach stole green apples when his love for her was still pure and untouched, a treasure now annihilated by the cataclysmic kiss he has just witnessed.

When he first arrived in the camp, and after Lego destroyed his watch, he thought he wouldn't last more than two days. He expected to die from hunger, cold, and melancholy—he knows how death operates, who it comes for and when: it's drawn to those already abandoned by the world, the ones nothing can save. That was who he was, a member of the sickly race, a truly condemned soul, until, that is, he laid eyes on Bleach, until he heard her uncanny song and let her light absorb him. She rescued him, and in those first seconds, he made up his mind that they would grow old together, they would marry, they would live holding on to each other, never apart, not even enough space between the two for the wind or a flea to pass. Bleach made his life in the camp not only tolerable but magical. But then she made it unbearable.

His legs are weary, he'd forgotten how far the house is— with Bleach the trip had seemed so easy—but finally he sees its gable, topped with moss, then a figure bending over in the field, alone, as though waiting for him; he remembers her skirt and her round face that night in the Ravine, her desperate questions and her tins of food. She wants so badly to know. And he, Tick-Tock, will tell her. He's the one who will break the promises, upset the balance, who will set the whole city on fire.

* * *

The sky descends on the fields like a huge cloak. Bent double, Gloria picks zucchini that she gathers in the fold of her skirt. Gently, she chases away a beetle; it glistens as it scuttles off. The stems teem with insects. Beneath the clouds of mercury, their backs of precious stone shimmer.

She looks at her knuckles and her fingernails blackened by the earth of Fort Détroit, a heavy soil, shifting, consumed. Her hands have been transformed since her arrival here: her tendons stand out, her bones have realigned, her palms that used to be smooth and flat have creases now. Fingers that take, seek, dig up the past. Nearby, a chattering of starlings slashes through the light. She remembers the images of long ago, in a book of her uncle's, showing a sky darkened by a flock of passenger pigeons. Back then, the birds lived in such huge colonies they blotted out the sun. In order to protect their crops, the first European farmers would kill as many as thirty thousand in a single hunt. Given their immeasurable numbers, no one could ever have imagined how fragile the species would prove to be, how rapid its collapse. No one imagines the extinction of the dominant order.

Just as Gloria prepares to leave, her task complete, a small figure appears, walking in her direction, barely disturbing the tall grasses. As he approaches, she recognizes the boy she saw on the night of her trip into Parc Rouge, the child who was so quick to scoop up the cans of food.

Her heart skips a beat, as though to avoid frightening him

off. His bony body, his drenched clothing, his protruding ears—it's as though he's an elf who's just emerged from a burrow. Once he draws even with her, he stops and waits for Gloria to come to him. She crouches down beside him. The boy cups her ear with his hands.

"I know where they're at."

Gloria quivers. "Who?"

"The girls you looked for."

"In Parc Rouge?"

"Uh-huh. But you won't find 'em, they're hided good."

"They don't need to hide," Gloria says in a rush of breath. "Please, tell them they've got nothing to be afraid of anymore. I'm their grandmother, here waiting for them. I want to take care of them."

"They won't come back. They couldn't."

"Why not?"

The boy backs away from Gloria's ear, looking at her at last, and a glint flashes in his eye that she can't identify, something hard, somewhere between anger and triumph.

"'Cause they killed somebody."

"What? What makes you say that?"

"I heard them say it. They're hided from the police."

For a few seconds, Gloria believes she's gone blind, an impression that blocks out the others at first, as though to protect her, to keep the world from crumbling before her eyes, and to keep her heart from evaporating into the air of Fort Détroit. Then she recovers her sight. She's on her knees in the soil, her basket of vegetables gone, the boy as well. Her legs tingle, demanding that she get up, but her stomach turns. She vomits onto a stump ringed with the mark of claws. Her eyes stare at the scratches, she wipes her mouth, then, in one brusque motion, gets to her feet. The starlings take flight the way water erupts in a splash.

* * *

Her hands covered in dirt and snot, Gloria pounds on Jonah's door. The skin of her knuckles is scraped raw, sunlight shatters her back. A few feet away, black heat pulses from the pile of tires lying in the yard. In her mind, the smell of overheated rubber will forever be associated with matricide. She would never have thought that such a thing could have a smell, a shape, or even a place in her consciousness.

"Jonah," Gloria says, "it's Judith's mother. Open up!"

A blurry shape starts to move inside, an eel waking up on the bottom of a lake. The door yawns open. The man is incredibly skinny; his face shows not only the shape of his skull but the contours of his jaw, the hollows between the bones. He is dressed in linen, and wisps of thin brown hair fall onto his shoulders. He looks like a prophet.

Treading slowly, he advances onto the porch then drops down onto the top step. Gloria is unable to sit. Blood keeps bursting in her body, a bomb that recharges as it detonates.

"Tell me what went on in that house."

Gloria realizes she has yelped at the sight of a cat bolting from beneath the balcony. As for Jonah, he doesn't bat an eyelash. He looks at his hands that he turns this way and that and opens and shuts as though his knuckles were some miraculous, impenetrable mechanism.

Gloria resumes, striving to keep her voice under control. "Is it possible my granddaughters could have reached the point where they'd turn on their mother?"

This time, he looks up. "It was them?"

Gloria doesn't move, fists clenched. Tears the texture of petroleum cling to her eyelids.

"That's what I figgered," murmurs Jonah.

"Why? Why?"

The man frowns and looks down as though the words he's searching for are lost somewhere in his overly-long body. Gloria feels like giving him a good shake.

"When I was around, Judith was careful," he starts slowly. "My parents used to beat me, so she knew it upset me. But I'd still hear her. Cassandra was almost as tall as her mom, but she'd never have returned her blows. She knew what was in store for them. She was scared of that happening. Foster families, group homes…Mathilda doesn't look to the future as much, she lives in the present. But she always listens to her sister."

Gloria's heart is thundering. This man knew her granddaughters, knew Judith so well. Growing paler by the second, he continues, "Judith had sold everything for what she could get. Her stuff, her daughters' stuff. She had nothing left. So…"

"So what?"

"She decided to sell them."

"To sell what."

"To sell her daughters."

The words make no sense to her.

"Sell them?" she repeats.

"Yes."

"How? To who?"

"To people lookin' for teens."

Now it's Gloria's turn to drop down next to Jonah. She has nothing to hang on to, can find no way to extract meaning from the words she has just heard.

"She didn't say a thing to me," Jonah adds, wiggling his toes inside his sandals. "I heard it. I hear everything. I know you've been by here twice. I know you saw the old man die in the street. I know that the witch fixed you. All from listening. The girls heard it too. Not long after, Judith died."

Slumped between the prophet and the pile of tires, Gloria's sobs spew forth. Crying had always been a relief, but now it's as though her face is being torn apart. If only she could melt away, a puddle soon to be sucked up by summer then spat out into the strait, strangled by the passing of ever more miserly years, clenched like the hand of some close-fisted man. Time that gives nothing, offers nothing but crosses to bear and the earth shifting beneath you.

Beside her, she senses Jonah get to his feet with barely any effort, like the release of a balloon full of hot air. His hand is the touch of a feather on Gloria's neck.

"Judith did have a heart. You won't think so. But she was my friend. Then one day, my friend's heart was swallowed up."

Silence unfurls in the wake of this last pronouncement as though to give her time to heal. But even in a city such as Fort Détroit, there can never be enough silence for that.

* * *

Rue Cécile-Tousignant vibrates almost imperceptibly; the arugula's leaves tremble on their slight stems. Solomon tells himself this is either the beginning or the end of an era. Or both at once, a death and a healing. He swipes at his eyes with long dirt-encrusted fingers. Caesar is dying. The man he has known for as long as he has known his own name is about to leave this world, and his last pronouncements

197

appear in a frenzy of asparagus shoots re-entering the soil and of green beans returning to their stems.

The vibration becomes a hissing that gradually starts to take on other inflections. Mouse-like voices sound, *He's here—no, there—he's everywhere, anyways*. Solomon quivers but is careful not to turn right away. As with any frightened creature, you must wait to be approached, to be incorporated within the boundaries of their world.

"We're here," a reedy voice pipes up behind him.

Solomon pivots carefully. He instantly recognizes the boy who likes books, the stutterer. The long-haired little girl who pees like a boy is there too. And Magic, of course. She advances, the spokesperson for the three, perhaps for ten or twenty children more who rely on her boldness.

"You can show us how," she states.

It is neither a request nor an order. It is permission granted. The children will allow Solomon to teach them something. He nods gravely, intuiting that this is a first for these youngsters to whom no adult has ever taught a single thing—other than fear, perhaps.

"What made up your mind?" he asks.

Magic pulls a face. "The others're all on about war."

"And they're playing in my scrapyard," adds the girl with the long hair.

"We like eating more."

"Perfect," says Solomon. "That's good. What do you wanna start with?"

The three little ones exchange a glance. The book boy takes the lead.

"F-from the b-beginning. Wh-what's the t-trick?"

"What trick?"

"To t-telling plants to p-push out s-stuff that's g-good to eat?"

Solomon remains mute, preferring silence to answering with a question even more abstruse than the one he's just heard.

"Yeah," continues the long-haired girl. "In the forest, plants don't got fruits. What'd you go and do to yours for them to give you some?"

At last understanding, Solomon opens his hands and it's as though the entire greenhouse has spread its arms, as though all the life it holds has left silence behind.

"First, I'm sure there're all kinds of plants that make fruit in the park. You just have to find them at the right time. Second, you have to choose what to grow."

The little boy opens his eyes wide. "Huh? Y-you're the one that ch-chooses?"

Solomon smiles. As gently as possible, he lays his hand on the boy's small bony back. The child gives a start but lets himself be guided to the seed library, followed by the other two.

"Look," the old fellow begins.

* * *

She's been keeping watch for two days now. The soft woman is no longer soft. She's not hard either; she's like a flame. Her energy pierces the walls of her house, pierces the light and the sounds, and the dog watches, dazzled. She is like those toads that tolerate increasing heat, never trying to escape, till they're consumed.

The woman cried a lot, she yelled and broke a few objects, she grabbed a cold box that stank of death like she wanted to destroy it, clutched it to her belly, then held it out as far as she could and finally put it back where she found it. She tried to sleep, but her blood was boiling; she tried to have a bath, but the water scalded her.

Halfway through the second night, she steps out into wind swirling with feathers and lashings and looks at the dog, asking the animal something with her eyes. The pitbull is tired, it's increasingly hard to get her body to move, but she knows, just as she knew the day a killer entered the yellow house, that only she can do this. It is up to her to respond to this woman set on fire by life, by the insane love humans carry. So she jumps up, twirls round and round, yips three times, and the woman's expression undergoes a transformation. With great difficulty, the dog manages to start up at a trot, then a gallop. The woman dashes after her, follows the animal down disintegrating streets, and together they run; two females weighed down by age and motherhood, they leap as though the moon could beam them up. They only return at dawn, one's skin glistening, the other's fur dripping with sweat and dew. The former collapses into the armchair with its lumpy stuffing. The latter waits, making a pretence of staying alert, holding out for a few more seconds; then, once she is sure the other is asleep and has gone from flames to glowing embers, she lets herself drop, tumbling into her fatigue, deep into wolf sleep.

* * *

Raquel was right. The treatment she gave Gloria a few weeks ago has transformed her. Catatonia and utter dejection are no longer part of who she is. They've been supplanted by a restlessness that propels her forward, even if only to turn circles under Iggy's alarmed gaze.

As though in response to her mindset, the house across

the way is clearly reconstituting itself, although *reconstituting* is not quite the right word. Rather it's as though it is sprouting again, slowly rising from the earth, both ancient and new, something nothing can conquer. They make a good pair, she and the house, Gloria thinks, combing as best she can her hair gone frizzy with the heat wave: one burning from the inside out, the other rising from its ashes.

Caesar succumbed to his illness despite Theo's best efforts. With a dozen other patients suffering from the same devastating symptoms, the nurse is exhausted. But he continues to care for them, keeping them hydrated and their fevers in check. He does what he can in the face of the unknown.

Gloria meets him outside his clinic where he is talking in hushed tones to Caesar's family: a statuesque woman, undoubtedly his daughter, and her two small boys. Gradually, the other neighbours and friends arrive—Eunice, Block, Sweetie, Alain, Clarence-with-the-toupée, Ulysses, and Solomon. Raquel is not here; no one has seen her for a while now.

"I hope she didn't catch the same bug," says Sweetie.

"Oh, please, she'll live to be a hundred," Eunice responds.

"No one lives to be a hundred," Block retorts. "This city polishes off its people long before then."

* * *

Solomon, Ulysses, Alain and Caesar's daughter carry the makeshift coffin, a wooden plank bearing the emaciated body wrapped in a sheet. The small group starts down Avenue Leblond slowly and hesitantly as if no one knows the way. Like the other members of the IAO, Caesar asked to be buried in one of their fields. As she walks, Gloria thinks of Judith's ashes. If she could burn them a second time, she would.

Eunice advances, head down, obsessed with the cracks in the sidewalk. Gloria's feet are burning up in her sandals, and she feels as though thirst has lodged in their soles, in her toes. She takes her friend's hand. Their palms warm on contact.

"You okay?" they ask at the same time.

"I'm okay," they answer, still in unison.

They walk at the same pace, heavy with worry but in a rush to reach the next stage.

"With each new discovery," says Gloria, "I realize that all the signs were there. Judith's addiction, the violence ... Everything was laid out for me, but it's as though I couldn't grasp the meaning till someone else told me."

"Did you have any clue what the girls had done?"

"No, but ... you know that recording, the call to 911? I think that's what I heard. In Cassandra's voice. It wasn't the tone of someone panicking. It was another kind of shock. Someone struggling to get her head around what she'd just done. Can you believe it, she wanted to sell them?"

Eunice shakes her head. "Human trafficking's been a flourishing market here. From day one."

Tin-plated clouds roil in the sky. A thunderstorm is brewing. The procession steps up its pace to make it to Caesar's last resting place before the storm hits. The hole has already been dug, the body is easily lowered, as though drawn by a magnet located in the earth's core. Imperceptibly, the small group shuffles back, out of fear no doubt of being dragged under by this same soil that eats living beings. Eunice and Gloria stand at a remove, staring at the sky rather than the grave. They can't take anymore. Eunice is impatient, almost exasperated with death. Gloria thinks of her daughter, of the children, unable to dissociate what Jonah revealed from

202

what she saw in Parc Rouge, as though Judith were responsible for putting all those kids there, as though she had sold every single one of Fort Détroit's children. Her eyes turn to the grave; almost immediately superimposed on its image is that of a bathtub and of two girls holding a body underwater. Cassandra, Mathilda, their existence contaminated. They, too, are underground, buried alive.

* * *

Eunice curses all the way home. She left before it was over. The minute Solomon's speech veered from Caesar's ancestry to a discourse on the Glorious Thirty Years, she knew the storm would have time to sweep through the city and away before the funeral oration came to an end. She thinks of what Block said earlier about the city polishing off its inhabitants. She thinks of her father—of all the other dangers that could have befallen him if it hadn't been the driver—of Marina, gone to live in La Traverse—initially to be closer to her daughter's school, but also perhaps to safeguard them, herself and her loved ones?

Thunder booms at the gates of the city as she starts up Avenue Leblond; the wind brings a chill. She tries to hurry, but something is slowing her down—confusion, a lack of closure, a weight she's dragging behind her like a ball and chain; it's as though her feet are mired in a too-thick soup. Out of the corner of her eye, she catches sight of someone even wearier than she is. At the foot of a giant bird made of tin cans, Raquel stands motionless, her arms crossed over her chest.

"There you are! The others thought you'd come down with dysentery. I told 'em no way, germs are too afraid of you."

Raquel doesn't respond. As she draws closer, Eunice sees

that her elderly neighbour is crying. Tears look out of place on this face marked by stubbornness and the bodies of others, like a crack in a diamond.

"What're you doing here?"

"What's it look like? I'm mourning the death of my beloved, that's what I'm doing!"

"What beloved?"

Raquel clucks in irritation. "Caesar, who else? All our lives, we loved each other, and I couldn't even bring myself to go to his funeral."

"You and Caesar?"

The old woman pulls herself up, eyeing Eunice haughtily. "We loved each other from a distance; we weren't meant to be. He wouldn't have been able to share me. And I'm not meant to be with only one man. But I was, in a way. It's the man of my life who has just left us."

Eunice refrains from rolling her eyes. Raquel staged the exact same scene on the death of Mikel, the old shoemaker from Rue Young, and of Yehudi Steinberg, the owner of what used to be the Boushel fruit shop. You'd think she'd had several lives, like a cat, with a different man every time, an impossible love for each possible world. Above them, the metallic bird seems poised to flap its wings. Eunice had never noticed it before. Urban art grows like weeds here, without explanation, as if by pure magic. A resounding crack reminds her of the storm's advance on the city. It shakes them both, Eunice and the tearful widow.

"C'mon on, you old heartbreaker. I'm taking you home."

Arm in arm, the two women hurry on to Avenue Clyde beneath the threatening sky and the crickets' stream of abuse. Suddenly, a roar buries all other sounds, a peremptory call.

Raquel and Eunice look to the end of the street where a large, colourful, pug-nosed shape hurtles toward them. Beneath the engine's din, a muffled voice makes guttural pronouncements through a loudspeaker, incomprehensible words whose judgmental tone nevertheless filters through. The rig races by too quickly to see who is behind the tinted windows. But the giant letters on the bus's side are perfectly legible. *URBAN DECAY TOUR—DÉCOUVREZ LES RUINES DE FORT DÉTROIT.*

Without warning, Eunice's knees buckle; she finds herself on all fours on the sidewalk, her fall cushioned by the dandelions flooding the pavement's cracks. As the bus vanishes round the corner, Raquel peers intently at her. Eunice grabs the hand that, with surprising strength, pulls her to her feet. The mainspring of her thoughts has just shifted.

* * *

What disappears with the death of a friend? Solomon wonders, standing in the field threatened by the storm. The funeral is over, the survivors have left, Caesar's body has been buried in the earth to which he devoted his last years. One of the things we lose, thinks Solomon, is the person we were with them, the parts of us they brought to life. With such an old friend, we are also stripped of the memory of what we once were. There is no one left to remember twenty-year-old Solomon, crazy in love, asking Caesar to be his witness at a wedding that never took place. No one is left to describe the thirteen-year-old boy who shot dice on the streets to pay for his music lessons, who fled from high school bullies, who threw rocks at the police. No one is left to remember the expression on his face when, at the age of five, he was sat down at an upright piano for the first time.

Suddenly, another image is superimposed on Caesar's, a powerful one. The sky was exactly the same as today's. The zucchini and fine-skinned Principe Borghese tomatoes were at their best, bursting with colour and juice, ripe for harvesting. Solomon was alone in the field, and hail was on its way, threatening to destroy it all. He started picking as fast as he could, panic-stricken, convinced he'd never finish in time.

Then Judith appeared out of nowhere, wearing jeans cut off at the knee and a T-shirt her skinny body swam in.

"A race against the clock?" she said in a voice that sounded slightly hoarse as though emerging from slumber. "Let me give you a hand."

Without waiting for Solomon's reply, she grabbed a wooden crate and began filling it. Her movements were deft; nonplussed, Solomon watched her for a few seconds before rallying and resuming where he'd left off. They worked side by side in silence, as though it was the most natural thing in the world, both of them deep in a sort of moving trance punctuated by the scraping of the soles of their shoes along the parched soil and the rumble of thunder. Once he'd picked the last zucchini, he turned, ready to run for shelter. Judith stood motionless at the far end of the garden, her eyes turned to the sky. A huge smile crossed her face. Looking up, Solomon, too, caught sight of the clouds that had separated, as though torn asunder by a blow from a giant axe. To the east and to the west, the storm lashed out at the earth, but here the sun whispered over the grasslands, and Judith's pale skin drew on it as though on a spring of living water.

"Thank you, you saved me."

She shrugged, then grabbed a box full of tomatoes.

"Of course, help yourself!" Solomon was quick to add. "Take some zucchini, too."

"Nah. My girls can't stand zucchini."

Beneath the overcast sky, Solomon watches her walk away on frail legs, treading on what will become a grave for Caesar, his friend, who a few yards farther down, keeps on weeding, and the whole of Solomon's life is crammed into a field that suddenly feels too narrow, too deep.

* * *

With a determined step, Gloria follows the trail that tacks between the abandoned parcels of land in Seigneur-Printemps, the district north of Chesnay. That morning's horoscope gave her the courage to set out: *The gates are about to open. Keep digging, barehanded if necessary and until you bleed if that's how it must be. Your animal spirit guide: the raccoon.*

Since hearing the revelations from Jonah and the boy with protruding ears, she cannot seem to see the horizon clearly, whether that of the city that hides her granddaughters or that of her inner self, where a dike holds back shame, compassion, and disgust, together in the same vortex. Listening to nothing but the wisdom of the stars, she has resolved to persevere, to continue launching appeals until an answer surfaces, until something peels away from the morass of Fort Détroit.

She stops outside one of the living, an old cottage that shows signs of frequent comings and goings. Methodically, she sets down a bag of cookies to which she ties a canary yellow envelope, her letter to the children of Fort Détroit, its ultimate addressees being Cassandra and Mathilda. In her note, she alludes to the fact that, even though she knows their secret, she is still intent on welcoming them home, that they need not fear reprisals or the police. A bottle sent out on the sea of the city. Then, onto the fence that borders that same living house, one already papered with torn missing persons posters, she staples a sheet of paper, a green one this time. While the envelopes propose a solution, the poster has a question for anyone who might have information related to the death of Eunice's father. Eunice griped about the idea, then the wording, then the colour. But eventually she agreed. The bottles are their best hope.

When Gloria resumes walking, the papers rustle in her bag; it's as though they, too, are alive. And, in a certain fashion, they are: open to the possible. She has already sown some thirty posters and fifteen letters in both Chesnay and Perlemère, always accompanied by a small treat, except where something else can be used as a draw for hungry children, like rare tins of still edible food, or the inside of Solomon's greenhouses. In fact, that is where she is headed now.

The facilities on Rue Hameder are empty. The air sizzles, as though simmering in the noon heat. Gloria advances down the meandering rows of bedding plants—the old folk of IAO seem to be having trouble finding true north these days. A penny on the ground catches her eye. Gloria picks it up, squeezes it in her palm, and makes one wish for Eunice and another for Cassandra, Mathilda, and the children of Parc Rouge. There are too many people to rescue and not enough lost pennies, never any shooting stars. Gloria squeezes her eyes tight, then kisses the front face of the coin and buries it in the earth.

At the end of the row, tiny fruit flies weave silky patterns round the raspberry bushes, whose fruit has begun to glisten. Gloria hangs another letter there, between red and green, between sweet and barbed. A message infused with love and ringed with the residue of violence. The tone is confident even though Gloria feels as if she's wading through a swamp. Although she is as determined as ever to draw the girls out of the woods, beyond that certainty she knows nothing. How does one look after children who have gone so far, so young? Will she manage to redeem Judith, to redeem herself? Will she one day be able to think of her daughter without feeling like self-immolating on the spot?

She emerges from the smothering heat of the greenhouse and heads west down Rue Hameder. On the last wall still standing of one burned-out house, giant graffiti commands: *KEEP THE FAITH*. "Okay," murmurs Gloria, then staples a small green poster there. As though in response, there is a rustling overhead. She looks up to discover a family of raccoons, their fur bristling with sunlight. They're asleep in a linden tree, inexplicably maintaining their balance on its branches. A semblance of peace settles on her shoulders. Anything is possible, she tells herself.

* * *

"The bubble burst in the Sixties," says Solomon. "Everything was harmony and prosperity before then. According to the newspapers, that is. Harmony was mainly reserved for the WASPs, and prosperity, for the Americans who always felt at home here. Everybody else lived in crowded slums. Immigrants were corralled in districts that were built too fast and went up in flames at the slightest spark. No one would've rented a room to an Italian or a Ukranian, even less so to a Chinese man. People said it was their own fault if their buildings were always burning down. Shacks thrown together with faulty furnaces ... As for the Blacks, a municipal bylaw banned them from living outside their own district. My grandfather spent seven nights in prison for signing a lease in Perlemère in thirty-nine! White Francos had more freedom to move around, but like the other proles, they lived among the rats and got saddled with all the dirty jobs."

"What are *proles*?"

"Proletarians, plebes, the underemployed. That's how French became the language of the poor, the language of the people. It was like a secret code bosses couldn't understand."

"Pfft!"

Solomon interrupts his history lesson to study Magic, who's patting the earth down hard around a cucumber plant.

"Careful, Magic. If the earth's too tamped down, the plant won't do well."

"That's not even how the French gotted here," she retorts.

"Oh, really?"

"It's Nain Rouge who brung the French here. Everyone talked English at first. But Nain Rouge did come visit all the orphan babies in the city and 'stead of letting 'em learn English, he'd put French words in their heads. When they got to talking, it came out in French."

"Nain Rouge, huh?"

"Well, yeah, 'course," Pretty adds as she weeds the row of cauliflowers. "Even his name: *Nain Rouge*. He never called hisself *Red Dwarf*, get it?"

"Children, the city was founded by the French. Antoine Laumet de La Mothe Cadillac. That's why there's French in Fort Détroit."

"No way," retorts Pretty. "Cadillac's a car. They invented some musketeer guy to sell more of 'em."

Solomon turns, half confused, half amused. "Where'd you get that one from?"

"Vishnu told me."

"Vishnu?"

"Don't b'lieve everything you hear, Monsieur Solomon. My pepper box's empty. Can I get more?"

The old man heads to the lean-to, listening to the creaking of his joints. The presence of these lively, impatient youngsters makes him feel his years. He lifts up a rack of bedding plants and carries it over to Pretty, who is hopping from one foot to the other. The children's pace astounds him. They can do more work in an hour than an adult can in half a day. Then, out of the blue, they'll lie down and fall fast asleep, like cats, and wake up all in one go, ready to return to their unfinished task.

They've spent the week doing the rounds of Solomon's fields and greenhouses, working so efficiently that he has decided to entrust them with a plot of land he'd planned to leave fallow for an extra year, having no time to look after it himself. Since it's quite close to their camp, Solomon suggested they choose the plantings. It will be their field.

"B-but wh-what about the r-rebellion?" continues Stutt, who doesn't want to miss out on the story.

"Right, the rebellion. It started with strikes, demonstrations. But with change not happening fast enough, it ended in an actual uprising. Like when you get a pot boiling that's already too full."

"M-makes a r-real m-mess."

"Exactly."

"Were there any dead?"

"Uh-huh, dead and wounded, mainly people of colour, as per usual."

"Did you got wounded?"

Solomon scratches his head. "Uh-huh. Wounded then arrested, like just about everyone in my family. But the worst part is what came years later."

"What?"

"The wealth drain. That's when the rich people took off with their businesses and their money, leaving the poor to cope with unemployment, a busted infrastructure, polluted neighbourhoods, a bankrupt city. Fort Détroit was left on its own with no one to help. The Americans didn't want to invest here anymore. The government made a show of giving a hand to the folks still around but didn't keep it up, and, basically, they couldn't care less 'bout a gang of immigrants and illiterates, inferiors who wouldn't keep their mouths shut. We ended up quarantined to this day."

"Quarantined?"

"When you isolate someone."

"Oh, punishment."

"Yeah, that's right, punishment. They punished us 'cause we asked for more."

"We just done that. To a troublemaker."

"What'd he do?"

"Said stuff he shouldna. But he gotted his lesson."

Together, the three children turn to the Tour de Lys, which looms to the west like a giant bone blanched by the sun. Solomon tries to make out what the children seem to see so clearly, but all he notes is the haze of summer's heat that flutters to a steady beat. Tick, tock, tick, tock. The children start digging again.

* * *

Eunice has had her nose buried in old newspapers for so long that even her ideas are spattered with ink. Clarence, who collects the local dailies for some obscure reason, agreed to loan her last year's. With wavering patience, Eunice combs through them, looking for cases similar to her father's—accidents, hit-and-runs, pedestrians left for dead in the middle of a boulevard—in the hope of identifying suspects. It's a laborious task that drives her crazy. Beside her, the dog lies panting on her father's robe, lethargic after a night spent turning circles in the kitchen. Just as Eunice moves to April's issues, the back door bangs open. Eunice straightens up. Two young girls appear in the living room. Dirt emanates from them like light.

"Didn't anyone teach you to knock?"

"No," says the one who, under her layer of filth, is blindingly pale.

Indignant, Eunice turns to the dog. "And you? You didn't even bark! Some watchdog."

"'Course she's not gonna bark, she knowed us," says the little one, whose cheeks are so grimy it's as though she's wearing a mask.

"Plus, she's gonna have babies," adds the other.

"What?"

As if to corroborate the words spoken by the pale as pale girl, the dog gives a moan and resumes panting.

"See how she breathing?"

"Uh-huh, she's been like this since last night. She's hot."

"Not hot her. She having babies."

"That's how come we're here."

"Bleach seed her through the window."

Eunice has to admit the dog has been acting strangely for

the past few days. Her old aunties always used to say a woman goes a bit mad in the days before she gives birth. Eunice studies the eldest of the two girls.

"Are you Bleach?"

"Uh-huh. And this is Rasca, Priscilla's best friend."

"Priscilla?"

"We comed to help her."

Eunice doesn't move. Her limbs are tingling, she feels as if a wind is sculpting her from the inside out like a sand dune. Babies are about to be born.

"What needs doing?" she asks.

The two girls exchange a glance. "We don't know! *You're* the woman!"

A few hours later, every one of Eunice's towels is stained and five tiny puppies are squealing into their mother's belly. The sixth was stillborn; without a word, Bleach and Rasca carried it out to the yard, resolute young gravediggers accustomed to burying young lives. Crouched in front of the litter, Eunice sobs. She caresses the puppies' fragile flanks and wrinkled heads and cries over her existence, her own birth, and her father's end, the ties linking her today to so many more dead than alive; she cries over the incurable state of grief and the beauty of life's first moments, the tininess of the clumsy paws, the doings of these beings who know nothing as yet but still recognize exactly where to go to feed, to begin their lives.

Behind Eunice, Rasca and Bleach stand, waiting for her tears to stop, as though her meltdown is the most natural thing in the world. In the pantry, Rasca has found bread on which they nibble as they think up names for the newborns based on the patterns of their puppy coats and the shape of their ears; the mother no longer exists for the girls, their minds spontaneously eliminating everything that cannot be fathomed. Eunice alone murmurs in a tearful voice, "Good work, my girl. You've done well, Priscilla."

Bleach is the only one who hears, beyond the tender words, a desperate cry that rings through the neighbourhood, having sprung, it would seem, from the Tour de Lys.

* * *

She tears through the air, the smog, the pollen, and the spells. Bleach loves Fiji with all her heart but refuses, as Fiji is well aware, to let a child die of heat exposure, hunger, and solitude, which is likely why the leader has kept from Bleach the fact that she had Tick-Tock imprisoned after he confessed to revealing the sisters' secret to their grandmother. Officially, he's accused of espionage and treason, not that anyone knows what that means or what he betrayed exactly; Fiji probably had him confined to prevent him from revealing even more secrets.

Lego and Wolfpup refused to carry out the sentence, Lego because he's on strike and Wolfpup because she's given herself over heart and soul to planning the Attack. It's both bizarre and beautiful to see her collaborating with Pow-Pow despite the way the two have always loathed each other; now they scheme together, draw up plans, and protect their store of explosives as though it were the last sack of potatoes in the universe. So Yatim and Method were the ones who carried out the leader's orders and confined Tick-Tock to the top of the old tower, where no one will find him since no one goes there anymore given that no one ever knows whether it still stands or has been demolished or restored. Meanwhile, Fiji made sure there was no way Mathilda and Cassandra's new hideout could be found, pushing caution so far as to keep the secret from Bleach, just as she excludes her now from all of her thinking and decisions. That's what hurts the most: this gulf that Fiji has dug between them, ostensibly to protect them both. Maybe that's what pushed Bleach to follow Rasca outside the camp to the green house where the dog conjured wet babies in front of their very eyes, a transformational moment for both girls who, until that point, had never envisaged where their own lives began—only death preoccupied them, thus creating in their minds an impossible timeline: bordered at one end and infinite at the other. From now on, there is a beginning and an end, and the boundaries both reassure and overwhelm them. Fortunately, Bleach still has her wings.

After a half-hour of flight, however, those wings begin to tire and Bleach alights on the crown of a birch tree, scanning the horizon in all directions. To the southeast, the horrific structure on Île Gus haunts the landscape, while to the west, clouds advance—like opposing armies, marching into combat. Bleach remembers again the children's bodies in the river, sees them as clearly as if she herself had discovered them. Every evening, Method and Yatim tell the story, describing the unseeing eyes, the swollen flesh; they try to rid themselves of the images by speaking of them, by emptying them into the fire, but, of course, it's of no use: Method keeps wetting her bed, and Yatim cries all the time. Rasca is the only one who seems unscathed, wholly focused on two things only since her return: her brother and Priscilla. Too little to carry such a tale, she devotes herself to what keeps her upright.

Now rested, Bleach resumes her flight. The sky is overcast, she must find Tick-Tock before the storm hits. Beneath her shadow, grasslands and fields unfurl, then the green-houses where Magic and Stutt are at work, and, finally, the tower looms ahead.

Tick-Tock isn't hard to spot, his blue sweater flapping in the wind round his slender body. Fiji had asked that water, biscuits, and raw turnips be left for him. It has clearly not been enough. The moment he catches sight of Bleach, his eyes grow as big as his ears; it's as though the sky had just opened up before him. His bright red skin is blistered, and dried snot covers half his face.

"Bleach? What're you doing here? You're so beautiful! Were you flying?"

"'Course I didn't fly. You're hallucinating."

The boy tries to get to his feet, but the slanted floor and dehydration make him totter. Bleach catches him, her arms tight round the waist of her friend who sinks into her embrace.

"Careful, I'm gonna carry you."

"But where?"

"The camp."

"They'll kill me."

"Uh-uh. I'd be talking."

He looks up at her with a pleading expression. "I'm sorry, Bleach. I shouldna told. I just wanted to ruin it all. I was a jerk."

Bleach's wings have trouble lifting the two of them; some-how, they rise and leave the tower behind, but soon it's clear she will never be able to fly all the way to the camp. Tick-Tock is too heavy. Bleach brings them gently to the ground. They should walk, but her friend needs water, a bed, meat, and who knows if that will even be enough—his body is as limp as a mitten in summer's heat.

Just as she's about to give up, a black horse emerges like

an apparition from the woods. It's as though it has been waiting for them. Drawing closer, Bleach could swear that a bit of steam is coming from its nostrils and that its hooves leave slight scorch marks on the ground. It lowers its head as though urging them to climb up, and Bleach's wings sigh in relief as they fold together.

* * *

The puppies prevent her from sleeping, but it doesn't matter. Their yapping and roughhousing have become the workings of gears her existence requires. Her fatigue is luminous and draped over the wear and tear of the last few weeks. The demands of lives that are brand new.

Priscilla has regained her strength. She maintains order among her little ones with a single bark and keeps an eye on Eunice, who feels the dog's attentive gaze at all times, like an ear against a wall, a palm over a wound. The dog is both guardian angel and supreme authority of their abode.

When Gloria steps inside, she finds Eunice lying on the living room's beige carpet, being attacked from all sides by Priscilla's pups, chuckling amid nips and urine stains. Mesmerized, Gloria is reluctant to speak, refusing to break the spell. A newly repaired radio crackles with blues tunes as intermittent as the waves launching them through the city's skies.

"Ulysses is sick," she announces finally.

Eunice sits up. Her childlike air deserts her; in a matter of seconds, the adult has regained possession of her being.

"Holy shit."

The puppies scatter like shrapnel.

"Solomon?"

"He's okay. The children keep him going."

Gloria looks around. "Have the little girls left?"

"They resurface every day. I think they're gonna take the babies—once they're weaned though. It'll be good for 'em to have dogs."

"Uh-huh. And it's good for the dogs to have children."

"Is Ulysses getting treatment at Theo's?"

"He's staying home for now. They're taking turns watching over him."

"If this keeps up, the whole city'll end up below ground."

The women contemplate in silence the same thought of a Fort Détroit divided, the earth's surface separating identical yet inverted worlds. One city in the sun, another underground, thousands of lives milling about on either side of the scorched divide, each one with its fables, its worries, its memories, and its future.

"I'm done putting up the posters. Three hundred in all."

"And still no leads."

"No. What about you in *Le Citoyen?*"

"Nyet. I'm waiting for news from Francelin, he went to the Seigneur-Printemps police station for information. But I'm not about to hold my breath. The first two stations were a bust. It's like there are no cops left inside. Actually, there's that at least."

Gloria stands to get them some water. It comes out of the tap all cloudy.

"It's gotta be boiled today. I've got some cooling in the fridge."

"Maybe we're at another stage," says Gloria as she fills the glasses.

"The stage for miracles?"

"Exactly."

The puppies show up, racing with utmost determination between the chair legs and the cracks in the linoleum. The simple fact that new beings have been born on Fort Détroit soil could be enough to prove the possibility of a miracle, thinks Eunice. With all the stories of abandoned dogs— starving packs among which nature's ruthless law is said to prevail—the fact that Priscilla was able to give birth to such a healthy, joyful litter is a good sign.

Emerging from her thoughts, Eunice turns to look outside, surveying the field where a shadow passes, too big for a bird, too small for a plane. She exchanges a glance with Gloria. The plot thickens.

*　*　*

Parc Rouge's features are rather bleak. Great swathes of grass meant to be a gathering place for neighbourhood softball games and large picnics under a sky studded with clouds in the way of children's drawings. Instead, the place has turned into a wind tunnel. The lawn has dried up, the benches have burned to the ground, the area is strewn with fluttering litter. All the same, Gloria has grown attached to the greyish-green landscape, as quickly and fiercely as one discovers one still loves those who have done the unspeakable. Forgiveness, she muses, pacing back and forth on the sprinkling of grass, is not something that needs to be cultivated, maintained, prompted to slowly sprout. It is either there or not; it appears in an instant, fully formed, irrevocable. Gloria knew she forgave Cassandra and Mathilda even before Jonah's explanations, from the second the big-eared boy whispered their secret to her—maybe even earlier, before everything blew up, before she was told over the phone, during a call ridden with stat-

220

ic, that her daughter had died and her granddaughters were missing. She had probably forgiven them the day of her husband's funeral; forgiveness was in the air when she rocked Cassandra over the cold nights following her birth; it was already present in the belly of the pink, wrinkled baby she gave birth to thirty-nine years ago. It perches on the roof of her house and flies over Fort Détroit like a silent, unbending angel.

Every day since her trip into the forest, she has walked along the trees, scanning the underbrush, sometimes plunging into the anthill that harbours its orphans, but not too far, knowing full well that the minute she crosses the invisible frontier into their domain, their defences will spring up and Cassandra and Mathilda will be even more inaccessible. In the crackling of dead leaves, she thinks of Judith, so distant now, catapulted light years away by the inhumanity of her actions. Despite what Jonah had said about her daughter's heart, it's the word *inhuman* that has been tumbling through her mind for the past two weeks. Now she wonders if a propensity toward such a cataclysm is not, in fact, a hallmark of *Homo sapiens*. Animals—dogs, for instance—do not self-destruct; they want what life has on offer and do everything possible to engage fully.

There is also what Judith cannot be held responsible for— despair and addiction. Between two gusts of wind, Gloria comes to the realization that she doesn't even truly blame her daughter. She has lost Judith, both her body and her memory, like a planet gobbled up by a black hole. But she doesn't hold her responsible.

Only she is left, she who blames herself a thousand times over as every new sordid detail comes to light. Of course, it is always the mother who shoulders everything, she who creates the lives which will then, either through her fault or not, collide with others round the world's sharpest corners. She will have to absolve herself as well.

A great squall passes, an invisible train shaking the trees. One after another, they bend then right themselves, toss for another second or so then steady, tall dancers with skinny arms. But one spot refuses to straighten, swaying long after the wind has died down. Gloria freezes, then takes a step back, unsure, and watches as two small figures in grey rags emerge from the woods. Her heart races.

* * *

Rasca doesn't know what is allowed, if her brother has the right to leave, if he can return, how they will punish the bad kids without him, but she knows he has to get out of here. Lego has got to leave the forest, cross the treeline, that border that takes you by surprise, like when you've been pushing and pushing hard against something and it suddenly gives way; he has got to go through that transition from the dense, leafy universe of the Ravine to the vast, airy world outside. He has only left the camp twice since winter's end, each time to carry out a mission he never wanted to be entrusted with and from which he returned even grimmer than before. Rasca understands nothing of the problems facing the big kids, the ones who cry or get angry for hidden reasons, but of one thing she's sure: nothing can heal a bad mood better than time spent playing with baby dogs.

She leads Lego through the brush like an adventurer guiding a tenderfoot, holding branches aside for him, pointing out obstacles, warning of a wasp's approach, sure of herself, expert, and he follows without question. He no longer has the strength to dig in his heels. The Ravine creates so much anxiety for him that he wakes up at night feeling as if he's suffocating. Half the time, he can't even count on the presence of Adidas; like almost everyone else, he has been recruited for Yatim and Method's plan, which has been endorsed a bit too enthusiastically by Fiji. Before setting off to work in the greenhouse, Stutt showed him a page in a book that looked like it had been dug up from the Earth's core, in which an elderly king named Henry advises his son to wage war on outsiders to keep his own subjects from revolting. The story, tough going and complicated, nonetheless proved to be a revelation for Lego; for the first time, he has understood what Stutt sees in books: a sense of discovering a reality impossible to conceive of beforehand but that, once grasped, reveals itself to be age-old, weighing on the mind as only truths one has been unaware of can. Words reveal things that are already there.

He loathes Fiji. He despises her for having authorized the demented Attack that will only prolong her reign, already past its best-before date. He hates Yatim and Method for returning from their mission bent on waging war and curses them for having dragged his sister along on that nightmarish adventure. He resents the whole camp for voting in favour of such a pathetic plan for revenge, particularly Wolfpup, who shelved their burgeoning revolt to subject herself once again to Fiji's will; he's upset to be the only one who sees things clearly. Actually, not quite the only one—a few others have recognized a fiasco in the making and pulled back. Even Rasca, who seems oblivious to what's in the works, spends most of her time outside the camp. As for Lego, he has stayed put because he's incapable of seeing himself as a deserter, for one, and for another because he thought he could talk some sense into all the imbeciles who think they can take on a giant and come away unscathed.

But this afternoon, when Rasca approached him in front of the hopelessly damp campfire, when she held out her hand and asked him to follow her, he decided to listen to his heart. It wasn't easy, his heart has been overpowered for such a long time by all the orders and the rage, but the minute he followed his sister, a huge part of his being, the rough, tough part, broke away; he heard it drop off behind him, shed like a dead branch.

Now daylight can be glimpsed through the leaves. Although the sun beats down virtually non-stop in the summer, Lego feels like he has been living in the dark. Rasca slows down, then lets him pass, opening her arm ceremoniously toward the world of light. Playing along, Lego raises a foot high, ready to take the solemn step forward at her urging. He touches the grass, looks up and finds himself face to face with the grandmother.

* * *

Magic waits, a shovel in her hand. With the tip of their spades, Stutt and Pretty are already poking at the pile of putrid matter with relish. They're about to cover the crops in compost.

"That's right, Stutt, dig over there, where things are further along," Solomon urges as he pushes a wheelbarrow toward them.

The three children don't take long to fill it.

"It stinks!" Pretty exclaims with a look of delight.

"Sure as shootin' it does. And it'll be long, hard work."

"We'd gotta do that too?"

"If you want a good crop you do. There are easier ways, but the conditions have to be just right."

"Wh-what other w-ways?"

"Fire, for instance."

"Fire?"

"It's called slash-and-burn. We set fire to the whole field. The old folk did it that way 'stead of sawin' down trees. It works on fallow fields, too, or where plants are done for the year. The fire turns them into fertilizer that goes straight into the ground. It works, but it's hard on the soil. On cities, too, for that matter. You know, Fort Détroit was kind of made out of slash-and-burn."

"*Fire, fire, fire, can't go no higher, flame, flame, flame, your soul's not the same,*" chants Pretty.

"*Embers, embers, embers, Fort Détroit remembers,*" continues Magic, joined by Stutt, "*ash, ash, ash, now is the backlash.*"

Solomon looks at them, surprised. "What's that children's ditty? I've never heard it before."

"It's the fire rhyme," answers Pretty, as though it is self-evident.

"Wh-when was the f-first f-fire?" asks Stutt.

"In 1703, we think," answers Solomon, "with the fire that destroyed the Pontchartrain fort that Cadillac had founded a year earlier. It happened again in 1747, when the Wendat burned down the Assomption mission. In 1805, according to legend, a huge fire was started by a distracted baker. Then in 1887 and 1901...It got to be a tradition: we set fires when we're happy, we set fires when we're not, we set fires when we've got nothin' better to do. It got so the city itself stepped in. It burns itself down. Houses combust spontaneously, entire blocks go up in flames at our city's will."

225

"Nah, that's us."

Solomon stares at Pretty. "That's you what?"

"The fires that start on their own, that's us."

"You secretly start fires."

"Not *us* us. Other kids."

"The k-kids who're d-dead."

"Every time a kid dies in Fort Détroit," explains Pretty, "there'd be a fire start somewhere."

"I...I never noticed that," Solomon says carefully.

"That's 'cause there are too many. It's not easy to notice no more."

Slowly Solomon shakes his head. "What about when an adult dies?" he asks, thinking of Caesar and Ulysses, who is on the decline.

The children shoot each other a quizzical glance then shrug.

"Wouldn't do nothing, I think," declares Magic.

"Or m-maybe a d-demolition," Stutt speculates.

"Like the concerette place they're gonna knock down. Bling."

Solomon whirls to face Pretty. "Do you mean the Shling?"

"Yeah, that's it. There were lotsa people out front this morning. Big machines, too, and some shouting," the girl explains.

"They w-wanna kn-knock it all d-down."

"That can't be! They're making it new again."

"That's what the mad people shouted at the helmet guys. They had a kinda fight."

Abruptly, Solomon plants his shovel in the ground. Instinctively, the children back up. Then, seeing Solomon's eyes redden, they move in closer again.

"Was the Bling your house?"

The old farmer rubs the bridge of his nose, sniffs. It's like he's shrunk by a foot.

"In a way, yes."

"But we seed your house, that big, weird shack. You'd got yerself two?"

"No, it's just that . . . I'm very attached to that place. It's special in the city. That building never did burn down, actually; it's been around since 1870. I was there all the time in my other life."

"You'd got yerself two lives?"

Solomon gives a sad little smile. "At my age, I've had a lot more'n two. One of them was a musician's."

"How come it's over?"

"'Cause I don't have a piano to play anymore."

"There was a p-piano at the Sh-Shling?"

"Uh-huh."

"And you played there?"

"Exactly."

"That why you was bawling?"

"I'm not bawling! It's that damn compost that's got my eyes to watering! Enough—back to work, you bunch of slackers."

The children start shovelling again, side by side, up and down, their gestures synchronized as though they were each thinking exactly the same thing.

* * *

They don't really exist. She licks them, nurses them, feels them snuggle up to her spine at night and pant come sunrise, but their presence isn't real. Only the things that stay put are real. The others, temporary, changing, are not. Her little ones are impossible to hold fast, either in time or space. They're continually moving, growing, transforming; from one second to the next, they become different beings. They

227

are rivers, never the same. They are the light from stars that died a thousand years ago. Soon, she well knows, they will leave—they never belonged to her. Babies are transitory beings, and their closeness is an illusion.

By association, she, too, feels unreal. Her belly has emptied itself of foreign lives, only to be filled again with milk. The borders of her body have become fluid; she is fractalized, clouded by dreams. Entire stretches of her days are relinquished to the unseen. She dreams herself deep in blue waters, which are entirely deserted yet full of signs, and wakes suffocating, parched, unable to recognize the beige carpet and the human scents surrounding her.

She is brought back to herself by the woman's feet, sometimes swollen, sometimes tough and woody; they anchor her in reality. Looking at them, she remembers where she is and what she wants. She wants to run beneath the stars, weave between notes of music, mate and kill. Inside her is yet another body that demands other actions: that she lick the little ones, nurse the little ones, watch over their games, and growl rare but crucial lessons. But soon, she guesses, seeing their gaze sharpen, their ears prick up, their legs lengthen, it will all be over. They will vanish into the confusion of the world, amid vultures and prey, and the moment they disappear from her field of vision, they never will have existed.

* * *

The two children have camped out in the field for three days, between the romaine lettuce and the Better Boys. They sleep without a mat or blanket, the boy hugging the little girl close to keep away the dew. In the morning, they eat a tomato for breakfast, rummage about in the strawberry plants and ask nothing of Eunice or Gloria although the former always has a glass of milk for them and the latter bakes them muffins and cookies that overheat her kitchen and turn her face red. From time to time, Bleach comes to visit—she seems to live everywhere at once—and they spend hours playing with the puppies. They let them nip at their fingers and pee on their shoes without making the slightest attempt to train them, and they persist in removing them from their mother, in a hurry to see them weaned from what they seem to consider a degrading habit.

Ever since Gloria's visit, the camp's daily routine has been shattered, and she suspects that her incursion into the park is not the only reason. Something is up; she can tell by the pauses between the words spoken by the little ones she sees. She did try to ask them about her granddaughters, but, despite almost living together now, they rarely speak to adults, simply take what's offered before reinstating between them and their new neighbours a space the size of a football field, a no-man's land where, at dusk, the shadows of foxes and stray cats are visible.

To go over the situation, the neighbours have organized a meeting. A hypercharged atmosphere reigns in Eunice's kitchen. The arrival of the children in the neighbourhood is the emergence of life—of lives on the edge, damaged but exuberant all the same.

"It's obvious something's gotta be done," Eunice begins. "Those nippers saw Gloria, they've figured out there are good people hereabouts, and have jumped at the chance to get out of their hole. We can't let 'em down."

"A hole, a hole—you've never even been there, Eunice," Block points out.

"Have you seen how they're rigged out? Plus, Gloria, she saw their camp."

"It's mostly their tents that bother me," Gloria clarifies. "I don't know how they make it through the winter."

"Sounds like they build a big communal hut," notes Solomon.

"I didn't see it when I was there. It can't be all that sturdy."

"That's exactly why we're here," concludes Eunice. "Solomon has got things under control foodwise, which is great. But we've gotta think housing. Francelin, in your stock, is there an abandoned building that's not too run down? The kind it'd be easy to patch up before the weather turns rough? It's gotta be big."

Francelin scratches his pink-patched chin. "There's no wanting for big places round here. What's rarer is material, new wood, hardware. And the plumbing's often shot…"

"For now, plumbing's not a must," decrees Eunice. "I'm sure they know how to make do with outhouses and boiled snow. This first year, the goal is to make sure they're kept warm."

"In that case, I might have one could fit the bill not far from here. Rue Amir. The fireplace still works, so they'll be able to heat the place."

"That's good news."

"It'll take some labour."

"That's what I'm here for," Alain pipes up.

His right eye can barely open. He came across a thief not far from a factory in the east he'd gone to looking for work. His wallet and his earring didn't make it back.

"With Block, Eunice, and Gloria, that's probably enough of us."

"Great, we're in business then!"

"Wait a sec," Block interrupts. "Did you ask the kids what

they think? Maybe they don't wanna stay inside on Rue Amir for five whole months. If they wanted to live in the city, they'd do it. It's not like there aren't lots of spots."

The five others look at each other. Eunice radiates annoyance, while Francelin already seems to have discounted Block's objection with a wave of his hand.

"You're not wrong," states Solomon. "They've been through a lot, those tykes, and they've gotten by figgering stuff out on their own. We can't just show up and impose our solutions on them. That won't work."

"That girl with the white mane, I heard her say they lose three, four kids every winter," Eunice replies. "Are we supposed to stand by and let 'em drop like flies?"

"Just as many died when they lived in houses," mutters Block.

"Maybe if we get a place ready for them, they'll decide to come on their own?" Gloria suggests.

"I don't much feel like going to all that trouble for nothing," Francelin protests.

"Why don't we ask them what they want?" Block cuts in.

Six heads turn to look outside. The girl with albinism has joined the other two. Sitting cross-legged in the middle of the field, she's braiding the little one's hair while the boy, half-lying on the ground, plays with the puppies.

"Go on, Gloria. You're the nice one."

"We'll all go together."

Slowly, as though to avoid spooking a herd of deer, the mini-committee advances toward the children. The minute the adults come level with the group, the three children freeze as does the puppy; they stare at the grown-ups with an impenetrable expression. The youngest girl breaks the silence.

"We want."

"What do you want?"

"A place for the winter."

The six adults stare at her open-mouthed.

"My brother heared you," she explains.

"We hear it all," adds the girl with the white mane.

"He's your brother?" a surprised Francelin asks, pointing at the boy.

"Well, yeah."

"But you...he's Black and you're white—"

"So?" interrupts the boy. "You look like marble cheese, and nobody says nothing to you!"

Francelin touches his two-toned face and scowls.

"But not too far from camp. Else some won't come," adds the little one, glancing at the white-haired girl.

Solomon reaches into his pockets, extracting bright cherries and holding them out to the children.

"We'll see what we can do."

* * *

Eunice contemplates the horizon. Too often she forgets to notice just how beautiful her world can be, especially at this hour, when the light takes on a reddish hue. It's like honey pulled from a hive. The sky is pink—"It'll be a hot one tomorrow" her father would have said—and on the ground, the plants seem to exude a breath both cool and blue, like marble. Her backyard and Gloria's could be temples. Without warning, she has a vision of Judith again—as clear as an icon.

It was seven or eight years ago. Standing in her yard, its ground veined with dirty snow, all Judith wore was a robe, open to reveal sharp ribs and small breasts. Glimpsing her

232

from her kitchen, Eunice raced out to urge her back inside. But once on the porch, she paused. An Italian aria flowed from her neighbour like water from a spring, transforming the entire space into a hallowed hall. A spot in the centre of Eunice's chest grew warm. Her mouth rounded, her features relaxed, Judith sent her voice sweeping through March's mild air. Her song, absorbed then reflected back by the humidity, was projected to the four corners of the neighbourhood, while her long, dirty hair wafted round her like a cape. At that precise moment, she was a queen, and the city of Fort Détroit—its armies of unemployed, its inner circle of addicts, its penniless nobility—was blessed by her voice. Then Eunice shook herself. The temperature was three degrees, Judith was half-naked, something had to be done.

Just then, Cassandra stepped outside, followed closely by Mathilda. Judith still sang, but her eyes were open now and she gave a little smile. Timidly, not daring a bold approach, Cassandra closed the folds of the grey robe and knotted the belt around her mother's waist. With a gesture as sweeping as the notes escaping from her throat, Judith drew her eldest in and hugged her close. Eunice wondered what one would hear with an ear glued to the chest of someone singing opera. Could the notes be perceived in their every detail, or was it more their underside, their secret meaning? Cassandra let herself be rocked while, a few metres away in the slush piled up along the fields, Mathilda danced, spinning round and round. Eunice tiptoed back inside.

* * *

He knows he's still dreaming, yet he can't stop moving forward through this space that is both outer and inner, a

233

scorious moorland and a place on his body burning with such intensity that it opens up another horizon, a territory within the territory. As he walks, he realizes the burn is pain, and the pain is a war and a mistake, an exploit; on his leg, he carries vengeance taken, sheer, idiotic terrorism. He walks, both within and without his body, and features of the landscape jut like teeth from the earth; chimneys, pylons, cisterns, furnaces, decanters, pumps, reactors, pipes, conveyors, taps, hydrocrackers—rigid structures—eat up the world and vomit it out raw and undone, only to suddenly burst into flames.

This is no ordinary fire. It's as though the flames' dance has been sped up; in the thick of that urgency, Adidas draws closer, feeling not the heat of the inferno, only immense satisfaction, a revolution accomplished a thousand times over, again and again, until everything is crushed, avenged, until victory. The smoke whirls at a speed equal to that of the fire, evil flies to the sky where birds chant loudly, and when Adidas claps his hands, the birds fall; the sky chokes on the sins of the earth.

By the blaze, he looks down at his leg and sees it gaping open, its skin split, its muscles separating, bone piercing through, and blood flows with the secrets, memories flow with the marrow, the sticky delirium of horror. He is going to die. They are going to die. Human shadows surround him, dark and indiscernible against the absolute backlight of the fire, and he sees them gradually engulfed by the flames, then vaporized; he reaches out to grab for them, stop them from falling into their own trap, but one by one they elude him, sublimated by the heat that distends the universe.

Adidas wakens covered in sweat in the night riddled with sound. The camp no longer sleeps.

* * *

The cicadas' song is so dense that Solomon has to push through to advance, as though the air itself has been mineralized. Or maybe it's that he's the one dreading what awaits him at his destination. Yesterday, near day's end, the authorities made known their verdict. After failing to find the Shling's owner, then briefly discussing the matter with citizens bent on doing everything possible to save the concert hall, it was announced that their decision would be upheld. The famous club would be razed. Immediately, the instruments of demolition returned to station themselves in front of the building. Solomon decided not to witness what was to come.

But this morning, he's angry with himself, like someone who regrets not staying by a dying person's side. He picks a few of the red prairie-fire flowers growing along his cornfield. They are sad-looking and don't seem enough to pay tribute to the galaxy that has just died.

He would never have thought that the destruction of the Shling would rattle him to this extent, not now that he has become someone else. A farmer's life is made of new beginnings, the eternal return of winter, then of spring when one has to start all over again, successive deaths quickly muted by the chorus of births. But this farmer has not wholly erased the musician in him, the man who only lived for beauty and the quest for communion.

A patch of yellow daisies pulls him from his thoughts. He picks one, three, six, resisting the desire to question each petal on the future of the city's musical soul. Then his gaze alights on familiar leaves amid the wild grasses. It's not the first time he's noticed them; three days earlier, the same shapes appeared in a ditch along Rue Cécile-Tousignant, a familiar motif breaking away from chaos. This time, he decides to find out for sure. He tugs on stems limp from three days without rain. The root breaks through the earth and appears, round and purple. Solomon holds it before his eyes, stupefied. How was a beet able to grow here, three miles from the field in which its sisters are planted? By searching further, he finds another half-dozen, huddled together like expatriates. His first reflex is to pick them, but something stops him— a certain respect faced with this incursion of domestic vegetables in a wild setting.

He vows to discuss it with Ulysses when he has a chance. Once his friend is back on his feet. For now, it's almost impossible to communicate with the tall, wasted man who spends his days in bed, feverish, delirious.

On his way, Solomon also comes across cantaloupe flowers, baby eggplants, and a lush patch of Thai basil. More mysteries unfolding.

Eventually, he reaches the vicinity of the Shling, over whose streets and alleys he used to reign back in the day of The Clocks, the quartet he belonged to where he was known as Digits. The block's distinctive smell, a combination of dry-cleaning chemicals and pancake syrup, clings still to the bricks despite the fact that both Ninon Breakfasts and Cortez Cleaners have shut down. The memory is so evocative that, when he catches sight of the Shling's shadow at the end of the street, he thinks he's seeing a mirage. But, drawing closer, he realizes it is well and truly standing, this building with its bricks painted black that lists as though built straddling two tectonic plates. The demolition has not yet taken place.

Solomon finds himself out front, on the exact spot where, the day before, he wept at the sight of the heavy machinery.

A small crowd has gathered. Everyone looks not at the sign for the Shling but at a row of tortuous shapes, sombre and smoking, almost organic, like giant mushrooms.

"Don't get too close," one onlooker cries. "It's dangerous."

These are the instruments of demolition. Their bodies are deformed, and their yellow paint has turned a dull black that should be on the city's coat of arms—the sign for burning.

"What happened?" Solomon asks those assembled.

A woman carrying a large heavy shopping bag leans toward him to whisper in a conspiratorial tone, "No one knows. The machines got here yesterday, and this morning this is what they looked like."

"Word is that one of 'em was the city's last demolition crane," adds a young man sporting green hair.

"We all dreamed of doin' it," adds the woman. "Someone figured out how."

Briefly, Solomon glimpses a familiar shadow in the alley, hears a smothered laugh. Slowly, he starts after it, rounds a garbage bin where rustling can be heard. Behind it, their hands deep in bags of stale-dated chips, crumbs spotting their chests, his three protégés giggle along with a boy whose face is covered in soot.

"What're you doin' here?"

The kids shrug.

"The machines, did you see 'em explode? Are you okay?"

"Yeah, yeah."

"What could've happened? Last night, they were untouched."

"We didn't see nothing."

Magic gives him her usual frank stare. "All we know is, so long as machines keep coming here, they gonna blow up."

Solomon feels a vertigo he has rarely experienced in his lifetime, an upending of certainties that comes when one system of beliefs gives way.

"It's you?"

"No way," retorts the boy with the blackened face. "We're just kids, how d'ya think we'd blow up ten-ton rigs?"

The laughter that ensues gives off a scent of salt, vinegar, complicity, and triumph.

* * *

Reassured and disappointed, Eunice wipes her hands. Clothilde's engine did manage to run for a few seconds before stalling again. At least now she's got proof the old rattletrap is not brain dead. Putting away her tools, she drops a wrench. The bright ring of metal against concrete creates an almost immediate echo, a sharp cry followed by a shrill laugh. Eunice looks up. A tiny man walks slowly down Avenue Leblond carrying a bottle. He's wearing an impeccably cut but worn suit of scarlet felt, its elegance extending to the silk square in his chest pocket. Reaching the intersection, the man turns to her, a grimace distorting the features of his red face, then spits on the ground before snickering again. Eunice feels she should shrug it off, but something makes her blood run cold, countering any usual reaction of indifference. The red-faced vagabond makes her want to shut her eyes tight, hide behind a shield. When he disappears, it takes her a few minutes to get a grip on herself. Finally, she starts moving again, puts away her toolkit, and closes the garage door. It's time for the seance.

Usually, she steers clear of any shenanigans, devil's work, or other such nonsense that holds sway in Fort Détroit, particularly at Raquel's place. But Gloria insisted: she had to try, they

needed a third person, she could feel that something important would come of this. Eunice would rather die than admit it,
but she, too, has a premonition—or as close to one as possible
for as pragmatic a person as she—an inexplicable desire to
witness what, in the past, she would have called a masquerade.

Once night has fallen, Raquel ushers them inside amid the
fragrance of incense and sweetgrass. She has placed a round
table in the middle of her living room, as well as three chairs
and three candles on a purple tablecloth. She welcomes Gloria and Eunice in a hushed voice, as though the room were
already teeming with spirits that mustn't be disturbed.

"Have you got your questions ready?" Raquel asks Gloria
as they take their seats.

Gloria nods. Raquel doesn't bother asking Eunice; either
she assumes she has nothing to say to the dead or her questions seem obvious to Raquel. They are, of course; there's
only one question to be asked, only one answer being sought.

The ambiance in the room changes with the lighting of
candles, like a medal suddenly shining in the glow. Raquel
invites them to repeat a prayer of welcome for the souls of the
deceased, to which she adds a warning aimed at any evil spirits.

"Each of us has a bridge to the other world today," she
says next. "Gloria has her daughter; Eunice, her father; I
have Caesar. We'll call on all three."

The summoning of the dead begins. In turn, the women
repeat their names, an endless litany in which Eunice joins
with sporadic conviction. After a quarter of an hour, Raquel
interrupts the merry-go-round.

"Okay, this isn't working. There's someone here who
doesn't really believe, and it's not hard to guess who that person is. Eunice, if you can't get on board, go wait in the kitchen."

"Okay, okay, I'll make an effort."

She takes her neighbours' hands again. Eyes closed, she asks herself once more what she's doing here. Either her friendship with Gloria has reached the full-on solidarity stage or she's gone bonkers. Despite which, she tries to focus, thinking of her father, his songs, his voice stretched thin with the years; she gives herself over to that music and to the huge loss left behind.

"It's working. There's a spirit among us," Raquel whispers.

Eunice opens her eyes. Although there is no draft in the room, the candle flames flicker. A strange warmth radiates through her limbs.

"Spirit," appeals Raquel, "who are you here for? Did you come to speak to Gloria?"

The candle before Gloria goes out.

"Are you Caesar?"

Another flame dies, this time in front of Raquel. Unnerved, both women turn to Eunice.

"It's for you, Eunice," Gloria breathes.

"Are you our friend Eunice's father?" Raquel asks in a sombre voice.

The flame flickers, and Raquel gives a start.

"Yes! You said yes!" Raquel exclaims excitedly. "I hear you, spirit."

Turning to Eunice, Raquel invites her to speak. Eunice, confused, starts to stammer; the incense has gone to her head, her certainties have dissolved.

"Uh...Papa, are you all right wherever you are?"

Eyes shut, Raquel nods slowly. "Yes, he says he's all right. But...not at peace."

"Is that 'cause of the way he...the way you died?"

Once again, Raquel nods, looking like she's under a spell. Tears well up in Eunice's eyes, not from sorrow but from overwhelming astonishment.

"Papa, do…do you know who ran you down in the street?"

Raquel doesn't budge, concentrating as though the answer is coming through at a ponderous pace. Then, opening her eyes, she holds Eunice's gaze.

"It was a bus. It was *the* bus. For the ruins. The hunter of ruins brings about ruin," she utters in a deeper tone, in a voice not unlike Eunice's father's.

Eunice jumps to her feet so abruptly her chair tips over. The last candle flickers out just as she leaves the house. Gloria runs after her—abandoning Raquel returning slowly to herself—and finds Eunice out on the porch, trembling.

"Are you okay?"

Before Eunice can answer, a huge roar invades the sky. For the space of a few seconds, the universe disappears, there is nothing but the noise, all the rest is dark, irradiated. It's like a megalith collapsing. Instinctively, the two women huddle together. Raquel joins them, panting as though she's just run a marathon.

"What was that?"

Gloria and Eunice don't answer. Something hangs there between them. Then, as one, they race off in the direction of Parc Rouge.

* * *

Five days without rain, five days without a storm. The air quit moving. Now that explosion has ripped open the white sheet of time. Above the city, every molecule has come to life. Something titanic has just been shattered, shattering

241

the entire city in turn with the roar of a mythological beast, of a fractured god.

Rain counters by returning, pouring down. It bombards the city's sagging roofs, the open wounds, the ground turned hard by drought; it hammers the hunched shoulders of passersby. Creeks, rivers, sewers swell and push against boundaries with their round and frothing fingers. Gutters overflow, transporting petals, syringes, cockroaches, plastic, hair, cigarette butts, dust particles, and love letters. The world streams by.

In the fields, wisps of straw curl inward. Flowers fold up on themselves, become buds again, vague suggestions of colour. Vegetables return to their stems, and those stems shorten; roots plunge deeper into the soil, and seeds return to their sheaths. The trees, if they could, would dive into the earth, but they are the sentinels, the guardians of a silent and essential history.

Nor does civilization waste any time before reacting. In short order, conveyances arrive via water, land, air, their headlights raking surfaces. To the southeast, the wound glows red, spews its venom. The beast will not die before taking a few more victims, devouring their hearts.

* * *

When Eunice and Gloria reach the park's edge, the storm has broken and helicopter searchlights sweep the area. Two green trucks, hard to make out in the pounding rain, bark out equally hard-to-decipher orders. To the south, an incandescent shape radiates, thrusting thick smoke through the downpour. Out of breath, the two women scan the scene. At first, all they can see are the soldiers patrolling the site, bearing weapons and lights. But, little by little, they recognize among the crowd of curious onlookers the figures of Block and Sweetie, Alain, and Solomon with his three terror-stricken pupils. Two small rockets hurtle in their direction: Rasca and Lego, who, like them, came at a run as soon as they heard the blast.

"Didya see 'em come out?" cries Lego above the din of the helicopters.

"No," shouts Gloria at the same volume. "No one!"

Rasca runs over to ask Magic. She returns shortly.

"She says they'd be on Île Gus. They're the ones attacked it."

"Oh my God."

"We gotta find 'em 'fore the police do."

"I called Francelin," says Eunice waving her phone. "He's on his way."

And indeed, a few moments later, a shape comes to a halt on the edge of the park; headlights flash off and on through the downpour.

"That's him!" she yells. "Quick! Follow me!"

All four race toward the car that takes off with them inside, army trucks passing every minute.

"We've gotta get to Île Gus."

"The way'll be blocked."

"Try through Fieldvale."

For almost an hour, the car they're in circles, looking for an access point, illuminated wherever it goes by wild flashes of fire. In the back seat, Gloria hugs the children, shivering in their wet clothes. Eunice peers into the night with a barn owl's gaze.

Suddenly, between two clumps of trees, she glimpses movement.

"Stop!" she cries.

A half-dozen of them are walking as best they can, their faces blackened and striped with trickles of water, their legs mud-splattered, their clothes in tatters. Some are bleeding, others hacking as though they have tuberculosis. Eunice and Gloria jump out and bundle them into the car while Francelin carries in a boy with a deep gash on his leg.

"Take them to Theo's," Eunice orders.

The car only has room for half their number. Gloria, Eunice, Lego, and Rasca will wait for it to return. One of the survivors stays behind, the tall girl in hole-ridden ankle boots who addressed Gloria the night she ventured into the park.

For the longest while, no one speaks. Helicopter blades continue to whip through the air, but the search now focuses on the mouth of Rivière Rouge. Rain still beats down on the forest's trees whose crowns look to be in flames because of the reflection from the fire. From the pine grove where they're hiding, the night looks opaque, brutal; it smells of mud and hot metal.

"Didya blow it up?" Lego finally asks.

Fiji shakes her head. "Not everything. One bomb didn't go off."

"Bombs?" Gloria says.

"Where're the others?"

"The minis're in the camp with Whale and Tick-Tock."

"Tick-Tock?"

"It's okay. He wants us to forgive him bad. He'll take good care of 'em."

Turning to Gloria, Fiji adds, "Your granddaughters are okay too. In a cave. No one'll find them."

"Where? We have to get them out of there."

"Not now. It'd be dangerous. For everyone."

"Pow-Pow? Wolfpup?" Lego continues.

Fiji bows her head and starts to cry. Lego wants to hit her.

"Answer, Fiji!" Rasca insists. "Where they being, Wolfpup and Pow-Pow?"

Lego hugs his sister to him.

"They're dead, Rasca," he says. "They're dead."

A sudden noise billows behind them, a superhuman breathing coupled with furious galloping. Something big and strong is bearing down on them at top speed. Eunice shoves the children to the ground. A second later, a dark, smoking mass jumps over them in one giant leap. Raising their heads, they see a large black horse racing off. It seems untouched by the rain, as though its coat repels water.

"Did you see that?"

Gloria has no time to answer Eunice. Francelin is back; the car partially engulfed by rain slows to a stop in front of them. The five passengers climb inside and huddle together as though all they had left was the proximity of the others, their breath, their prayers slicing through the sky.

* * *

With the morning, the sun laps up raindrops and fear. Behind Gloria and Eunice's homes, small clothes with holes in them dry on the lines, on lawn chairs, on fences. The kids are still asleep; they spent part of the night at Theo's being cared for, heaving sighs despite their injuries as though they were the ones doing the nurse a favour. Afterward, Fiji, Yatim, Pretty, and Stutt settled in at Gloria's while Eunice's house was given over to Rasca, Lego, Magic, and Adidas. They put

Adidas in the La-Z-Boy once Theo had stitched up the long laceration in his calf. Propping himself up, the boy wore the triumphant air of one who has overcome pain through sheer force of will. Theo had nothing to use as an anesthetic. As for Method, she refused to sleep inside and headed out into the storm, a four-foot-tall veteran. The others collapsed onto beds and couches without waiting for either Gloria or Eunice's permission or directions, leaving the two women unsure as to who was calling the shots here, the adults or the children.

Even now, as they drink their morning tea of chicory root on the porch, they try to get their heads round the bizarre sense they're living in an occupied zone.

"Can we come in?"

Block stands facing them, Sweetie beside her. They're carrying a tray of cookies and a cardboard box. Eunice steps back to let them inside, not unhappy to have someone else take over after their sleepless night.

Once the children had fallen asleep, Francelin dropped by to bring them up to date on the situation: The army has established a perimeter around Parc Rouge. The explosions destroyed half of the island's foundry. Other than the unofficial deaths of the two small guerrilleros, no one else was injured. Solomon stayed on in the park through the night with his protégés, who were determined to keep watch to see if any others might leave the camp. After six hours, the farmer managed to convince the kids to return to his place to rest. Francelin drove them back to Perlemère at dawn.

As Gloria nods off in a sodden rocking chair, Eunice slips inside. In her living room smelling of feet and things burning, she comes upon an unexpected scene: the children, not the least bit wary, sit around a relaxed and smiling Block, who is busy chatting with them. While the puppies turn circles round her, she pulls from her cardboard box small-sized clothing that, if it doesn't look exactly new, at least seems to be clean and in good condition. Choosing a short-sleeved pink sweater, she holds it up against Pretty to check the size. Pretty pulls it on, then asks if she has shorts, to which Block responds with an enthusiastic dive back into the box. Rasca has put on a flounced dress, Lego a sweater sporting a fake-tie print. As for Sweetie, she is busy massaging Adidas's foot to help him get rid of his pins and needles. The children seem calm and at ease, as though the drama of the day before had dissolved with the morning's sunshine and the ministrations of the grown-ups. Then Fiji makes her entrance.

Her face grey, her stature eroded, the queen sinks deeper and deeper into the couch as though her flesh is made of an extraordinary matter so concentrated it is heavier than lead, denser than sorrow. She looks at no one, barely breathes. Without saying a word, Block sits down beside her and lays a hand on her shoulder.

* * *

Morning filters in, its bright light penetrating each crack, each fissure in the floor, each gap between small branches, and all the wood creaks, moans, liberates the anguish of the night, almost masking the words of the trees that, in the midst of sorrow, seek to comfort. Whale gives thanks to them in a whisper. The trees have already done so much. If it hadn't been for them, the children who'd stayed behind in the camp would have been found.

As soon as the trees called attention to the invasion, Whale sounded the alarm, which Tick-Tock and the minis didn't question—not many questioned Whale's word now, not since the relaying of Terror's death even before that expedition had returned. Straightaway, Tick-Tock began to panic, blubbering that they'd all be arrested, that he'd always been headed for prison, that it would serve him right because, deep down, he was nothing but a coward, but what would become of the poor minis . . . Whale, on the other hand, knew immediately what to do, as though an until-then unused part of the brain had kicked into gear; at Whale's urging, the minis climbed into the trees while Tick-Tock, more than happy to follow someone else's orders, quickly hoisted up what remained of their supplies, the cleanest blankets, essential objects—pocket knives, matches, bottles, pots, weapons. Every time he bemoaned a lack of room, Whale created more through a system of ropes and pulleys worthy of a tall ship, hanging bags made of old clothes, and using the canvas from the best tents to form hammocks so they could all sleep on high, even Bleach, should she return. Unlike Tick-Tock, Whale wasn't worried about Bleach; she had a knack for turning up where she was most needed—and she'd have no trouble escaping the soldiers' clutches.

Once the work was done, Tick-Tock turned to Whale in distress. "Do I really have to?"

With an aching heart, Whale said they had no choice. Under the minis' curious and anxious gaze, crying the whole while, Tick-Tock did something he would have exulted in doing only a few weeks earlier; he emptied a can of gas on all that was left—the chipped furniture, the rickety huts—and, in the grand tradition of Fort Détroit, he set fire to it all.

As soon as the camp was razed, rain muscled in, extinguishing any glowing embers, remorse, or suspect odours while overhead the little survivors sobbed, most because the place that had saved them from hunger and predators no longer existed, and others because it would have to be rebuilt. Whale, however, shed secret tears over the deaths of Pow-Pow and Wolfpup, still incapable of telling the others what beloved Cybele had just revealed.

As expected, the soldiers did find the little that was left of the camp—a glass bottle, a silver spoon, some cigarette butts, a muddy cap. They decided it must have been a meeting place for vabagonds, never thinking for a second to look up into the canopy where a half-dozen children shivered under a torn tarp, praying that the men in uniform would fall into the poo hole and drown.

Now everyone is asleep, and Whale can play over the events of the night with peculiar pride at having been up to the task, feeling for the first time that a reclusive existence did not rule out the possibility of usefulness. The forest rustles, water droplets splash on leaves, peace seeks a way, and there is something out of the ordinary in this beauty, something reassuring that Whale takes a while to grasp. The birds, silent since the river's poisoning, have begun to sing again.

* * *

Solomon has never seen the likes of it. Neither digging through his memory nor consulting his manuals on botany provides him with an explanation. For the umpteenth time, he looks up, questions the sky still clogged with what remains of the black smoke. In burning, could the factory have given off a substance that killed the fruit or provoked a kind of wasting disease? he wonders, knowing full well such an explanation makes no sense. The vegetables are neither dead nor underdeveloped: they have regressed. The apricots, almost ripe two days ago, have returned to their budding state. The carrots are now nothing but a pale filament; the corn is a tiny prayer between giant husks. At first, the potatoes seemed to have completely disappeared until, out of exasperation, Solomon began to dig furiously. Along the row of baby potatoes, he discovered the first tuber more than two feet down. As though they had gone into hiding.

As for the children, they don't seem the least bit surprised by the turn of events. Pretty simply called the situation "a pain," while Stutt asked the farmer how he fixed the problem the last time. Solomon stammered out a few vague words, unable to articulate his helplessness. It's the first time he has been at a loss to find something in the past to inform the present. He pulls a card from his Tarot deck in the hope of seeing an axis, a line of conduct somewhere, and lands on the Wheel of Fortune. The card linked to the future and fate.

Walking home, his stupefaction increases tenfold at the discovery of new crops growing spontaneously in the fields. These ones don't seem to have been harmed by the explosion; the jalapeños, for instance, gleam almost arrogantly. On impulse, he leaves the trail and plunges into the tall grasses. After some twenty steps, he lets himself drop down among a host of plants he recognizes, having spent time in his youth along railroad tracks and behind yards in the company of tomcats and rebel girls. Tiny flowers with petals finer than eyelashes, miniature creepers delicately strangling their neighbours, and pods that burst on contact, projecting their seeds everywhere like fireworks. Solomon takes a deep breath. Although the plants' odour is far from pleasing, he is delighted by the scent: it is somehow indifferent, free. He thinks of Ulysses, of the concoctions and liqueurs he extracts from this other vegetation; he thinks, as always, of Caesar's death. Then he thinks of his own death—it's the first time his mind has dared go there. Through all the disasters and disappearances woven into the history of Fort Détroit and despite the personal failures, violence, and injustice he himself has endured, he never felt his own existence to be compromised. Throughout his life, he has been immortal.

He turns his gaze east, where a few seconds earlier all he could see was the horizon buzzing with insects. A cluster is suspended there, laden with small, swollen, near-black berries. Elderberries. This early! The wind shakes the branch, as if in greeting. All of a sudden, the taste of Ulysses' elderflower liqueur returns to him. Solomon walks over to the bush and reaches for what seems like forever, as though the distance between his palm and the fruit keeps subdividing, but he knows he will touch it eventually and then everything will grow quiet and the sky over Fort Détroit will change colour.

* * *

Francelin's guess was ten days, and Eunice's, a month, while Gloria thinks it possible they may stay forever. For a week now, the soldiers have kept a tight perimeter around the park, forbidding entry. Should anyone leave, it would be an admission of guilt. Bleach is the only one who has found a way to come and go without being spotted, which has made it possible to confirm that the children still in the camp are safe and sound. Stutt is convinced Bleach has dug a tunnel there, while Yatim thinks she has an invisibility cape; Lego is furious at her for refusing to reveal her secret to the rest of them. As for Cassandra and Mathilda, it's impossible to glean any information on them, despite Gloria's constant badgering. According to Bleach who, at Fiji's request, brings them supplies, the older sister is "quite happy with their hideout, but less than before" and "the little one doesn't eat much." Gloria agonizes over it and wants nothing more than to plunge into Parc Rouge to carry off her granddaughters, but she has no idea where to look and, as Eunice reminds her on a regular basis, any such intrusion would endanger all the children still in the camp.

Those who have made their way out cope with varying degrees of acceptance. Some can't wait to return to their home, refusing the food offered by Avenue Clyde's residents who take turns making huge meals; those children prefer digging through garbage cans or sleeping under the stars. Others seem to take to the comfort inside the homes. Most of them are in a decent mood, but every one of them breaks into uncontrollable sobs at least once a day, some hit the others or break objects or run off only to return the next day; they yell, climb, and turn the house upside down— Gloria feels as though she spends all her time picking up the pieces. Calm descends every once in a while with no explanation, so abruptly that it becomes a cause for concern. At those times, Gloria walks from one room to the next looking for the soundless catastrophe and, finding nothing, takes a seat to catch her breath while lingering doubt remains.

When she does manage to fall asleep for a short while, she is visited by strange dreams. A beggar in red straddles the back of the racing mother pitbull or lurks by the cave where Cassandra and Mathilda are hiding. When he tries to enter, a flock of bats appears to chase away the intruder. The bats then turn into winged, coal-black horses, spewing flames through their nostrils.

No matter how often she questions the children on the subject, she receives nothing but sibylline answers. They all seem to know of the existence of the horse, who Rasca swears is their "saviour." Fiji nods gravely at the comment. The young girl, who Gloria understands to be the band leader, has pronounced barely a dozen words since her arrival. She spends hours shut up in the pink bedroom where she sleeps on the floor, and her face is always streaked with tears.

Yatim and Pretty are more talkative; they prattle on night and day, only stopping to fill their faces with anything that includes white flour or sugar. That's why, when their chatter dries up one afternoon, Gloria is filled with her usual sense of foreboding. She heads upstairs, more convinced by the second that something has happened. At the top, she bumps into Pretty who, eyes downcast and followed by Yatim, is about to descend with a limp object like a small piece of grey fabric clutched between her hands.

"What have you got there?" she asks.

Pretty opens her fingers, revealing Iggy's inert body. "He did die."

"What?"

"We squeezed it with our fingers."

No contrition shows on either the little girl's or the boy's face, not even fear of a scolding. They killed a rodent, that's all.

"But you knew that's my tame field mouse," Gloria exclaims.

"Mice aren't to be tame. They're wild."

Before Gloria's stunned gaze, the two children continue to the bottom of the stairs, head out the back door, and throw Iggy's body into the tall grasses before diving into the fields themselves, they who are simultaneously prey, predators, wild creatures, and resistance fighters.

* * *

The stars are enough, Method tells herself, looking at the corner of a ramshackle house; no need for a blanket, mattress, hot milk, or an ugly woman telling you when to sleep. At the far end of Avenue Clyde, the child lies down under her moonbeam, annoyed. It's like the others have already bought into house-living and forgotten the Ravine, their tents, and the fabulous swirl of campfires, sleepless nights, battles, free will. Here, the rules have started: don't eat with your fingers, don't put the radio on too loud, don't bite, don't throw objects, don't run carrying scissors, don't draw on the furniture, don't forget to wash. The minute they agreed to the anti-lice shampoo, she knew: if they knuckled under for that one thing, they'd knuckle under for everything else. She herself would give anything to curl up again in the bosom of the forest, in the heavy, pungent jumble of the group, but instead, she sleeps alone on rotting porches, exposed to rats and the wind. Better that than a house, she tells herself over and over, like a nursery rhyme lulling her to sleep. Better that than a house.

She has dozed off briefly, or maybe for a long time, when a sound pulls her from sleep, like something falling, a bulky object being shed—a coat, a bag, a moral code. Alert, she nonetheless keeps her eyes shut, a proven ruse: she needs to understand what's going on before springing into action. Soon, heavy breathing materializes next to her, then the sound of a zipper. A shiver runs from her toes to the top of

her skull, then her throat and her whole body close down—
she remembers perfectly what will follow. Maybe she has a
chance of getting out of this, after all, she's outside, that's one
of the reasons she avoids houses and enclosed spaces; she can
leap up, launch herself through space. A hand lands on her leg,
neither brusque nor gentle, just there, and she doesn't twitch.

When she opens her eyes, the man's face is only visible for
a fleeting moment, such a brief appearance she isn't really
sure she saw it; already he's sprawled face down next to her,
as though the two are napping side by side, the little girl and
the soldier, and it's only after he has fallen that the sound
reaches her, a short irrevocable *crack*.

Method sits up. On the other side of the dead soldier
stands the woman everyone calls Block, a name that suits
her, her shape that of a block of wood, even the short hair on
her head making her look like a log; her skin seems rough,
her core hard and warm. Stowing her gun back in her belt,
she looks at Method dispassionately.

"Sorry, didn't mean to scare you. I'll look after the carcass."

Method studies Block, then the soldier's body gradually
being devoured by a red stain.

"We got a place for dead wolves," she says.

"Uh-huh," replies Block. "I know where."

* * *

Ulysses has been lying on his back for so long his skin seems
to have slid down, drawn toward the floor like a steep slope
collapsing. His forehead is damp and burning, chills course
through his muscles, his mind is confused. But he has not
yet slipped into the unconscious state that engulfed Caesar.
Solomon makes an effort to prop him up, piling pillows

behind his back. With each move, Ulysses flutters his eyelids and gazes into space.

"Thank you. Thank you, dear friend. Oh, thank you."

Solomon gives a sad smile. The invalid's shock of hair, pure white, is as thick and abundant as ever; he feels like plunging his fingers into its long cascade.

"The vegetables have disappeared, Ulysses. There was an explosion, and they disappeared."

"Hmm…An explosion."

"Maybe you felt it. There are soldiers everywhere. Parc Rouge is like an occupied zone."

"I was a soldier once."

"I know."

"A failed soldier."

"It's like it's had an effect on the plants. The explosion."

"Scared."

"Exactly! You ever seen that happen before?"

Eyes staring straight ahead, Ulysses lifts his index finger, then his whole arm, which starts to move, swaying to an unheard rhythm. Like a deaf orchestra conductor.

"Weirdest thing is," Solomon continues, "it hasn't affected every garden. I started finding stuff growin' in the scrub. Places no one goes; it's almost impossible for anyone to have planted or sown them there, or even for the seeds to have travelled that far."

"Happy he who like Ulysses has journeyed far and wide."

His index finger dances as though such limply articulated words were a cheery melody.

"Eggplant, hot peppers, beets…"

"Spontaneous love," Ulysses murmurs.

"How come they didn't disappear?"

256

"*And regained after years of wand'ring, the land of his youth.*"

A delicate melody builds with the words. His finger dances a bit longer, then drops. Solomon rubs his eyes.

"The salt of the earth," continues Ulysses. "Eventually, it flowers. It can't help itself. It's like love that way. Like children."

"You know I'm teaching a few of them? The next generation."

"Me, I had children. Never saw 'em again."

"I know."

"Never."

"They do a good job. Come from Parc Rouge, y'know? The wildlings. We've done some fine work since you took sick."

"But all this is them."

"All what?"

"The gardens. The budding. The things playing hide-and-seek. The bombs on Gus."

Solomon is speechless. He hasn't told Ulysses that the explosion happened on Île Gus.

"It'll come back. You gotta be patient. Play cards meanwhile. Caesar doesn't cheat as much as me."

"Caesar's dead, Ulysses. Just you and me left."

Solomon wants to say more, make a wish, a petition, but his voice gives out. He grits his teeth.

"It'll come back," Ulysses says again. "This place isn't made for disappearing, it's a place for resurrection."

Solomon nods. Tears run down his cheeks. He grabs a paper bag from the bedside table and pulls out a cluster of black fruit.

"Look what else is growing in the scrub. Elderberries."

At last, Ulysses turns toward his friend and looks him in

the eye. He lays an awkward hand on the fruit. As though that contact were enough to comfort him, the invalid closes his eyes and smiles.

"Yes. This, yes."

* * *

Her foot is bothering her. Lately, her diabetes has turned into an unpredictable matter: elusive mercury. One day, she feels light and could dance the Charleston; the next, she feels as if the ground has turned to dough. Eunice has learned to judge the state of her condition by averaging out her days. All in all, she manages to stay on course; even today, with her feet in marsh-mallow filling, she fares all right handling a rosary of plates that are dirtied as fast as she can clean them. The children are in her father's bedroom rummaging through a toy box unearthed from a neighbour's basement. Their voices mingle, reaching her as a fog of interjections. There are moments when other folk become impossible to tell apart. Especially when they're knee-high to a grasshopper and their chatter never lets up.

But through the haze, something stands out. It's a song she knows, a stone until then engulfed in the well of her memory.

"Jean qui pue qui danse, Jean qui pue qui danse."

Bursts of laughter ring out after the chorus. Eunice wipes her hands on her shorts and heads toward Adidas who's hopping, one leg still bandaged, toward the washroom.

"What's that you're singing?"

"Uh…your tune."

"My tune?"

"You're always singing round songs. Especially that one. That's how I learned it."

"I sing that?"

"I change the words a bit. A stinky dancing Jean is funnier than a dancing Jean Petit."

Eunice watches the boy shut the door to the bathroom, refraining from yelling "Aim for the toilet!" for the umpteenth time. There's no point. Every evening, she wipes half a litre of piss off the linoleum.

She lumbers off, filled with consternation. Can it be that her father's songs have lived on in her without her realizing it? In the room, the kids jabber away as they play with the old toys. Seeing them, you'd never think that their camp is under siege, that two of their own are dead, and that they've just carried out a bombing. Their souls are elastic. Eunice holds back, half invisible in her own home. The children, even the most timid among them, have grown accustomed to her presence, which means they carry on as though she doesn't exist. Which has the advantage of allowing her to eavesdrop on their conversations.

"Any apple sauce left?"

"L-look, l-little t-trucks!"

"No, Rasca eated it all."

"Little *tits?*

"Rasca, what a fat pig!"

"Tru-trucks!"

"We gonna help Magic in the field today?"

"Yah!"

"No!"

"Let's play grumpy bird!"

"Me, I'll gonna build our house with Marble Cheese and Block."

"You're not good enough."

"It's hot out!"

"Am so, more'n you! Better know I learned how to do the hammer."

"It smells old guy in here."

"I wanna go for a swim."

"That's 'cause it'd use to be a old man's room."

"Oh, yeah, the one got runned over by the bus."

Hearing these words, Eunice shudders. "What'd you just say?" she asks, stepping into the room.

Yatim looks down as though he is the driver being accused. "The . . . the man who lived here. He got runned over by a bus."

"A bus? Are you sure?"

"Three of us seed it. Didn't we, Adidas?"

Back in the bedroom, installed like a pasha, Adidas nods. Eunice's hand clutches at her chest, clawing desperately as if to dig straight to her heart.

"Do you mean that big colourful bus? The one that gives guided tours of the city?"

"And not the first time," says Lego, looking stern. "One of us got runned down by it last fall. On the edge o' the park."

"A mini, on top of it all," Adidas adds.

"Was it your dad, that old man?" Rasca asks.

Eunice's hand moves up to sweep her forehead. "Yes. He was my dad."

The children respond, eight small ovals nodding slowly in the damp air like balls bobbing in water, memories in a great white lake.

* * *

The minute he opens his eyes, he sees them. In one of the books Stutt reads out loud, the person back from war keeps saying, "The minute I close my eyes, I see them." Yatim can tell that the person who wrote that story has never really experienced horror because, if they had, that person would know it's just the opposite: it's when you *open* your eyes that you see them, the people who died, the ones you hurt or couldn't save, the ones you liked without realizing it and will never see again; they live among us, like dreams outside sleep. Wherever he goes, the dead appear to Yatim—he looks to the right and the compact figures of Pow-Pow and Wolfpup rear up in front of Île Gus's foundry; to his left surfaces the mass grave floating on the Rouge; and, before him, Terror, arms raised, laughing his maniacal laugh, and the sight rips him in two, one part of him still wanting to strangle the kid, the other realizing how much his crazy ideas will be missed and to what extent his barbarity was precious to them all.

On the expedition's return, he let himself be guided by Terror's signature fury, his wielding of a sledgehammer in answer to the world: the factory had taken their own, so they would turn on it. Simple, logical, absolute. But now that it's been done, Yatim is no longer sure of anything; he wonders if that is really what needs doing or whether they shouldn't back off. The others tell him to keep quiet, that he's too late, they don't accept the possibility that he might want to backtrack; they don't understand that the ghosts have contaminated Yatim's tongue, that the future and the past are in fact like two dots on an ever-spinning sphere. Despite their annoyance, he insists. Is violence a good idea? Is one great act of destruction equal to hundreds of small deadly blows? Will it solve the problem? Seeing army officers patrolling the west side of the city like lead soldiers, he's far from convinced, and part of him, maybe the part where Terror has taken up residence, wants to mow them down while the other part wants to throw up its hands—after all, what's wrong with living in houses that have beds, breakfasts, and toilets that get rid of poo, snot, and blunders? At the thought, his eyes fill. Why is it so easy to be here, in the world of grown-ups, after doing everything they've done in order to escape it?

Above him, a hawk wheels in search of its meal. Everyone is bent on survival. "Terror, what should we do?" A membrane buried deep inside him transmits an obscure answer, an elusive truth he wishes he could sink his teeth into. Unless, that is, the soundwave comes from elsewhere, from beneath his feet? The city is a river of questions.

* * *

In her desperate search for the slightest sign of life from her granddaughters, Gloria decides to do a tea-leaf reading. The kettle's whistle wakens Fiji, who is asleep on the couch. "Fire!" she cries before collapsing back into her pile of blankets. Gloria pours the water, drinks the tea, then turns the cup, staring at the bottom. The leaves scatter to outline a message, a path, a direction. It looks like a hammer ... thinks Gloria, or a swan. Every time she makes something out, it's as though the pattern slips away and changes shape. *A bridge. A bear. A propeller.* Outside, the children play a sport they've invented that involves trying to score a goal with your feet while using wooden sticks to hit your opponents. *A hand. A crab.*

A cool breeze blows through the mosquito screen. After making them wait for months, summer is now on the wane. It's like a roller coaster: climbing up for what seems like forever, then hurtling down in a flash. You find yourself either looking forward or looking back, while the moment itself doesn't arrive. You are never really on the summit of the ride; you are never really in the thick of summer. *A shovel. An urn.* Gloria pushes the cup away from her and goes to check that her daughter's ashes are still in the wardrobe she moved them to, away from all the chaos. Nothing has budged; the grey box is there, straight then crooked like a question mark. Gloria places her hand on top. The metal is warm, polished by uncertainty, and the second she touches it, tears fill her eyes. *I still don't know what to do with you.*

Upstairs, the beds are unmade—which is not actually the proper term; *dismantled* might be more like it, as though the children had deconstructed the very concept of a bed. Gloria picks up the leftovers going rancid in corners, balls up the damp sheets. In Judith's room, the floor is strewn with marbles. They sparkle in the sunlight; their reflections climb the walls, tracing a huge moving heart by the window. Suddenly, a presence gives her a start, and she turns. Bleach stands behind her, appearing out of nowhere as though she has hatched from a heap of dirty laundry.

"What'd you be doing?"

"Housework. Do you need something?"

"My marbles."

"Oh, they're yours," Gloria remarks, watching her pick up the small glass spheres, which seem to roll toward her hand as though her skin is magnetized. "Bleach," she resumes, "I wanted to ask you something about Cassandra and Mathilda…Do you know if they've received my messages?"

"What messages?"

"I left letters all over town, I hoped they'd make it to them. But with the park being closed…"

"Ah, the yellow papers! Yes, they did made it."

"Are you sure? How?"

"Well, they're words. They make it."

Gloria wrings her dishtowel. "If that's the case . . . What did . . . Did they say anything?"

Her expression impenetrable, the child shushes Gloria with her red eyes, an index finger to her lips. A cry rings out outside, and Gloria briefly turns to the window. When she looks back at the room, Bleach has disappeared. A few seconds later, she sees Bleach join her friends' game, more quickly than seems possible.

Stepping cautiously as though to avoid marbles or children's toes, Gloria heads for the bathroom. She perches on the edge of the tub, the inside of which is coated in a thick grimy layer, and starts scouring. The same sound, like a human breath, ruffles the space around her; it's as though someone is whispering a secret to her. She repeats the operation, scrubbing the white surface again, and the murmur resumes: "Selves." Or maybe "solo." Or "sisters," or simply "soiled."

In the filth, she traces the letters of her name, then Cassandra's, Mathilda's. The word *Judith*. She contemplates all four, side by side like friends, relatives seated at the same table, waiting to share a meal or pictures from their travels. Things could have been so normal.

She runs the water, scrubs the enamel surface, and rinses the residue left by ten small bodies, erasing the names which no longer hold the same meaning. Then she plugs the tub, fills it with hot water, and plunges the soiled sheets, the dirty towels, and her squalid fear inside. Her fear—a small, innocent-looking object, no bigger than an egg, no heavier than shame. She clutches it in her palm and holds it underwater; she scrubs the sheets the way she wishes she could do with everything else. Anguish resurfaces, it too scrubbed clean, as raw as fresh fabric.

* * *

The Shling is illuminated with candles. In a city such as this, that fact alone is almost sheer provocation, but the generator that feeds the amplifiers has reached capacity. The light of the flames works its magic, creating music within the music, long auburn notes in the silence of expectation. The instruments thunder quietly as the musicians set them up, adding to the patient hum.

Solomon chose a seat at the very back, spurning the table in the first row that Gloria has reserved for them. He looks at their heads bowed low from the humidity: Raquel's brittle mane, Gloria's long locks like an Italian saint's. Leaning back, stage right, Francelin contemplates with satisfaction the resurrection he has been part of. As for the children, they expressed little interest in the reopening of the facility they were, in all likelihood, instrumental in sparing, but out in the alley, Solomon thought he caught sight of small shadows sharing a clove cigarette. His hands are shaking, his mouth dry, incongruous stage fright. He hasn't seen a full house in this hall for thirty years. Bodies warming air, instrumentalists leaning over tuning pegs, murmurs of conversation and notes seeking each other out, beads forming on glasses in the heat wave. The scene is so marvellously anachronistic.

The violin begins. Solomon didn't recognize the violinist until he started to play. He can't believe his ears. A combination of French-Canadian reel, jazz, and klezmer lament, a dancing, soulful music he'd left so far behind him he'd forgotten its very existence. And here it has resurfaced, intact, magnificent.

The violin is joined by the double bass and by discreet drumming, and the music leans more toward jazz until the accordion crashes into the melody, leading it closer to Cajun, then a guitar rents the air with melancholy. One part of Solomon falls asleep, another awakens. He can feel his hands jiggling on his knees and tears rolling down his cheeks. Up front, his friends' heads bob in time to the music. Solomon wonders if Raquel feels as he does, that he's tasting a fruit that was no longer thought to exist, one that holds in its flavour an entire universe.

The musicians finish their piece, begin another, the elderly gentleman on guitar takes the mic, delivers a song in which *fou* rhymes with *true*, the crowd applauds, tempering their enthusiasm, as though to avoid frightening a mirage. The pieces follow one after another while Solomon's head still spins, his spirit swiftly ascending and descending the scaffolding of his memories. Then, upstage, the drummer stands and shields his eyes with his hand as though from an imaginary sun. Immediately, Solomon guesses what is about to happen; he wedges himself into his seat, the candles' flames flicker, faces turn to him. The percussionist feigns surprise—he has probably known from the start that Solomon was here, huddled in the shadows, terrified of revisiting his former lives.

"Ladies and gentlemen, one player was absent when this evening began, but the gods of the strait have provided. One of the best pianists ever to perform on the Shling's stage is among us and, with a bit of encouragement, he could very well agree to return. Solomon—Digits—come join us!"

He knows there's no point in refusing. The audience will clap and shout at the top of their lungs, they'll make a commotion until he gives in, he who, deep down, has already given in. He is rusty, it will sound all wrong—he was never a virtuoso, for that matter. But he did know how to shape a good melody. The love radiating from the audience did the rest.

In a stiff trance, he gets to his feet and steps over purses, flasks of homemade hooch, and motorcycle helmets to climb onstage. The piano, by some marvel, has not changed—the same key in cracked ivory on the lower F, the same anarchistic graffiti on the music desk. He sits.

"It's been tuned," the bassist with the Senegalese accent assures him.

A numb Solomon turns toward the audience. By the stage, Gloria and Raquel stare, the first with stupefaction, the second with utmost confidence. The other faces are blurred, like water troubled by wind, but he can feel the children's gaze, that of his friends, living and dead, and even of the woman who taught him how to position his fingers on a keyboard with a light but firm touch, eager and deferential. He feels the whole of his life teeming in his hands, a chapter of his past suddenly let loose in the room. He can't do this.

Then a figure advances from the back of the room, hunched as though in apology for being late. The man walks up to the front row and slides into the chair between Raquel and Gloria. When the new arrival looks up, Solomon finally recognizes him with certainty. Ulysses is here.

His old friend pulls from his belt a small paper bag from

which he extracts a dark berry, which he pops into his mouth with a flick of his finger. Under the amused gaze of his two companions, he winks at Solomon. Solomon turns his attention back to the keyboard. Behind him, he senses the musicians' boundless solidarity, their silent urging, *you can do it, vas-y, we've got your back*, and he places his long fingers on the keys the way one touches a brother's shoulder after a years-long absence; the moment he comes into contact with the yellowed ivory, he stops shaking. He stamps his foot three times and, at last, after a lapse of more than thirty years, the music flows through him.

* * *

It is not like Eunice to leave her house in the middle of the night. Even when she was young and bars, parties, and demonstrations were still a possibility, she stayed put, a homebody before her time. There is no way today, at almost fifty years of age, in a city overrun by coyotes and soldiers, that she's about to start roaming the streets by the full moon.

The children are another story. It's against their nature to stay indoors from dusk to dawn. They go out whenever, sometimes till daybreak, then collapse onto their mattresses, the carpet, or under the kitchen table and sleep till one of the others yells loudly enough to waken them. Eunice lets them be, choosing her battles. To her mind, making sure they use toilet paper and don't burn any furniture seems sufficient. So the kids continue to come and go as they please while she guards the fort at night.

But when Lego arrives at half-past midnight with a piece of information so important that she demands he hop up on her bed to tell her, all principles evaporate.

"Where, did you say?"

"Over there," he says pointing to the east.

Eunice hurries to get dressed, putting her pants on inside out, her T-shirt front to back, and follows Lego outside. They take several tools from the shed—a pickaxe, a baseball bat that Lego swings like an expert—then head east. They walk for half an hour, following twisting shortcuts during which the boy seizes the opportunity to tear down a few missing-children posters even though they're illegible. Eunice and Lego end up in a large grey parking lot in the middle of which colourful letters stand out, as glaring as in full daylight: *URBAN DECAY TOUR—DÉCOUVREZ LES RUINES DE FORT DÉTROIT.*

"That's it."

"That's it."

"There's no one inside?"

"Who cares?"

With a growl, Eunice walks round the huge vehicle and raps on the door, at first gently, then with more force. Above them, bats circle, making little Martian-sounding cries in the halo of the only lamppost. Lego waits impatiently.

"Okay," Eunice decides.

The furor that follows has an element of the supernatural in that it defies fatigue, disease, and the wear and tear of time on joints. Eunice leaps high and, with a wild swing of the pickaxe, smashes the bus's side-view mirror to bits. On the other side of the colossus, Lego tackles its windows, then its flanks, riddling the metal with hollows and dents. Eunice follows his lead, then goes after the tires that she bursts one after another; her strength grows tenfold with each blow, but it isn't enough, more is needed, the bus is too big, impregnable.

That's when a rumbling starts, a greedy hum that advances from all sides at once, and for a few seconds, Lego and Eunice fall back, afraid they'll see soldiers or furious tourists appear, but no. Out of nowhere, a swarm of children armed with iron rods, crowbars, pipes, and lightsabres arrive at a run, roused by who knows what instinct, a sixth sense that quite naturally guides them to ventures such as this one, and now it's an ill-assorted army that takes on the man-eating bus, striking it and making its entrails hiss. Amid their collective frenzy, Eunice can no longer see clearly, she pulverizes, smashes, destroys. In the melee, she thinks she catches sight of Gloria, maybe Solomon, the raging shape of Nain Rouge shod in burning clogs, and up high, above what no longer resembles in any way a bus, the shadow of her father; it's as though he's dancing on the roof, his feet maintaining his balance on the crumpled metal. In the dirty dawn, a spark shoots out from who knows where, and slowly, with a kind of grace, fire consumes what remains of the vehicle. The attackers retreat, form a big circle around the flames, and a dusky light settles on the trashed parking lot in the centre of which evil continues to burn.

* * *

The storms continue. Fiji has forgotten what it was to endure them in the camp—how did they ever find shelter in those hole-ridden tents? Were they really wet all the time? The days grow shorter, the heat dissipates with the passing of the army's helicopters, and, already, Fiji's thoughts have turned to winter. She muses over her second, her third life. All the other lives she has ruined. She should have seen just how dangerous Yatim and Method's plan was, should have put the brakes on, but with Terror's death and the carnage on the river, the idea of revenge had set the Ravine on fire and, for once, there was an agreement of sorts, a collective will; for once, things seemed simple, black and white, and she strode into the darkness without a second thought. Wherever she goes now, she carries the burden of those three bodies.

Block has shown her how to use a drill, how to change fuses, how to insert screws in gypsum and two-by-fours. For three days, they install partitions to carve out dormitories in the wintering house. The grandmother helps them, less efficient than Block but more patient, except when she asks questions about her granddaughters, to which Fiji has no answer.

Francelin shows up, his arms weighed down with various wires and sections of pipe in the hope he can connect the house back to both the electrical grid and the conduits to drinking water in order to offer the kids "a minimum of comfort." Fiji doesn't bother saying it would be next to impossible to find anything more uncomfortable than their freezing winter hut where the children were plagued by phlegm and fever. She doesn't know how many of them will use the house or who will agree to spend the winter in the city—for now, most have just one thought: to return to the Ravine. But it's the least she can do after the attack, the lies, after having hidden the keys to Paradise in her pillowcase and kept her age secret by binding her breasts with duct tape.

"Starting to look good," Block exclaims, backing up to admire their handiwork.

They've divided the central room, with its fireplace cleaned by Alain, into several alcoves to give everyone their own space to sleep in, either alone or with another person when it gets extra cold. The bedrooms upstairs will be kept to house anyone who's sick and avoid contagion, a concept Theo hammers away at at every opportunity.

"What corner will you choose?" the woman asks.

"None," says Fiji. "I'd not be living here."

Block looks hard at her. "'Cause of your age?"

Her eyes glued to the floor, Fiji nods. Broad and sturdy, Block walks over to the young girl. Gloria can be heard sawing upstairs while Francelin utters apocalyptic curses in the basement.

"Just like me," she says half under her breath. "It was hard for me, too, when I got too old."

Fiji says nothing. Francelin's grousing curbs her urge to cry.

Block says, "It's hard for everyone, but it's even worse when you're the leader. It's not just that you don't know where to go. You don't know who you are anymore."

Stunned, Fiji looks up at Block's craggy face. In response to the girl's unspoken questions, Block gives a sad half-smile.

"We were the first. It was twenty years ago. The camp was a bit farther downstream back then. I laid down the law for years. I was the one who came up with the age limit—some kids were getting ideas. When my turn came, I had no choice but to go."

Fiji reaches out to touch the woman's arm as though the adult standing before her has turned into a mirage, an apparition that needs to be felt to be believed. The Ravine's first leader.

"What'd you do? After you left?"

Block lets out a noisy breath, her forehead knit. "It was a tough slog. For a long time. Lucky for me, I wasn't alone. Sweetie came with me. No matter that she was still young enough to stay. She never deserted me."

The woman casts a glance behind her, then leans over so their faces are level; she lays a hand on Fiji's shoulder and it's as though a door has opened. "If you want, Fiji, you can come live with us. No need to roam the way we did. We can take you in for a while, long enough for you to land on your feet. As long as you need."

Fiji's whole body, each and every one of her molecules, surges toward the hand enveloping her shoulder, her whole being crowding toward the future, toward a gentler way of life, toward the possibility of something else; she's dying to throw herself onto Block, to melt into her solid chest.

"I don't know," she says.

"You could bring your pal Bleach with you."

Fiji conjures up the crystalline form of her friend and her vertiginous power over time, except when it comes to changing her age.

"No," she says. "Bleach's a fairy. She'd not be made to live in a house."

"What about you?"

"Me, maybe. Maybe so ..."

*　*　*

All Judith's possessions fit into the pickup. Scattered throughout the house, there had seemed to be so many. But once piled into boxes in the back of the truck, it's as if they're reduced to almost nothing, a few books, a bundle of clothing, two or three stray toiletries in a case.

"Sure you don't want some furniture?" Gloria asked a second time.

Judith shook her head. Her father pushed her into the truck's cab before Gloria could offer anything else, silverware,

273

linens, anything that might make her feel like her daughter wasn't leaving empty-handed and wouldn't find herself in the big city with absolutely nothing. For once, Judith answered as though reading her thoughts, "I don't need anything but music, Maman."

The plan was fuzzy. She'd arrive in Fort Détroit after the deadline for enrolment in a community college. What's more, all the vocal training schools had waiting lists. But Judith thought that by showing up in person, she'd be able to persuade them to accept her. If not, she'd spend the semester singing in cabarets or on the street. She would sing on her own in the tiny studio she'd rented sight unseen, knowing nothing of the district it was in. Gloria made her husband swear to stay on a few extra days to make sure she lacked for nothing and to fill her pantry: "rice, canned food, anything that will keep." At that time, Fort Détroit was more populated, more restless, a great dance of knives. On a seeming whim, Judith had decided that that was where she would become somebody—unless the idea had been germinating for much longer and she'd never breathed a word of it to anyone. On the cusp of adulthood, she still said little, either through words or actions, a placid expression almost permanently plastered onto her face. Gloria hadn't thought she was capable of such a daring move.

She hugged her daughter through the open window of the pickup, cried into her newly-dyed blond hair and reiterated her warnings: "Don't walk alone at night. Hurry and make friends there. Don't swim in the lake. Visit museums. Don't drink too much, protect your vocal chords from cigarette smoke. And no drugs. Don't go near them, okay?"

"I promise, Maman."

"I love you."

The engine was running, and Gloria hadn't had time to add "I'm proud of you." She hadn't even had time to think it, to formulate the words; it was too difficult to reconcile loss and ambition. The pickup disappeared along the gravel road as Gloria kept staring, convinced that Judith hadn't looked back even once.

Stepping inside, she found the house changed—incomplete, lacking. How could so few objects change the look of a place? Suddenly dizzy, Gloria plunged her fingers into a pot holding a spider plant, then raised them to her mouth.

* * *

She is nothing but sense of smell. Or else the world is nothing but scent. Night fell a thousand years ago, she has been alone forever, or almost alone—she has a shooting pain in one ear, and twelve spots that burn on her abdomen, like tiny teeth gnawing. She licks her belly, detects no presence there, resumes her journey. The area reeks of smoke. Even where there is no smell of fire, there is the smell of fire. If a queen had to be chosen here, that scent would be she. There are also whiffs of something else: trash, mud, rust, gamey flesh. Sex, everywhere, all the time. But these are the grand notes, and the dog is not interested in the obvious. It's the more discreet veins, the hidden or marginal fragrances that captivate her. Pollens and their complicated interactions, crumbs of food, traces of blood. The passing, along well-defined routes, of humans whose age and frequency she can detect; sometimes, even the walker's state of mind is evident, especially fear. The same goes for coyotes, cats, badgers, and garter snakes. Only birds don't let themselves be defined.

The house is an interesting case. The dog knows it well; she spent time there before the fire, she has haunted its charred ruins. Now that it has resprouted, its smells are ambiguous, contradictory. The green perfume of fresh wood, and another denser fragrance of earth cracked open to expel the new growth, whiffs of smoke and soot still, and, underneath, something both pliant and crumbling: human cooking. The dog has never seen anyone living there, even less so making a meal; nonetheless, the place is redolent of warm dough kneaded with intoxicating herbs, grilled animal, and women's hands. Enough to make you want to lick the walls.

Across the street, the yellow house and the green house give off other exhalations, muddled and exhausting. The places continue to overflow with little humans, the same ones the dog knows well but who, jammed inside cubes, have become unbearable. She lifts her muzzle. The effluvia of the forest is still blocked by something hard, metallic. She'll head toward the grasslands. They scent of creatures on the move, they smell of life.

* * *

Gloria has come here every morning since the explosion. She saw the army arrive, spread out like an oil slick, poke around for imaginary terrorist cells. She stationed herself along the perimeter to observe the soldiers as though, by keeping an eye on their operations, she could guarantee they wouldn't discover Cassandra and Mathilda. She walked as far as the mouth of the Rouge to survey the rubble of the factory on Île Gus. The devastation of the facilities there is staggering. It looks like a dismembered dragon. Accord-

276

ing to rumours, the company is considering abandoning the plant. Rebuilding would take too long and wouldn't be worth the effort.

This morning, she saw the soldiers' trucks leave, some north, some south, called back to their masters. Their mission is over. They have intimidated the already distressed population without elucidating a single thing. This afternoon, news of the siege's end spreads throughout the city. The children gathered up their few possessions and, without fanfare, headed for the park.

Now that the day is coming to a close, they converge, calmly and haphazardly, on the park's grasses along the edge of the woods, whispering again of secret squalls. All the exiles are there. Lego, Rasca and her stuffed bear, Adidas and his healed leg, a stoic Fiji, Method stamping her feet impatiently, an exceedingly dishevelled Yatim, and Bleach flitting from one to the other, present yet above it all. Three hyper puppies turn circles round them. Her shoulders back, her step confident, Eunice joins Gloria. Solomon is there as well, flanked by his three apprentices. Standing off to the side, Block and Sweetie turn a kindly gaze on Fiji.

The forest comes alive. A great breath brings the boughs to life, opening space. All the children stop talking and the adults follow suit.

"They all gone?"

The question comes from amid the branches, high and imperious, as though posed by an owl.

"All of 'em!" Bleach cries.

Then, like flames flickering to life one after another, faces surface in the shadow of the woods. The children appear, radiant but cautious—they stay at the edge of the trees, don't advance onto the grass—several are quite small. Shouts ring out—"Magic! Stutt! Adidas! Tick-Tock! Rasca! Little doggies!"—and like two seas meeting, they merge, exiles reuniting with resistance fighters, punching shoulders, doling out damp hugs.

"You're grown!"

"Your hair stinkers!"

"It's the shampoo!"

"The little doggies're cute!"

"What's shampoo?"

"Did you killed any soldiers?"

"We gotta home for winter!"

"It's gonna be a castle?"

"It's such a castle."

"Tick-Tock, you weren't dead?"

"Who're the old guys?"

"No, I was Whale's second."

"Grown-ups that helped us."

"Tick-Tock was just about a hero."

"Then Whale saved us."

"How come Fiji don't come over?"

"Fiji!"

Everyone turns toward the tall girl who has held back. Finally wearing clothes that fit, she seems even older. Bleach draws close, takes her hand, which Fiji squeezes without looking either at her friend or at the dozens of eyes trained on her. She scans the crowns of the trees.

"Whale! You there?"

On the ground, all sounds hush; everyone pricks up their ears, even the dogs.

"Yes," the owl's voice finally replies.

"Bleach'd told me what you did. How 'bout *you* lead the camp?"

"Do I gotta come down to earth?"

Fiji thinks it over.

"Hey, don't tell me these kids can fly…?" Eunice whispers in Gloria's ear.

"We'd help," Yatim says. "We'll be Whale's soldiers on the ground."

Fiji takes a step back, as though to see the big picture. She draws in a long, shaky breath, a backward sob.

"Everyone okay with that?"

"Yes!" cry all the voices at once.

"Okay, bye then."

Letting go of Bleach's hand, the teen heads toward Sweetie and Block, who is weeping, already in her new role, suffering and harbouring dreams on behalf of another; the three walk off in silence. Leaves quiver in quiet applause.

Slowly, the children return to the woods, disappearing one by one past the treeline. A few say their farewells. Magic and Stutt are staying with Solomon. Pretty will keep learning but live in the camp. Some promise to return come winter; most aren't even thinking that far ahead. Rasca leads Lego, who has extracted the promise that he'll never be made to enforce the law again. Tick-Tock accepts hearty slaps on the back.

As she watches the comings and goings, the farewells and reunions, the resumption of bickering, Gloria is projected outside herself, a feeling she has often experienced since that first foray into the woods, as though for an instant her being has flowed into another—Eunice, Solomon, or one of these children who have brought her closer on her quest, briefly enabling her to forget her sorrow. Dusk wraps round their feet, hot and cold, then locks onto the forest's jagged facade, pink, purple, increasingly blue, and the small bodies nesting there shimmer like precious jewels in a vast mane.

A little farther south, other shapes emerge, wary, hesitant. Gloria doesn't pay them any mind, the whole park seems invested with tiny lives, as much of children as of insects and trees. But suddenly, Eunice squeezes her arm and points at a spot between the trunks. Something stands out, a bright yellow object moving like a puppet's hand. Feeling light-headed, Gloria focuses her gaze on the yellow and lingers there to steady herself while Eunice, tentative, backs away. The yellow spot is attached to a hand, and the hand belongs to an arm, and the arm to the body of a young trembling girl, and behind her stands another, shorter child who has adopted a defensive posture. It looks like they haven't eaten in days—their cheeks are sunken, their skin coated in chlorophyll and dirt—but Cassandra and Mathilda are here, alive, and out of the woods.

IV

We know that we are beyond repair.

ALEXIE MORIN

After Judith's death, Cassandra started getting headaches, and every time her sister tells her to shut up, there's a stab of pain, like a heart beating against bone. Finally understanding why trepanation exists, she dreams of piercing her skull; if only the bone in her forehead could be perforated to free the hurt like air from a balloon, pus from an abscess. At times, the migraine is blinding, and in the darkness of the dazzlement, Judith reappears beneath the bathwater. Cassandra sees herself leaning over her mother's body, trying to kiss her, unable to cry, and, for a horrifying fraction of a second, the dead woman's eyes jerk open as though to say she will never be fully gone and to announce, with all the spite of a drowned woman, that she will haunt her forever. It's a paradox that she'd be the one damned when it was Mathilda who carried out the deed, but that's only normal since, deep down, Cassandra wanted it; behind her fear and everything she wished she didn't know, she had already been killing her mother in her dreams. That afternoon, she said nothing; she watched without lifting a finger, letting what needed to be done—a thing only her sister was capable of—play itself out. The fact her younger sister feels no remorse may be a reward for her courage. Or else Mathilda has always been this way, forging ahead, never stopping to think, forgetting as she goes; Mathilda, who has to be reminded to brush her teeth, to look both ways before crossing, to hide her money, who has to be told again and again the important stuff: *Maman'll be in withdrawal, careful, Maman's going to have a visitor, let's go out, Maman's going to trade us in for something more useful.* Cassandra always knew how to decode any silence and whispers; it is Mathilda, though, who knew what to do with that knowledge.

* * *

The wind is both behind and in front of her, buffeting her from the left and from the right, and Mathilda feels as though she is in the centre, a place all gusts strive to reach in order to sweep it outside time, yet it doesn't budge; whatever force pushes her, she stays standing. It isn't hard. It's not hard when you're running flat out, and all that spring, Mathilda gallops on gusts of wind, removed from it all; fleeing is an unencumbered act, she is never out of breath. Where she struggles is having to stay cooped up, as in the tumbledown house of mouldy stone, a place for tears which is not made for her, a place where she circles round and round like a bad idea. She doesn't know how her sister stands staying still, it's like she turns into a statue, she'd have thought she was made of marble if it weren't for the never-ending tears. Cassandra has always been a talker, and even not talking she speaks, it leaks from her like blood from a too-thin bandage; she's incapable of stopping the endless, infinite flow of things in and out. Since they left, she has said eight times a day, "We shouldn't have. This'll never end," and Mathilda has had it, she wants to hit her but is too hungry and can't spare the energy. More and more, her sister has breasts and thoughts that dig tunnels through her head producing tears and a dank silence that makes you want to throw yourself against a wall. Mathilda's fingers twitch and burn, she dreams of making her escape walking on her hands.

* * *

There were just the three of them the day Mathilda was born, her father had already died, and Cassandra's father had vanished. Judith had a gift for scaring fathers off, or for setting her sights on the kind who run away. In their household, flight was a bit of a recurring theme. Her sister's birth had been like a prison break, Mathilda fleeing the womb like a dungeon. Cassandra was there. She saw it all: she remembers protesting, refusing to have the umbilical cord cut; she can still see the woman carrying the placenta away like carnage on a tray. Judith instantly fell into a deep sleep while Mathilda howled, glowering, and Cassandra saw her sister as a saviour, a mystery, and a plague. From the vantage point of her three years, she understood exactly what this baby would be capable of. That has always been Cassandra's role: to see what lies ahead and to try to prevent it. At first, she shared her forebodings with Judith, but, over time, she gave up, there was no point, her mother was too distracted, or else she'd fall asleep as Cassandra spoke. Not that that stopped her visions of what was to come. At the age of five, she pictured what would happen if Judith died or forgot to come home after some party or other. At the age of ten, she anticipated the possibility of her mother ending up in prison and already foresaw the orphanage, the foster families, and her separation from Mathilda. At the age of fifteen, she foretold that their fate had reached a tipping point. Her sister is the only person who has ever listened to her. She tried to communicate through her eyes to neighbours and teachers, to ask for help, but no one ever picked up on her silent cries. There was only Mathilda, no one else.

* * *

They have a grandmother, and the grandmother's name is Gloria, like a hymn, and Gloria walks through the park carrying a picture of the two of them. She says she wants to see them, the kids yell at her, she says she wants to help them, she comes and goes; Mathilda feels her like a stickiness in the air, something that clings to her skin. She couldn't care less, a grandmother means nothing, doesn't exist, and she will never go back there. Cassandra clasps her head in her hands, words push up from inside and she buckles, she tells everything to the girl with holes in her boots and to the girl of white, and Mathilda wants to kill her, kill them all, the damn idiots making plans, thinking they can decide how things will unfold or shape the world with their words. Gloria. A name that disappears even as it's being uttered. They've been moved, they're stuck deep in a cave where it's too hot on hot days, too cold on cold nights, their sleeping bags have turned into rivers of mud; all of it eats away at Cassandra, who says they're going to die in their cavern, but Mathilda gets used to it, she doesn't feel discomfort anymore, there is nothing but the forest against her skin, nature expanding all around her, then one day a huge explosion and fear suffocating her sister. Mathilda is not afraid. She is where she should have been born, where her life hid waiting for her to approach. The soldiers are nothing but shadows she can send up in smoke if she wants to. The girl of white comes and goes, Mathilda can follow her or she can stay here; since being in the forest, her desire to flee has been transformed, mutated into a similar yet different desire. To roam. To follow a spiral not an arrow, a new beginning that advances slowly then returns, never passing the same spot. Her sister perspires at night and dries up during the day, thousands of spiders torment her, they lurk near Mathilda as well but don't bite, or else she doesn't feel them. She gives herself over to the day.

* * *

For the most part, living with an addict meant rooming with inertia. Although there were regular bursts of laughter and flare-ups, their existence was primarily ruled by long periods of torpor during which Cassandra could approach Judith's body. As a little girl, she liked to run her hands through her mother's bleached-out hair, trace the delicate skin between her thumb and index finger, the choppy lines on her palm. Her body was full of signs to be deciphered— bruises, scabs, abscesses—that Cassandra inventoried and counted, measuring the proximity of death. Sometimes, Judith woke during her ritual and Cassandra immediately knew whether she had to step back or stay put, whether it was a day for caresses or a day for rage, or perhaps a day for song, a godsend that became rarer over time. Her sister's body also held signs—scratches, trails of grime. Cassandra would encircle the baby's calf with her fingers, and, when- ever they went all the way round, she'd set off in search of bread that she broke into crumbs and stuffed into her sis- ter's mouth. She washed her, cut her nails, swaddled her when goosebumps appeared on her flesh and when puddles were covered by a membrane of ice. All surfaces could be read: the kitchen counter, tidy or cluttered; the mattresses, damp or clean; the sky, grey or black; the floor, creaking or silent. When she started school, Cassandra already knew how to decipher a dozen non-inventoried languages. Learning to read in French was a snap compared to all the rest. Sensing that school wouldn't last long, she came home every day and tried to convey to her sister what she had gleaned, but Mathilda ripped up notebooks and spat on pencils; she tore the toothbrush from her sister and slapped her hands so she wouldn't tie her shoes for her. As soon as she was old enough to talk, she wanted to do everything by herself. Mathilda never learned how to read.

* * *

There is always a goading inside her, a fire, a whip that never rests. Even unmoving, even in water or stretched out on ice, Mathilda feels it like a second pulse, this presence that beats an untenable time, a voice without words, white-hot tusks, the jaws of a dragon that galvanize silence. The creature is accustomed to having something to sink its teeth into, its daily ration of dark matter, but here, in this forest that bends to its every will, there is no adversary, no distance to overcome, zero cannon fodder. It isn't natural. Mathilda feels all wrong, the feral ball runs on empty in her belly; it needs a target, a bone, so she turns to her sister, eight times a day, and bites down, she has no choice, and her sister knows it, she offers herself up. Cassandra lets herself be devoured the way fields are violated by crops or houses go up in flames, and it doesn't matter because plants resprout, houses grow back, stumps transform sooner or later into new limbs, nothing really disappears, everything is already here, destroyed and resuscitated at once.

* * *

She has only ever known her sister to fight. Everyone her adversary, and she the winner always. Cassandra felt in her own navel every punch delivered, ashamed and proud to have such a fierce, unconquerable little sister. She herself has never struck a soul, she wouldn't know where to start, but sometimes she felt like she was a party to the attack launched on the children of the wealthy suburbs who lost their way in the inner city, on the rare students of the run-down school, on the adolescents who chased them down deserted streets, and, once, on Judith's male friend who stepped into their bedroom in the middle of the night. With men, Mathilda knew instinctively where to aim: in the exact same spot they used to destroy little girls. Cassandra never helped, and Mathilda never blamed her; each had her role to play in their mutual survival. Judith didn't put up a fight in the bathtub—it was as though she expected her life to end that way. Or else, she was too stoned to realize what was happening. Mathilda placed one hand on her shoulder, the other on her forehead, and pressed down. Judith sank easily, and Mathilda had no trouble holding her underwater. The bubbles left her, taking with them what little awareness remained; her face was pale, her stomach, too, as were the tub and the walls. The death of a woman is a pale, easy thing. Cassandra watched the scene from the doorway, realizing and not realizing what was happening, and once it was over, she began to hyperventilate, this was a crime, a catastrophe, she had seen it coming, had done nothing, and now it was too late. Wiping her hands on a towel, her sister simply looked her in the eye. At that moment, Cassandra could have sworn her younger sister was the taller of the two.

* * *

This is the first time she has dug in the ground. Normally, what happens below the earth's surface is of no interest to her, it's a kingdom for insects and crypts, the living and the dead. Horizontal motion—running, the wind, the throwing of stones—is what interests her, not vertical forces—drilling, burying, germinating, disinterring. But in the forest, everything is different: what grows does so without permission and what dies does so without a sound, destroying what should not be destroyed and creating what should not be created. The soil makes you hungry. Ever since she was little, Mathilda hasn't liked to eat: in her eyes, food is a compromise, a rank accommodation between disgust and wasting away. Flour on her tongue never loses its dusty texture. Vegetables seem to her to contain a proliferation, a diseased growth, like a tumour; biting into one is like eating a parasite of sorts, a foreign organism capable of multiplying inside her. It's been worse since the explosion: food comes to them rotten, spangled with a viscous film. Cassandra eats gingerly, detaching from the miasma chunks she convinces herself are free from rot; she is rapidly wasting away, consumed by her lamentations, poisoned by the moribund supplies. As for Mathilda, she turned to the forest. Without a second thought, she crawled out of the cave, breathing in the smell of earth washed and hollowed out by the storm. An epiphany: soil contains everything—roots, walnuts, fallen fruit, larvae, even stones whose texture doesn't stop them from yielding to Mathilda's appetite; she takes it all in and grows stronger, turns into something more sturdy, anchored, all-powerful. As her sister fades, Mathilda becomes increasingly herself.

* * *

One day there will be rain for long stretches of time, kilometres, years of rain, which will create new lakes and new rivers, streams of water that will feed on the earth, and the world will be cleansed. One day, the ground will long to open to reveal hidden treasures, buried veins, to let the sun caress what darkness held prisoner too long. One day, fruit will speak, tell of its own weight, its honey, the dreams it dreams at night. One day, entire sections of the city will collapse to let in the sky. Empty shirts will fly, fluttering like flags, wounds will open inside wounds to illuminate them, one great word will eclipse all desires, curses, songs, committals, ruses, bolts from the blue, wayfarers brought down by the light. The animals will sort themselves out, they will create new paths, feeding trails. There will be noise, voices that don't say it all, pages of rhythms to order time, one single bell to bring space alive. We know nothing till we know. We cannot understand until we can. The future invites itself in, tiny, almost mute in our hands, then takes up all space. The future whispers our names, without others knowing, whispers as we sleep an incitement to prescience: "Cassandra."

* * *

The first envelope arrives via the girl of white, and the yellow of its paper seems to be even more yellow in the white of her hands. She holds it out to Cassandra as to a magnetic pole toward which all messages converge. Cassandra pulls out a letter, her pupils jump from one syllable to the next, then she refolds the piece of paper and slides it back into the envelope, and her gaze continues to leap like a deer. For once, she says nothing, bites her cheeks—she has little in the way of cheeks left to bite—then dozes off. And that is when Mathilda strokes the envelope, the words curling there, a closed door. A few days later, three other envelopes reach them, the girl explains that the kids find them everywhere, those who can read say they're about them, Mathilda and Cassandra; the girl hands the damp bundle to Mathilda who passes it over to her sister. Cassandra says nothing, but—Mathilda can tell—their words are needles making their way to her heart; she turns circles, gnaws on her hair the way she did in the time of Judith, and foretells of cyclones in her sleep. Soon, still more envelopes arrive; they no longer need a messenger but appear on their own, carried by the wind and in the beaks of crows, they hasten to the threshold of their cave. Cassandra doesn't need to read them, she knows what's inside; Mathilda doesn't ask her what that is—it doesn't matter, it won't stop her sister from being mesmerized, and when an idea worms its way inside her like this, time opens, the universe moves. Cassandra has an amazing aptitude: that of doing nothing other than thinking, yet still managing to change the world.

* * *

A house made of yellow paper. In fact, that was their home: a flimsy, frail abode that only stood thanks to the strength of its folds. Despite herself, Cassandra has begun to wonder what the place would look like now without Judith, without the never-ending parade of addicts, a home with a healthy heart that would pump life and light into its rooms, a grandmother's heart. She hadn't thought she remembered her, but since the letters, memories have taken shape like sculptures emerging from a ball of clay. She was the one in the cemetery at the end of the world, unmoving next to a grave, the woman in black that her imagination had transformed into a stele. She was a crumbling voice on the telephone that Judith didn't answer; the only flowers growing in the yard, the organization inside closets that was slowly eroded by the laws of chaos and addiction. And something else, an older memory, primal, warmth, scent, pressure on the body; a sensation in the hollow of her palm at night that makes her want to close her fingers round a stick. With the memories, desire has returned—for a bed, a hot meal, a shower—sprung from the envelopes like yellow lightning. She felt like crushing the stack of letters tormenting her, but the second her skin touched the paper, the future spoke in its many voices, a choir accompanied by an organ. She will live again in that house. She will confront the tub, learn to live with the crucible of their transgression; in the clouded rooms, she will reconcile walls and cracks, ceiling and windows. What's more, she hears that a day will come when the house will have something else to say. Years of fear and guilt will be overcome by years of restitution. Then, there will be a swing in time. It came to her all of a sudden, and she could have revelled in it, or at least felt relief, but something murky remains, a black hole in her field of vision. She has seen the house, its frail porch, its roof of moss, but one area remains indistinct, like a partially burned photograph. An enormous blind spot engulfing her.

* * *

She takes her big sister by the hand. The time has come; they can no longer stay here; Cassandra will go mad, and Mathilda will grind her to bits. Finally, the soldiers have left, the way is clear. This is what needs to be done—Mathilda always knows what needs doing, decisions come to her ready-made and with absolute certainty, and she slips them on like rings on each finger. Cassandra understands, she knows her sister's sense of direction, which is why she follows her without question—in those moments, the eldest is like ripe fruit that needs only a touch to be freed. As soon as they set out, as soon as the cave disappears in a green rustling, joy floods through Mathilda like nothing else can, other than anger, perhaps, or sunshine. Each leg lifts in turn, light, as though controlled by strings; beneath her feet, the earth murmurs, the wind weaves through trees. Nothing is more beautiful than a forest left to itself, nothing is grander than walking a spiral there, inhabiting it concentrically. With each step, she feels Cassandra grow calmer: her psychosis of the past few days simply needed fresh air, a direction, and to leave the woods behind. Mathilda is at peace as well, even though her world is about to be upended again, even though amid the trees an empty brightness grows. At last, they reach the boundary, where the landscape shifts, and Cassandra shoots her sister a questioning glance. Mathilda reaches into her pocket, pulls out a tattered yellow paper that she presses against her sister's chest. Cassandra doesn't budge; through the myriad strings attached to the letters, there is an element that still escapes her—Mathilda can see clearly the enigma hanging over her, but does not dwell on it. They are where they are meant to be. Mathilda pushes Cassandra out of the woods, and she lands on a greyish patch of grass where a woman with a moon-like face and doe eyes awaits them. The woman's skirt billows in the wind like a ship's sail, her hands wringing in front of her round belly. Cassandra drops the letter.

* * *

The touch of her body is incongruous, both foreign and intensely familiar, like a place that once belonged to the girl, a space that must have contracted or warped over time. Her grandmother hugs her tight, and at first Cassandra thinks she's sobbing, then identifies a series of sighs, a mix of affliction and relief, thousands of small promises. They say nothing, there is no room, everything is too highly charged. Further along stands a thickset woman, short hair, determined chin, and Cassandra recognizes the neighbour and gives a timid wave. The woman returns her greeting, her expression kindly and sad, and in that moment Cassandra foresees that the two women will protect her with their lives, a feeling so new she just about stumbles. But she doesn't fall. She is where she should be. Yet a niggling doubt continues to gnaw at her, inexplicable anxiety—she feels like she has forgotten something. In the empty park under the setting sun, Cassandra freezes. She needs another push, the cruel and perfect hand of her sister. She turns. Mathilda has not budged from the woods' edge. With arms crossed, she observes her older sister, her expression serene in its certainty, and, finally, Cassandra understands. Mathilda will not be coming with her. During those weeks of biding their time, her sister has turned into another, a huntress, a hermit. She has turned into a girl of the woods. And with the same implacable majesty found in each of her actions, she has decided to stay behind in the forest. Cassandra looks at Mathilda, this creature barely bigger than a wolf, who owes her survival to her sister just as her sister owes her her own, her only definition of love, and part of her awareness founders; her being, already severed in two by Judith's death, is severed again, leaving her with only a quarter of what she was born with. She moves toward her.

* * *

Her sister is tall. She hadn't realized it, seeing her prostrate in a cave, huddled round the taut thread of her memory, but here she is as tall as a chimney stack, broader, too, in the shoulders and hips; there are even breasts, buttocks, new contours come from nowhere, born of crusts of bread and raw potatoes. Mathilda looks down at her own skinny legs, her sunken belly, her feet swimming in runners that used to be too tight; the body that is hers seems to be subject to an opposing force that brings everything back to its centre, making her limbs shorter, more compact. Now, face to face, the two sisters look at odds, a seed and an apple, a child and a woman. Cassandra draws near and takes her little sister in her arms, whispers in her ear, "Mathilda," in a suddenly deeper voice, and Mathilda knows Cassandra has understood, has seen what she could not see before. Cassandra cries a little, and a drop of lava trickles down the nape of Mathilda's neck; she squirms, it tickles and burns, she can't wait to return to the forest. Gloria watches the scene unfold, and Mathilda prays she won't come over to hug her in turn; but the old woman holds back, and Mathilda thinks that perhaps she is invisible now, that her sister may be the only one who has ever seen her. Her sister's neck smells of dead leaves, flour, and patience; Mathilda breathes in deeply, and Cassandra frees her, opening her arms wide as though to embrace the whole of the woodlands, the forest that rumbles and grows, stretching farther already, Mathilda can feel it, toward the vacant lots and deserted streets, swallowing abandoned districts like walnuts, like stones. She need do nothing to return to the cover of the trees: the edge advances, catches up to her, brings her back to her brand-new life. The wind shakes the branches like an impatient incubus; unmoving, Mathilda keeps her eyes on her sister, who is slowly erased by trunks and branches. Just as she disappears, there is a snap like a cord breaking, and Mathilda wonders if Cassandra has heard it too. Yes. Yes, she heard it—of that, she is certain.

The storm bores a hole through the street, a great iron fist revealing a parallel world. A small crowd has formed round the hole to watch the rush of dark water several metres beneath the concrete. Block reaches out to Fiji to hold her back, but she herself can't help edging closer, fascinated by the current's movement. As for Gloria and Eunice, they encourage a fearful Cassandra to come admire the phenomenon. Theophilus and Francelin speculate over what could have caused the sinkhole at the corner of Clyde and Leblond. Ulysses and Solomon scan the sky in search of an answer. At a remove, Jonah smokes with a meditative air, his gaze focused on the gap as though on a portal into a new dimension. Half-whispering, Magic and Stutt wonder how long this river has flowed beneath the banality of houses. Raquel is the only one who doesn't seem surprised.

At first, they thought lightning had staved in the street. But lightning alone couldn't have drilled a hole through the asphalt. It was rain, tears, piss, and blood that worked on the ground, slowly pushing, opening a tunnel through the earth till the buried waterway assumed its rightful place again. It was only a matter of time before the pavement buckled and gave back to the light of day its own.

The clouds disperse, and sunshine streams forth, illuminating the subterranean river. Its water is limpid and enticing, bordered by sandy banks, moss, and ferns; it looks like there may even be fish. At that juncture, all the inhabitants of Avenue Clyde have the same thought: they take a step forward as though to drink from this unexpected spring that could perhaps restore their youth, make it possible to start all over again.

A cry rings out suddenly, made of laughter and squeals, and Magic and Stutt jump into the current, yelping with joy. The adults have a moment of panic: no one knows how deep the river is, if it hides sharp rocks, if the little ones know how to swim. But the water is shallow and free of hazards, and the two kids splash about with ease. Out of nowhere, other children launch spread-eagled, too, and with each body that dives in, the sinkhole seems to expand even more. Rasca is there, bathing her teddy bear whose fur has almost dissolved. Adidas, Lego, and Tick-Tock squirt water using their palms. Pretty and Yatim take turns keeping each other afloat on the surface; Method looks for frogs. Two newcomers, Godot and Carottine, hang on to driftwood and float—by the end of the day, they will know how to swim. Soon, the children no longer jump in from the street; they emerge directly from the water, like submarines, and multiply—ten, twelve, twenty small beings splashing about under the grown-ups' gaze. Between two waves, Gloria thinks she catches sight of Mathilda's curls—she isn't sure, maybe it's something else instead, foam, a reflection of the sky … She turns to Cassandra but discovers her granddaughter has left for home. Eunice finds flat stones to toss or skip across the water; Priscilla whines for the chance to retrieve one.

Although he has kept dry, Solomon feels drenched. Downstream, the spirits have gathered: Caesar, Eunice's father, Terror, Wolfpup, Pow-Pow, and all the others; Raquel sees them talking with their feet in the water, catching crayfish.

Eventually, Cassandra returns and approaches her grandmother, a metal container in her hands. Gloria grazes it with her fingertips, probes the adolescent's gaze. They agree. Cassandra steps to the edge of the sinkhole, her long arms extended over the river, and opens the urn. The children part. Judith's ashes tumble into the current that carries away her first life and starts her on her second. Cassandra returns to stand by Gloria, and together they contemplate the water rushing past, the universe changing from one drop to the next.

The river, as in a poem, sings. It sings a song whose lyrics are unintelligible yet which everyone understands nonetheless, a melody that transforms the world, that reaches into the very hollows of bones. The music flees, vanishes the minute it comes into being, but resurfaces, repeating itself over and over, always there and already gone, always ahead of itself.

The river flows, and what it ferries is impossible to grasp, to touch, anything born there instantly becomes an echo of itself. Objects thrown into the river ricochet, thoughts stay afloat to spell place names reviving history.

The river roils, it barrels toward the largest lakes in the world, it dashes toward whatever awaits that can neither be seen nor avoided, only welcomed, faced head-on.

One autumn afternoon in Fort Détroit, the last warm day of the season, the first hint of winter, a dozen figures lean over the edge of a sinkhole in the shape of a mouth gaping wide. In the heart of a city built on water, wind, fire, and dreams, a handful of adults watch a multitude of children swim in perilous living water. It brims with the promise of rivers and oceans, ferries more lives than the hand of any god. And into the unstoppable flow, the youngsters dive, hold their breath—one minute, three, ten; they keep not breathing for a hundred years, and their bodies disappear, carried away by the current. They reappear downstream, borne by the current as though the waves were an endless loop, and, by leaning over further, it is possible to see each object go by in similar fashion, vanishing then resurfacing, a branch, a feather, a chrysanthemum, a branch, a feather, a chrysanthemum, a branch, a feather, a child; they flow past again and again, each time slightly different but always themselves, and just when it seems like they have gone forever, they resurface, irrepressible. All around them, the future.

ACKNOWLEDGEMENTS

The Future would not have been possible without research done by ethnologist Marcel Bénéteau, in particular his books *Mots choisis: Trois cents ans de francophonie au détroit du lac Érié* and *Contes du Détroit*, where I discovered the fairy-tale Adidas tells on page 146, which was in turn found in Université Laval's Archives de folklore et d'ethnologie. I also owe a great debt to Tiya Miles's *The Dawn of Detroit: A Chronicle of Slavery and Freedom* as well as to Thomas J. Sugrue's *The Origins of the Urban Crisis: Race and Inequality in Postwar Detroit* and to Mark Binelli's *Detroit City Is the Place to Be: The Afterlife of an American Metropolis. Up the Rouge!* by Joel Thurtell and Patricia Beck provided me with essential information on the famous river the children navigate. Prior to any research or creation, the documentaries *Detroit, ville sauvage* by Florent Tillon and *Detropia* by Rachel Grady and Heidi Ewing spurred my imagination and fed my reflections. But the most invigorating and enlightening part of my research comes without question from the conversations I was privileged to have with historians and researchers Irene Moore Davis, Guillaume Teasdale, and Matthew Van Meter, to whom I would like to express my deepest gratitude.

* * *

My heartfelt thanks go out to Antoine Tanguay for his unfailing support, his merciless eye, and his indispensable optimism, and to the whole of the Alto team for their support and enthusiasm. Thank you to Christine Eddie for the relevance of her comments and to Christiane Vadnais for crucial assistance near journey's end. Thank you to everyone at Biblioasis for their work and their continuing support. Thank you to Susan Ouriou for her extraordinary translation.

Huge thanks go out to Dan Wells and Alexis Everitt-Wells for their encouragement and advice and the wonderful tour of Detroit they gave me. Thank you also to Emerson, Anson, and Imogen for welcoming me into their home.

Thank you to the Conseil des arts et des lettres du Québec for its financial assistance. Thank you to McGill University and the Mordecai Richler Writer-in-Residence Program that gave me an opportunity to spend precious moments with professors and students and helped me further my writing. Thank you to the Vermont College of Fine Arts for allowing me to work and stay at the Banff Centre for Arts and Creativity, and thank you to the brilliant students and instructors there, particularly Kim Echlin, who introduced me to Inanna's sense of time and her poem (mentioned on page 292).

Thank you to Lanan Adcock (advice on card-reading), Sabrina Leblond-Murphy (medical advice and travelling companion in Detroit), Claude Leroux and Alex Godley (advice on farming), and to Claude again for diving into the jumble of the manuscript on two different occasions. Thank you to my readers Catherine Chesnay, Robert Leroux, Chantal Maillé, Karine Michel, and Neil Smith. Thank you to Madeleine Thien for exploring reinvented cities and for our discussions that furthered the making of this novel. Thank you to Nicolas Dickner, Alain Farah, Dominique Fortier, Rawi Hage, Lazer Lederhendler, Sean Michaels, Charles Sagalane, Élise Turcotte, and Audrée Wilhelmy for their friendship and views on writing. Infinite thanks to Béatrice and Clément for their perspectives on the lives of the children of the Rouge and for their life's work; thank you again to my parents for their moral and logistical support during the writing of this novel. Thank you to the Achkar family, Sefi Amir, Patricia Boushel, Camille Champeval, Aisling Chin-Yee, Nancy Hameder, the Lacroix family, Jean Lavigne, Frédéric Lord, Luc Mikelsons, Michael Nardone, Laura Perlmutter, the Prud'hommes, Sarah Spring, Sarah Steinberg, Annie St-Pierre, and Dylan Young. You are the ones who help open life to writing and happiness.

ABOUT THE AUTHOR

Catherine Leroux is the author of three highly praised novels and an innovative sequence of short stories. Her first novel, *La marche en forêt* (2011), was a finalist for Quebec's Booksellers' Prize. Her bestselling second novel, *The Party Wall*, a translation of *Le mur mitoyen*, won the France–Quebec Prize in the original and, in translation as *The Party Wall*, was a finalist for the Scotiabank Giller Prize and the Dublin IMPAC Award. In the United States, *The Party Wall* was a prestigious Indies Introduce selection. Leroux's story sequence, *Madame Victoria*, won Quebec's Adrienne Choquette Prize and was a finalist for the Booksellers' Prize. The French original of *The Future* (*L'avenir*) won the Jacques Brossard Prize and was a finalist for the Imaginary Horizons Prize.

Catherine Leroux works as a translator and editor in Montreal. She was awarded the 2019 Governor General's Literary Award for Translation.

ABOUT THE TRANSLATOR

Calgary-based Susan Ouriou is an award-winning literary translator, fiction writer, and editor. She won the Governor General's Award for Translation (French to English) in 2009 for *Pieces of Me* by Charlotte Gingras. She has been a finalist for the Governor General's Award on five other occasions, most recently in 2022. Ouriou has published the novels *Damselfish* and *Nathan* and has edited two anthologies: *Beyond Words: Translating the World* and *Languages of Our Land: Indigenous Poems and Stories from Quebec*.

Biblioasis International Translation Series
General Editor: Stephen Henighan